The Charmers

Center Point
Large Print

Also by Elizabeth Adler and available from Center Point Large Print:

One Way or Another
Last to Know

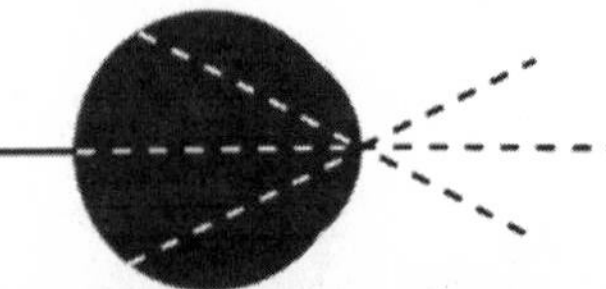

This Large Print Book carries the Seal of Approval of N.A.V.H.

The Charmers

Elizabeth Adler

CENTER POINT LARGE PRINT
THORNDIKE, MAINE

This Center Point Large Print edition
is published in the year 2016 by arrangement with
St. Martin's Press.

This is a work of fiction.
All of the characters, organizations, and events portrayed
in this novel are either products of the author's
imagination or are used fictitiously.

The text of this Large Print edition is unabridged.
In other aspects, this book may vary
from the original edition.
Printed in the United States of America
on permanent paper.
Set in 16-point Times New Roman type.

ISBN: 978-1-68324-055-6

Library of Congress Cataloging-in-Publication Data

Names: Adler, Elizabeth (Elizabeth A.) author.
Title: The charmers / Elizabeth Adler.
Description: Center Point Large Print edition. | Thorndike, Maine : Center Point Large Print, 2016.
Identifiers: LCCN 2016022642 | ISBN 9781683240556
(hardcover : alk. paper)
Subjects: LCSH: Large type books. | GSAFD: Suspense fiction.
Classification: LCC PR6051.D56 C48 2016b | DDC 823/.914—dc23
LC record available at https://lccn.loc.gov/2016022642

Acknowledgments

Of course, and as always, my thanks to Jennifer Enderlin, the best editor any writer could wish for. I consider myself lucky to have her insight. She always knows exactly how the timing should be to get maximum suspense and impact, as well as what they should be eating and drinking in the south of France!

My thanks also to all the team at St. Martin's Minotaur, who, with their hard and careful work, make the production of a book seem so easy. And of course to my wonderful agent, Anne Sibbald of Janklow, Nesbitt & Associates, without whom I would not be publishing my thirtieth novel, with my other novels in more than thirty published languages. Quite simply, she is the best, and when we're not talking plot lines, we are talking "kitties," hers and mine, who keep us amused, not to say "on our toes" chasing after them when they get a little bored and start swiping ornaments off shelves.

Last but not least, my husband of so many years we've stopped counting, Richard Adler . . . "without whom" . . . is all I need to say. He checks my every word, queries plot directions, retypes it all, and pours the champagne when it's finished. What more could I want?

A few months ago, my darling black cat, Sunny, got sick with cancer. Losing him was a terrible sadness; he was fifteen years old and so much a part of our lives. We miss his golden-eyed innocence, his pleasure in life. Our Siamese, Sweet Pea, is still with us, thank heaven, and becoming more vocal with age.

So, here I am enjoying the desert sunshine, and already writing the next . . . and then the next and the next. Please, enjoy them.

The Charmers

Prologue

The Painting

April 14, 1912

Walter Matthews

Walter "Iron Man" Matthews was propping up the first-class bar on the new luxury liner, the RMS *Titanic*, as it plowed steadily through the Atlantic. There were no waves, no wind. The ocean was flat as a board. A faint haze hung over it, under a sky so glittering with stars it outshone the great ship's own lights.

He was downing a double Macallan whiskey, his preferred pre-dinner tipple wherever he was in the world, be it on a boat or in a London drawing-room, in a Manhattan penthouse or a canoe floating down the Amazon, because of course in places like the jungle one must always take one's own supplies. It was the only civilized way, even though in the jungle one's boots might be being attacked by fire ants, and in the drawing-room one's soul attacked by someone's unlovely daughter "tinkling the ivories" as they called it, without a speck of emotion.

He placed the painting on the bar. It was a river scene by the artist J. M. W. Turner. He had fallen in love with its misty colors.

It was professionally wrapped in waterproof covering. "Just in case, sir," the art dealer had said with a faint smile. "One can never trust the ocean."

Quite right, Walt thought now as he became aware of a grinding noise and a sideways lurch that sent his glass sliding half the length of the mahogany bar and almost into the lap of another fellow. He waved an apologetic hand even as he slid from his seat because there was no more traction to hold him in place. Gravity had shifted and with it the enormous, new, unsinkable ship.

He was one of the first on deck. It was bitterly cold. A white cliff loomed beside them. They had struck an iceberg, formed by the cold waves of the Labrador current mixing with the warm waters of the Gulf Stream.

Ever the gentleman, he helped the ladies into the constantly moving lifeboats that lifted and dropped with the movement of the ship. He never let go of his painting though, kept it tucked inside his dinner jacket. He had been about to go down for dinner and of course had dressed appropriately for his position in first-class. He kind of regretted the dinner; it would have been good, solid fare, a bit Frenchified perhaps as they often were on the big ships, but he enjoyed that. And he regretted the Macallan, which had spilt all over the place, including on his hand-tailored Soames and Whitby jacket, even staining his pristine white shirt cuffs that were linked with circles of gold and sapphire, matching the studs in his starched white shirt front.

The situation was disastrous, he knew it; recognized what fate had in store for all of them; heard the screams of the terrified women on the lower decks, the wails of children and infants, the cursing of the seamen attempting to get the insufficient lifeboats lowered from the constantly shifting ship.

Now, the ship slipped even lower, tilted, stern-up. The lifeboats already in the water pulled away, afraid to be caught in the whirling downward current as the liner quickly began to sink.

"Mr. Matthews, sir, come this way." An officer grabbed his arm, tugged him toward the ladder over the side, leading into a small dinghy. But Walt stepped back when a young woman ran toward them, screams dying in her throat, fear written across her face.

Here," he said, grabbing her arm, "now jump." And he gave her an almighty shove that sent her dropping feet first into the orange dinghy.

"Jump yourself, sir," the officer beckoned him from the dinghy.

But Walt could see it was already overloaded and, holding the painting over his head with one hand, he jumped into the icy depths. The winter temperature was minus two degrees. He might last, at most, fifteen minutes. He grabbed onto the dinghy's rope with his free hand, splashing his already-numb feet in his good crawl stroke, wondering if this was, in fact, the end. How ironic, he told himself. And how much he would have enjoyed that dinner.

He knew he could last no more than ten minutes. But then, quite suddenly, from one moment to the next, the water grew substantially warmer, certainly now above freezing.

The warm Gulf Stream current was what saved him. He was picked up several hours later, along with the few other survivors and taken aboard a passing cruiser, the *Carpathia*, where he was revived with brandy and hot blankets, after which he took to his bed—a small lower bunk in a lower cabin—and, with the painting stashed under his pillow, slept the sleep of the saved. He was one of the few.

The painting would some years later end up in the rose-silken boudoir of his mistress and love of his live, the wonderful, beautiful, well, *almost* beautiful if you looked at her the right way—the glorious Jerusha.

Part I

The Present

1

Antibes, South of France

The Boss, as he was called by everyone, even those that did not work for him and merely knew his reputation, strode purposefully past the sea-front terrace bars until he came to the one he favored, where he pulled a chair from a table in the third row back, closest to the building. He always liked to face the street, the crowds, the other customers, keep his back against the wall, so to speak. Backs were vulnerable, his particularly so.

Despite the heat he was comfortable in white linen pants and a blue-and-white-print shirt, sleeves rolled up over his muscular forearms. His watch was neither gold nor flashy, though it was certainly expensive.

The chairs were small for a man his size, big, built like a wrestler. Most chairs were, except of course for the ones specifically crafted for his many homes. He was a man who liked his comforts, and coming from his background, who could blame him? Though you could blame him for the way he'd gone about getting them.

The waiter recognized him. Smiling, obsequious, linen napkin draped over an arm, and tray in hand, he inquired what his pleasure might be.

Lemonade was the answer. The Boss did not drink liquor, not even wine in this wine-growing country. The estates around St. Tropez in particular produced a benign, gently flavored rosé that slid down comfortably with a good lunch of lobster salad, or with the crisp and very fresh vegetables served raw with a house-made mayonnaise dip. They crunched between the teeth and had the added benefit of making the eater feel virtuous at not having had the hearty sandwich on the delicious locally baked bread many others were tucking into.

The lemonade came immediately, along with a bowl of ice and a spoon so he might help himself, decide how cold he wanted it, how diluted. He took a sip, and nodded to the waiter, who asked if there would be anything else. The waiter was told that there was not, but that he was expecting someone. He should be shown immediately to the table.

The Boss's original Russian name was Boris Boronovsky, which he had changed some time ago to a more satisfactorily acceptable European Bruce Bergen, though he looked nothing like a "Bruce." He had a massive build, exactly, he had been told, like that of a Cossack from the Steppes: mighty on a horse, saber in hand, ready to take on the enemy. Yet his face was lean, with craggy cheekbones and deep-set eyes, lined from a lifetime of scouting for danger, which was all around. In his world it was anyway. And now at the international property level where land was fought over for the millions it would bring, that danger was ever-present. He knew always to look over his shoulder.

The Boss certainly took on the enemy, though not in an overtly aggressive fashion. He was more discreet, more subtle, more specific in his methods. He had always known, even as a child growing up—or more like existing—in the cold cabin outside the town of Minsk in Belarus, that he was destined for better things. No forest cabin for him, no logging trees, risking life and limb with a power saw; no dragging great lumps of wood still oozing sap onto a tractor so old it no longer functioned and was pulled instead by two donkeys with long faces like biblical animals in Renaissance frescoes. There was just something about those donkeys that made Boris think that, like in the paintings, they should have golden halos over their heads. Sometimes there was an unexpected tenderness in him, odd in such a brutal man.

The donkeys worked hard, were obedient to his commands, alert when he gave them food, drank from the stone trough when he permitted them to stop, thin sides shivering, ribs sticking out. Until one day they were not pulling hard anymore, their heads drooped with weariness, too weak to go on. He shot them where they stood, butchered them, sold the meat door-to-door in the town as fresh venison. Nobody knew the difference, or if they did they never said because Boris was intimidating, with his height, his massive build, his intense dark stare.

It wasn't long before he realized the power that stare and his very presence brought to any scene, whether it was the local market or the city streets. He was from a poor family who'd given him a brief education and strived to elevate him in society. He would certainly have become moderately successful, a big fish in a small pond, but the one element in Boris's character that no one perceived but himself was that he was capable of doing anything. Anything at all to further his ascent into the larger world he knew existed and that he wanted to be part of. More than part of; he wanted to own it. As he wanted to own the women in his life. Besides, he enjoyed intimidating women, liked to see fear in their eyes. It pleased him. There was only one way to leave, and it was not out the front door.

It had taken several years existing in a number of Ukrainian towns, then on through Poland, Hungary, Croatia, and ultimately France, before he achieved his goals. And the place where he was most comfortable, of all the homes he owned, was the sprawling villa overlooking the Mediterranean in the hills in the South of France. Which is where he was now, in Antibes, at the café, sipping a lemonade iced just sufficiently to his taste, awaiting the arrival of the man known merely as "the Russian."

Everybody in the Boss's world had a name that was not the one they were given by their parents at birth. Those were long forgotten, buried like their enemies, or their victims, long ago. The Boss had given up carrying out any such distasteful tasks himself. Now, he employed men like the Russian to do them for him.

But the Russian was late. The Boss tapped his fingers impatiently on the table and the waiter popped up immediately next to him. He waved him off as he saw the Russian wending his way through the tables to where he was sitting.

He was a plain man, undistinguished in any way, which was crucial to his job. Nobody ever recognized him, nobody so much as remembered him. Medium height, medium hair, maybe receding a bit, glasses sometimes with wire rims, sometimes horn-rims, sometimes no rims at all. Often a Panama hat, open-neck shirt, never a tie unless it was a city job. Inexpensive jacket but not too obviously cheap, after all he made good money doing what he did. Didn't like to flaunt it on the job, was all.

He took a seat opposite the Boss, offered his hand, which the Boss did not shake. Stung, the Russian called over the waiter, ordered a dirty martini, two olives. It was barely eleven-thirty

A.M. and the Boss did not like it. A man who drank could be a dangerous man. He waved the waiter back, canceled the order, said to bring a double espresso and be sharp about it.

The Russian made no complaint, he knew better. He sat quietly, listening, as the Boss told him what he wanted done.

"There is a house in the hills nearby. In fact you can see it from here." He pointed across the arc of the bay to the greenery beyond, and a glimpse of a pink stucco villa. "In that house is a painting. Small. The artist's name is Turner. The woman who owned the house died recently."

The Russian nodded. He knew about Jolly Matthews's death.

"I immediately made an offer to buy the whole property, the hectares of land adjoining it, plus the contents, including artworks, most of which in my mind are worthless, but that the old woman enjoyed all her life. She was a social acquaintance, known to all as Aunt Jolly though her real name was Juliet Matthews. When she passed, I made contact with the legal representatives of the heir, a woman by the name of Mirabella Matthews. A writer of some kind of entertaining novels." The Boss was a snob about both art and literature, though he scarcely read anything other than the local newspaper, the *Nice-Matin*, and the *Wall Street Journal*.

"The heir, through her representative, has

refused to sell. I wish to build a fourteen-story condo on that property. I increased my offer considerably. Meanwhile, through subtle means, I found out the details of the contents, and that the one piece of real value is that painting. I want it for my collection. I cannot get it by legal means. Therefore, I am asking you to take care of this task for me."

The Russian nodded. It was the kind of work he did. None of it was legal, none of it could be mentioned, most of it was lucrative. He had removed jewels from vaults, pearls from necks, cars from underground garages. Everything had a value and there was always somebody willing to pay.

"I'll get you the painting," he said.

The Boss named a price. The Russian shook his head. "It's not the value of the painting," he said, then added, "sir," as compensation for what he was about to say. "It's what it's worth to you."

"It is worth everything," the Boss said. And it was. He wanted that land and the painting the bitch, Jolly Matthews, had denied him in her lifetime. He would have both now that she was dead. Of course the police were looking into her death, and rightly so, because obviously, with a knife in her back, she had been murdered.

Perhaps a robbery, the police were speculating. Maybe the house was turned over, that sort of thing. They'd never trace that knife, though. There were millions like it and the Russian knew every source. Jolly Matthews had gotten in the Boss's way, triumphed over him in life but not in death. All he had to do now was get his hands on her property.

Architectural plans were already drawn up, documents were ready to be submitted for planning permission, already promised and paid for, of course. Millions would be made by everybody, though the green hillside would disappear under a plague of small villas, most of which would be bought by people who intended them to be rented out and everybody knew that in a couple of years rental properties often became shabby and neglected, and would downgrade the area.

The Boss did not care about the future. He would make money from each part of the deal: the sale of the land, the construction of the buildings, the sale of those properties, the infrastructure—roads, water, electricity. And to top it all would be the fourteen-story apartment building, the max allowed even to him in the restricted area, and the top three floors, which would become for a few years his new home. His would be a magnificent view down to the sea, of the yachts, the palm trees, a view better than most everyone's. Not all though, because this was a rich man's playground, yet certainly better than many of his soon-to-be neighbors.

And to highlight it, he wanted the Turner. Of

course he could buy any painting he desired, and had. His walls were already adorned with a couple of Picassos, maybe not the best because they were, even for him, hard to come by and usually went through private, almost secretive sales. He had a few Impressionists, as well as some Italians: a Raphael, a Caravaggio, whatever his advisors recommended. None of them impressed him but they were expected of a man in his position. This Turner painting had become an obsession and he was a man who got what he wanted.

Right now, the thing he liked best of all that he owned was the fifty-foot Riva he sailed himself, at top speed the length of the coast from Marseille to Menton, leaving other boats awash in the great surge of its wake. There'd been a few insurance claims as a result but of course he'd settled quietly, out of court. In that sense, he was a man of his word, and held respect for his fellow sailors.

He was aware though, of how impressive he looked to those in the passing boats, with his great height, his white captain's cap with the gold braid and navy-blue anchor, his sun-browned chest, shaved of hair so he did not quite resemble a bear, which is what some woman had told him, mocking him, while he ran his heavy hands over her own lithe body.

Actually, he had liked the comparison; he'd chuckled over it, looking at himself in the mirror over the bed, a great bear, full of power. That was him.

And he wanted his condos on that land, and the painting, the Turner, on his wall. Everything Jolly Matthews had denied him in life would be his now that she was dead. And if that meant removing Mirabella Matthews from the scene, so be it.

2

Mirabella

My name is Mirabella Matthews, a name you might recognize as I am a well-known author of suspense novels. I'm on the train from Paris to Nice, attempting to ignore the fraught-looking young blonde sitting opposite, and whose problems I certainly do not want to hear, though I can tell she is dying to unburden herself. I turn my head away, hoping not to be the one who has to hear it all.

I am returning once again to the scene of the crime: the villa I had visited several times and which I have inherited upon the sudden and unexplained death of my Aunt Jolly, a tragedy that is taking me from an apartment in London to the shores of the South of France. They have not yet found out who killed her, nor have they discovered why.

She was simply gone, "in the twinkling of an eye," as they say, and I became a rich woman. I had not always seen eye to eye with Aunt Jolly, who disapproved of my youthful antics. She once invited me to stay and I stood her up for a more tempting offer from a man I could not resist. More fool me. It didn't last. Aunt Jolly's attention did. I learned the hard way, but then, don't we all?

The villa lured me with a magic my family home in Scotland never had. "Home" in my childhood was a Victorian turreted redbrick monstrosity, from which I longed to escape, especially after Mom "went over the wall," as Dad succinctly put it, with an American tourist, leaving him to cope with an obstreperous and angry ten-year-old.

It was my job to help clean out the stables, morning and evening. The horses knew I was afraid of them and would lean on me, trapping me against the wall, or do a nifty little back-kick that invariably got my shins. I hated it, but I liked the outfit, the tight little cream jodhpurs, the black jacket, and cute velvet helmet.

I guess when Dad had had enough, he sent me off to live for a while with what he termed "foster parents," though they were no relation and simply made a living from taking in boarders like me. Life there was not much different, except it was in Wyoming. Both were equally cold in winter.

After a couple of years they sent me back, having also had enough, I suppose. Back in Scotland, I wore a pleated tartan kilt fastened with an oversized safety pin to protect my modesty from the everlasting wind that blew it apart, displaying more, I'm sure, than anyone ever wanted to see. I also wore heavy woolen shooting socks, the kind made specially for men and days out in the woods and fields, gun in hand, ready to murder a few innocent pheasant, that I refused to eat when they showed up later on the dinner table. Every Sunday the family attended church where a lady in a feathered hat pounded out "Abide with Me" on an organ with many pipes. I can still sing every verse.

Needless to say it didn't last long. London called. And boys—well, men really.

In London I went through my gauzy, "hippie" phase, all fluttering skirts and softly draped tops with a large fake jewel or two prominently displayed on my bosom. This was when I met husband number one, about whom the less said the better. His only excuse was that he was as young as I was.

Then it was on to smart little suits and heels, very businesslike. I took a job as a receptionist at an agency for actors where I met some fun people, all of whom were as broke as I was. I also met husband number two. An actor of course.

After him, and I was still only twenty years old, came the "debutante" era: the dirndl skirt, the little white frilly collared shirt, the cashmere cardigan, and the flats, with a bag big enough to pack a weekend's clothes in, which I often did. Along with that look came husband number three. I never could resist a man with charm and he had it in spades. He also had money but I got none of it when I left, being too goody-goody to take any man's money. "Fool," was more like it. Obviously, I was having trouble "finding myself."

A couple years later I took the train to Paris, and then to Nice and Aunt Jolly. Well, that was *then*. And now is now.

And now, I guess, I'm just me. Or who I perceive I am currently. Like the characters in the books I write, I can change with the wind.

My Aunt Jolly was in her seventies, or thereabouts. We didn't actually know for sure because she never let on. Looking at her, she might have been any age between fifty and seventy; she was of medium height but stood tall. Her large, curious brown eyes were always interested in other people and she loved a good gossip, though never of the mean sort. She was a whiz at bridge and an evening tippler—two glasses of champagne—at precisely five each evening. A giver of good parties where the food was important and the wine was local, brought down the hill to the Villa Romantica on a wheelbarrow from the grower. There was always music in the background, along with the sound of the sea and the happy blur of conversation.

Elegant, chatty, pretty, Aunt Jolly was a delight to be with. Not a proper "aunt," more likely a second cousin of my late mother's, a couple of times removed, but beloved in the family anyway.

Jolly had never married, though there were

"gentlemen" as she demurely called them, and young though I was when I met her, I still remember that when I kissed her she smelled delightfully of some citrusy musky perfume that clung to her clothes and made me want to bury my head in her shoulder, simply to drink it in.

"Quite a girl" was how Aunt Jolly had described me, and I had always believed that. Oh, and she was rich.

I'm writing a book about Aunt Jolly's murder, though so far I have no ending since there seems no way to know the truth. Now, though, I am wondering if I might find something: a clue here and there, a word dropped in my ear, a conversation avoided, a meeting canceled. Normal enough day-to-day events, you might think, yet something had gone horribly wrong.

Verity

I'm on the same Paris-to-Nice train, looking at my opposite neighbor. She is wearing a brown jumper, a too-long and very crumpled linen skirt, sensible black shoes with a cross strap, and little white lace gloves. No, not lace, they are crochet, ending just above the wrist bone in a tiny ruffle. She's not "made-up" but certainly powdered, and with a pale lipstick in entirely the wrong shade. Who wears that pastel pink anymore, unless they are from the 1960s, and this woman is not as old as that. She's maybe forty; certainly old enough to know how to dress for travel: a white tee and black pants with a simple cashmere cardigan thrown over the shoulders would be better. And if she can't afford pricey cashmere, well, then, a nice wool—you can get them anywhere now, even really cheap at the market in your local town. And her hair! Christ, the hair! Wild and red enough to be fake, though I guess it's not, and shiny enough to have been just washed and slathered with too much conditioner.

Ah, now she throws a glance at me, covertly inspecting me too. And what does she see? A blonde with her hair pulled back so tight it makes angles out of the cheekbones and also shows that the forehead is too high—can't help that, my dear, it's the genes; Dad had that forehead. I got Mom's legs though, long and with skinny thighs that look good in a tight skirt, such as I am wearing now; white Lycra, thoroughly unsuitable for a train journey, or any journey for that matter, but it was what came to hand this morning when I made my escape. From him. I wonder where he is, what happened when he saw I had finally bolted, made good on my threats. "Fuck her," he probably said. *The bastard.*

I stare at the woman, wondering what she is thinking about me. Can she read my thoughts? Read *me?*

Mirabella

What I am thinking about her is that she should not pull her hair back like that; she has a lovely face but it loses its sweetness when the skin is so taut over cheekbones I would give a million to possess. And by the way, I have a million and more, so that's no idle threat.

She looks like a runaway to me, clothes thrown together in a mad, anger-inflamed rush, fling all the rest into a bag, sweep out the underwear drawer, the sweater shelves, the jeans, which in fact I am surprised she is not wearing; she's definitely a jeans kinda girl. Good hair stylist, color perfect, just that proper shade of cornsilk with a paler strand or so around the face. Couldn't have been done better. No makeup. In too much of a hurry, as I thought before. Doesn't need it, lucky bitch; I can't set foot outside without my eyebrows carefully patted on with a brown dust then smoothed over with a wax pencil. See me without them and you'll think you're looking at a rabbit, or a mole perhaps. But my eyes are a nice blue, not deep, not pale, just, well, *blue.*

Now that Aunt Jolly has passed I'm the rich-bitch owner of a villa, and expected to behave like the discreet society woman I'm not, though I'll never wear a hat to those dull luncheons where the aim is purportedly to raise funds for starving children in whatever country is fashionable at the moment, but whose real purpose is to show off the latest outfit from the newest hot designer, and if every woman doesn't throw away those fuckin' red-soled shoes I swear to God I will kill them all. Same with that dreary handbag, y'know the one I mean. Copies gone rampant. I think they pick 'em up over the border in Italy for next to nothing.

And then of course, there are my gloves. Crochet, handmade by a local village woman who does beautiful work. I always wear them. It's not a habit, or for fashion; it's a necessity.

3

Verity

My name is Verity Real, though I'm changing that ASAP to Unreal. No, just joking.

I'm sneaking a look at Miss Frump again. This "chick"—I only call her that in jest, she is so far from being "a chick" it's laughable—is sitting there, her crochet-gloved hands folded neatly in her lap, with, I notice, an enormous sapphire ring worn on the middle finger of the right hand. Now that bit of ostentation is a surprise. I should not have thought she could afford such a thing, but of course, like the handbags, fakes come "good" as well as cheap these days. Her eyes are closed, she's not even looking out the window now, certainly not looking at me, though I know she is aware I am looking at her.

"So?" I finally say loudly. "What's up?"

She makes no answer. It's as though I'm talking to somebody not there. Without so much as a glance at me, she takes a notebook from her bag, the kind schoolchildren use, a composition book I suppose it's known as, then shuffles through the bag, a soft black leather drawstring of the type I personally find so difficult to find anything in, because it always seems to have dropped into the muddle at the bottom. Still, she manages to bring out a pen. A proper pen, at that. What used to be called, and probably still is, a fountain pen, which I seem to remember long ago had to be filled from a bottle of ink. Who in the world has seen a bottle of ink in how many years? *Certainement pas moi.*

Sorry, I slipped into French, not exactly my second language but a language I use badly, for effect, sometimes. When necessary. Or when I feel like bitching. I find French a good language for bitching, *trés* expressive while sounding sweet at the same time. The perfect language in fact; you can do whatever you want with it, unlike English, which always says precisely what it means even if you don't exactly mean what you said.

I watch her open the composition book and carefully smooth down a clean page. I notice there's no writing on the previous pages. She begins to write—smooth, firm, precise strokes, a pretty looped cursive. *Violet* ink! Haven't seen that in forever either. I'm trying to read it upside down, dying to know what's so important she has to write it now, immediately. Her eyes flick up and meet my guilty gaze.

"Oh, sorry," I manage to mumble, feeling the blush heat my cheeks, something I haven't felt in many a moon. Blushing was from my innocent era, a few lifetimes ago. Not that I'm old, a mere twenty-two—well, twenty-five to be honest and if I can't be honest now, when can I? Anyhow, lying about one's age when you are only in your twenties can lead to disaster later when you start totting up the years. Dumb, in fact. Besides, she's older, certainly not the same age as me. She probably would have written, "the same age as I." Or is that not correct grammar? I know I learned it at that smart boarding school I attended, though I'm not sure I learned much else except how babies were conceived. Not by me, I hasten to add, but you know how that young girly conversation goes, somebody always knew somebody who'd actually done it, though never themselves, of course. It went down well with the passed-around bottle of Stoli sugared with pineapple juice that tasted vile but we all pretended to love. Sooo sophisticated.

She smiled at my blush and to my surprise leaned across and offered her hand.

"I'm Mirabella Matthews."

The crochet glove was crisp, her hand cold.

"Oh my God, of course you are," I said, coming to my senses. "The writer. Oh my God, I just love your books."

She leaned back in her seat, still holding the pen over the empty page of the notebook. "Indeed. And which one did you particularly enjoy?"

Christ, she had me. I knew she was a bitch, just looking at her, so calm and friggin' collected, and full of herself, meaning her "self-importance." Now I really was being bitchy; she had not even so much as looked at me, not given me any cause for complaint, all she'd done was ask which book I'd read and of course I had not read a single one.

"You've got me there," I said, deciding honesty was the best policy, surprised when she laughed.

She put the pen carefully in the fold of the notebook, then ran a hand through that dense red mass of hair, a nimbus, an aureole. . . . I was getting poetic about a complete stranger who was looking at me with that quizzical expression that suggested perhaps I might be mad. Which I am, in a way. At least today I am. The runaway wife, the rich-bitch lonely girl, the envied one who has it all.

"I don't, you know," I said, answering some unspoken question. "Have it all, I mean."

She nodded. "Few of us do."

"I mean . . . well, I just walked out on my husband. Ran, actually. . . ."

"Running's much better, once you've made up your mind. I wish I'd done that, I should have run away from all three of my husbands. You'd have had a way to go to catch up, if you see what I mean."

"Ohh, ohh. I do. I so admire you."

"I can't imagine why. Meanwhile, where exactly are you running to?"

I gestured to the small bag nestled between my feet. Obviously there wasn't enough in it for proper runaway stuff, not "long-term," so to speak. "But now I want it to be forever," I said, fat tears running unexpectedly down my unmade-up face. "I can't ever go back to him."

She stared thoughtfully at me, assessing me, head to toe, exactly the way I had done her earlier. "I don't think it's safe to run away and not know where you are heading. Dangerous, in fact. Especially in your state of mind."

"But I couldn't stand him anymore." I blurted out the whole sordid story, my betrayal by the cheating husband. "I believed in him," I said. "I loved him. He was handsome, so charming, I was proud to be the girl on his arm. He knew how to make me feel good, y'know what I mean?" I said, "I have no money in my pocket, he's canceled all the credit cards. I have no jewelry to sell because I'd stupidly left it all behind in a gesture of defiance I'm now regretting."

She said, "What's your name?"

I told her, Verity. I saw something in her eyes, a warm woman-to-woman understanding.

Still I was surprised when she said, "Well, Verity, why not come stay with me? 'Til we can get you settled," she added with a slight smile to make sure I understood she was not offering me charity or taking me to the cops or the lost wives' home.

"I'll be alone this weekend, as it happens, and my villa will feel empty with only myself to rattle around in it."

Rattle around? Didn't that imply "large"? But that word, "alone," was scary, I mean did she have "designs" on me, or what?

"Think about it," she said. "Take your time, we won't be there for another half hour." And she took up her pen again and began to write.

Ten minutes ticked by. Another ten. I still had my Cartier watch with the diamond bezel. I hadn't been dumb enough to get rid of that because I always needed to know the time.

"So, alright," I said, loftily. Then, realizing I was being rude, added more humbly, "Thank you, I'd like to accept your offer. In fact I don't know what I would do otherwise, I didn't plan . . ."

"I know how it is." She smiled as she closed her book, put the pen back in her bag, tightened the black leather string around its top, and smoothed the crochet gloves she was remarkably still wearing. The sapphire ring glinted darkly in the sunlight. "I promise everything will be alright."

"I'm sure it will," I said, remembering my manners as a well-brought-up girl. "Young woman," that is, though right now she made me feel like a child again. And somewhere deep inside that felt so good.

"My car is at the station," she said. "We'll be at the villa before you know it."

I could not believe the car belonged to a woman who wore crochet gloves, no makeup and her hair in a red tangle: a gorgeous dark-blue Maserati GranTurismo convertible with cream leather seats hand-stitched to immaculate perfection. A chauffeur stood by, while a second man waited alongside a small white Citroen, ready to drive the chauffeur back while Mirabella drove herself.

"Thank you, Alfred," she said as the chauffeur opened the door to the Maserati for her and she slid behind the wheel. "My friend will be accompanying me," she added and he walked quickly around to the passenger side, took my bag, and held open the door.

She waved lightly to him, and he disappeared rapidly in the Citroen to wherever perfect servants disappear, into the ether perhaps, to be called on when required by Madame, though this "Madame" did not seem particularly demanding. I thought it nice of her to speak to him softly like that, and with a slight smile, though I guess he'd expected to leave her to go wherever she wanted in the gorgeous Maserati.

"Get in, Verity," she said, hitching up her too-long linen skirt, a foot already on the pedal. This woman waited for no one. I was in that car so quickly I had no time even to consider what I was doing, who I might be with—a kidnapper trading in sex slaves, a serial killer preying on young women, or a madwoman who wore a ring outside her gloves. Her flaming red hair flew behind her in the wind as she drove far too fast when we got to the corniche road that wrapped itself around the base of the mountains on one side and fell into the canyon and the sea a hundred feet below on the other. Ohh, that blue-blue sea, the blue of her eyes.

I crouched lower, clinging to the cream leather door so as not to be catapulted to my doom. We were following a gray car, a flattened, close-to-the-earth shape that suggested a Porsche, and which was itself following a small green car. My eyes were fixed on the Porsche and the road ahead; I was practically driving for her, edging into that curve, heading for the next bend.

Our eyes met in the mirror. Her face was pale, her mouth set.

"Take a look behind you," she said.

I looked. Nothing there. Wait. Yes, a motorcycle zapped around the bend. Black. My ex happened to be a motorcycle fan and I recognized the Ducati Monster by its exposed engine and frame, a classic, geared for speed and elegance, as was its rider, all black leathers and black steel helmet. There was no way to see his face, tell who he was, but he was certainly on our tail.

"Jesus," I said, the wobble in my voice telling how nervous I was. "What's up with him anyway?"

She did not answer but her foot pressed all the way down and we were off like a rocket. I closed my eyes and thought about praying. I repented my sins rapidly; I should not have left my husband even if he did behave like a bastard. I should not have called him a bastard. We went quicker and I thought even quicker: I should have taken the damn money, taken all the jewelry, gotten a good lawyer and sued the hell out of him. Instead I was going to end my days the victim of a madwoman whose red hair and crochet gloves should have given me due warning. I had ignored that gut instinct and now I was to pay the price.

"Hang on, my dear," she said, taking a hand off the wheel to brush her hair out of her eyes. I held my breath. Two hands were better than one even if it was a no-win situation. I decided to close my eyes. No point in watching the Maserati compete with the Ducati and the Porsche and a rapidly approaching sixteen-wheeler for road ownership when it was all doomed to disaster anyway. I did like this car though, loved the smooth feel of the leather under my desperate clutching hand, the way my head fit on the perfectly adjusted headrest. I even liked, no, at this moment *I loved* the way the seat belt gripped my chest, though I'd probably have no tits left whenever it stopped. If it stopped. I hung on.

And then the Ducati roared past, the small green car disappeared, the road stopped being underneath us, and we were flying, a glorious dark blue bird, smooth as on a test drive, through the air into the depths below.

Somewhere, somehow, out of the corner of my eye before I shut out everything and fled into unconsciousness, I glimpsed the Ducati tearing up that stretch of the corniche road, its faceless leather-clad driver speeding away without so much as a glance our way. The Porsche was gone, the green car was gone, he was gone, and so, I believed were we. I did not feel it would be to a better place. But then, I didn't have much time to think about anything.

4
Chad Prescott

The flight from Paris's Charles de Gaulle to Nice's Côte d'Azur was delayed. That was what Chad Prescott was told when he disembarked from his third flight in twenty-four hours, starting out in a small and very ancient Fokker biplane in a jungle airstrip in the Amazon that took him to Manaus, and from there, on a six-seater Lear to São Paulo. Which was where he had started out to begin with, several months ago.

It seemed longer than that, he thought wearily, taking a seat at the bar in the first-class lounge and downing a beer, his first in a long time. Well, his first *cold* beer. He'd had others but those he'd drunk in locations where refrigeration was erratic, if not completely unknown. He had the generator in his truck, of course, but that was used for medical situations, its energy not to be wasted on simply chilling a beer.

He ordered a ham-and-cheese sandwich. It came on a soggy roll but still tasted better than anything he recalled eating recently. There had never been much time to think of anything other than the job at hand.

Chad was what he'd always termed a "medical

man." Born in Chicago, where he later attended med school, to a French mother and a U.D. engineer father, who had died together in a train crash in Europe, he was used to international travel from childhood, to calling the place he happened to be at that moment, "home." He was a surgeon specializing in facial reconstruction, which is what took him twice a year to South America, Africa, the Congo—you name it—and where he operated on children with cleft palates, or without noses, or whose jaws were malformed. Job satisfaction rated high on his list, especially when he saw the amazed joy on the young patients' faces when they looked at the results in the mirror. He might not be able to give them beauty, but he gave them normality. It was enough.

His other job was as a consultant at a top Paris hospital, where he kept an apartment on the Left Bank. In Paris he needed to be near the river Seine, to keep it somehow always in view or at least around the corner, a walk from the Rue Jacob, or Bonaparte, or the Café de Flore. Sometimes he thought he lived on the terrace at the Flore; he couldn't count the hours he must have spent in those uncomfortable faux-cane chairs, sipping a glass of wine or a coffee, just watching the world go by. The contrast to the jungles of his other life—his real life as he thought of it—was extreme and he relished it.

Now though, he was heading for the place he loved best of all: his villa in the South of France where he was fortunate enough to own several acres—hectares as they were called—that protected the privacy he needed. Plus, he now owned the villa next door and its land, left to him by his old friend and neighbor, Jolly Matthews, who'd sent him a letter to that effect a couple of months before she died so violently, so tragically. He'd liked the old girl, they'd enjoyed many a pleasant evening together, conversation and the wine flowing, her tales of the past, of the famous musical star, the beauteous Jerusha, and life as it was then, before the crowds and the airports and the hustle and bustle.

He planned to invite guests to his villa, old friends, not many but enough; bistros would be visited; a swim in the cool blue Mediterranean of an early morning; good hot French coffee; a croissant rich with butter; perhaps even a mango from the tree he'd planted himself five years ago, if mangoes were in season. He wasn't sure. Out there, in the jungle villages, he kind of lost track of how the seasons passed, unless it was the rainy season and he found himself engulfed in mud. That was the way life was, but his work gave him the energy, the strength to go on. Still, it was good to be going home to perfect peace and quiet.

His flight was finally announced and they boarded. He was thankful he had spent the previous night in a hotel where he'd had the opportunity to take a proper shower and shave, though his hair badly needed cutting. He chopped at it himself every now and again. It was dark blond, floppy, thick, and dead straight.

He was tall, six-two, perhaps overly lean, but with a tight body gained from hard work and the deprivation of the jungle locations where he spent a great deal of his time, often forced to operate in the flickering light from a generator that sometimes went out completely.

He was respectable enough now, in his khakis and a white polo shirt picked up in the airport shop, his trusty Nikes, and a backpack so ancient it was certainly not recognizable as coming from Loewe, the prestigious Spanish leather company. His face was lightly tanned, well-seasoned he called it, laughing at himself, which made the lines around his dark blue eyes crease up and a furrow appear across his brow. He did not consider himself good-looking, and had no vanity. He was a medical man first and foremost.

Twice a year he allowed himself to "come home." The villa had been in his family for five generations, and was smaller than might be expected, never added to, never changed. It was basically still the simple white farmhouse it had always been, though now with modern comforts, like showers and electricity and a swimming pool. And a sort of beauty because Chad was a civilized man who hung his paintings on the walls and spent many an hour admiring them, and who filled his library shelves with rare editions as well as with paperback detective stories of the old-fashioned kind, which he found entertaining.

The villa itself was built from local stone for the first floor, and white painted wood for the second. There were no dormers and only a single chimney, venting the fireplace that divided the living area from the kitchen, an odd arrangement he found completely satisfactory because it saved time and effort. Log fires needed fueling and in winter he'd often fall asleep in front of the flames, drawing back his energy, his life.

The only problem with his villa was the driveway, which was shared with the house next door, the Villa Romantica. A dispute had been going on for decades about this, beginning with the original neighbor, Jerusha, the famed singer, actress, artiste supreme, and *woman-de-luxe*, mistress to many, it was rumored, and a superstar of her era. It was still unresolved but now that Chad owned the property, it was no longer an issue.

The flight attendant, a tall young woman with smiling dark eyes, showed him to his first-class seat, took his ratty old jacket—he had not had time to think about buying a new one—and offered him a glass of champagne, which, to his surprise, he found himself accepting. It was Taittinger, he noted with approval. He had not had that taste, felt that spritz on his tongue, the bubbles hitting the back of his throat in their sparkling way, in a long time. He enjoyed it but did not have a second glass. In fact, he extended his seat, turned out the light, put on an eye mask, and fell asleep.

He slept through the entire flight, waking only when the nice attendant shook him gently to warn him they would be landing in fifteen minutes. He went to the tiny bathroom, washed the sleep from his eyes, ran his hands through his hair, which looked even worse under the harsh light, straightened the collar of his polo shirt, and went back to his seat, where he confirmed on his cell phone that the car awaited him.

He knew Nice Côte d'Azur Airport like the back of his hand; he'd been using it for years, from back when it was still merely a small holiday link to the Mediterranean. Now it was a main destination from many countries. He always liked arriving there, with the quick glimpse of the blue sea, the avenues of palms, all long skinny trunks with a fluff of leaves at the top, the grainy pebbly strip of beach scattered with sunburned bodies in summer and a few strollers at the edge of the tiny waves off-season, when the beach shanties selling Fanta and ice cream and dried-up sandwiches in plastic bags were closed. He liked all of it. Anytime. It was home.

Chad came from a family of privilege with enough funds to maintain the Paris apartment, as well as his small villa. Even so, he remained a loner, though he did show up for the local cocktail parties in aid of what he considered "good causes," to which he contributed what he could. His sole luxury was buying artworks for his small "home"—though when he was asked if he was an art expert he always said he was merely a medical man.

At the airport, he picked up his Mercedes. It made him think of the odd way the car came to be named. Austrian diplomat and businessman, Emil Jellinek, had raced custom-built Gottlieb Daimler cars that he named after his daughter, Mercédès.

The car had been left at the airport by Chad's caretaker and guy-of-all-work, who had been with him for the past ten years and knew how to keep out of the way and how to be there when needed.

First though, Chad decided to stop for a coffee—a good, rich cup of French coffee—at a seafront place where he could sit at a terrace table and watch the Mediterranean change color, the people flaunting their bodies on the pebbly beach, and the world going by. The contrast to his work life never failed to amuse him.

And the fact was it made him happy. He was coming home.

Later, fortified by the coffee and a butter-rich croissant, he turned the Mercedes onto the corniche road, the very same road where the famous fifties movie star, Grace Kelly, had met her untimely death and that wound between the steep hill and the canyon. There was a smile on his face, dark glasses filtered the sunlight, the windows were open to the breeze.

He spotted the dark blue Maserati and the two cars in front of it, and the black Ducati with the black-helmeted biker that roared past him. And, as if in slow motion, he saw the Maserati with a woman at the wheel and a blond passenger next to her spin off the road and into the depths of that canyon.

Chad braked hard, got on his mobile, and called for medical help and the gendarmes. Then he got out of the car and stood looking down at the wreck. It was impossible to access on foot; they would need a helicopter. He remained at the side of the road, awaiting the ambulances and the cops.

5
Mirabella

When I came to, I found we were perched precariously, right-side-up, halfway down the canyon. How we had not tumbled to the bottom was a miracle, and we would need another miracle to get us out of there.

The car wobbled under me, then settled itself on the rugged chunks of rock that had stopped our fall. I put up a hand to sweep the hair from my brow, tugged at the seat belt that was cutting into my chest and which had probably saved my life, opened my eyes, and took stock. I could move my head, my arms, my legs.

I glanced sideways at my blond passenger. Poor girl, how unfortunate that she had accepted a lift. Running from a husband she called a bastard was one thing; facing her demise in a car crash with a total stranger was another. The first event you might survive; the second was unlikely, though thank God she did not appear to be bleeding all over the white leather.

Thoughts spun through my head. I had been forced off the road by a mad biker, who presumably wanted me dead. But why? Perhaps it wasn't *me* the Ducati rider was after, it might have been the small green car in front, driving slowly and a bit erratically along the dangerously winding road, veering over the center line practically under the sixteen-wheeler coming at us. A shiver ran through me as I recalled the Ducati shooting past, swinging sideways at the small car, until with a shriek of rubber on cement it had spun off the road and over the edge, and then the Ducati hit me and took off, faster, as they said of Superman, than a speeding bullet.

Oh, Jesus, had I just witnessed a murder? Or was it me he had meant to kill and gotten somebody else by mistake? But who would want *me* dead? Or the young blonde sitting next to me? Surely not even a bastard husband could want *her* dead.

No, it had to be *me,* the "rich bitch" in the expensive car, the woman with all that money she'd not even earned, simply inherited from an aunt who'd died violently and mysteriously. Me, Mirabella, the woman who now owned the villa where we were heading before this event. I could not bring myself to call the dangerous act "attempted murder." Not yet, anyway. I would have to deal with that later, try to think of who might have something to gain from my death.

Meanwhile, I had to get my head together, find my phone, get help for the other car, though there was unlikely to be any reception down here. Yet, wait, up at the top of the cliff, faces peered over the broken edge-rail, horror written all over them. I put up an arm, waved, saw them flinch with shock, then rush about, obviously trying to get help. I must wait; later I would find out who had tried to kill me. Or Verity.

The rescuers were soon here; some clambering on ropes down the slope while others circled in a small open-sided helicopter, swirling dust into my eyes so I could hardly see. "Saviors," I should really call them, because I knew in a very short while the Maserati would have continued its tumble into what seemed a bottomless canyon, where even finding our bodies would have been doubtful. Probably been just bits and pieces by then anyway, and since we both seemed currently to be all in one piece, I allowed myself the luxury of tears. In fact I was crying my eyes out, in front of all those TV and press cameras that suddenly appeared out of nowhere, the way they always do at scenes of disaster, though I doubted my demise would have counted as "a disaster," except to me.

I wanted a few more years if only to get to the bottom of what really happened to Aunt Jolly and catch the perpetrator, because I was sure as hell he was now also after me. But why? The same old same, of course: money or sex. I didn't think the sex was appropriate for Aunt Jolly so it had to be the money. The inheritance, which perhaps someone felt more entitled to than they thought I was. Well now, I wondered who that could be. Whoever it was would stoop to murder. Did I even know anybody like that? Of course I did not. This perpetrator had to be a stranger. The thought was even more terrifying than if it really was somebody I knew. Didn't they say better the devil you know than the devil you don't?

Suddenly a couple of soldiers in khaki jump-suits and rugged boots were dangling over us from a helicopter. One took Verity. I reached up to the other. God, I was so relieved that amid my tears I even kissed him; well, kissed his stubbly cheek anyway, saw him grin from the corner of my eye, heard myself laughing and sobbing at the same time as, terrified in his arms, I swung back up the canyon and miraculously was shoved into the hovering helicopter, rotors whirling, and looking to me like a bird of good omen. And oh boy, did I need one.

Minutes later I was on the ground again, laid out on a rough blanket that scratched my bare legs, and a man who said he was a doctor was leaning over me, checking my racing pulse, my thundering heart, my legs, arms, head. I hurt everywhere and just wished he would go away, stop bothering me. Though I did have sufficient wits left to notice how good-looking he was. Trust me to find a handsome doc when I most needed one.

He said, “You’re going to be alright, you’ll make it.”

“Oh, go away,” I said.

“Right,” he said. And he signaled to the ambulance driver and left.

Aunt Jolly, wherever you are now, I know what happened was because of you. I will use all of this, I will find out how, why, where, when; I will avenge you, my poor dear Aunt Jolly, so happy in your lovely Mediterranean aerie, needing no one but your dog and your cat and the tiny canary bird that seemed to live on forever. Its name is Sing, I remembered it as I flew like that canary out of the canyon to safety. It sang all your life. I hoped it was still singing, though you are gone.

6

A detective came to the hospital to question us, though Verity and I were in shock, still disbelieving that someone had run us off that road and halfway down a canyon.

"It's a miracle Dr. Prescott found you and that you are alive," the detective said in English.

He introduced himself as Colonel Rufus Barrada. He was fortyish, attractive, stocky, thickset, with a stubbled chin, deep eyes you could not read, and a thatch of dark untidy hair after he took his cap off. Those eyes bored into me from beneath brows as thick and untidy as his hair and I knew I was looking at a man who was not prepared to believe what I had to say, and that he thought the accident was my fault. I recalled the motorbike rider, the green car, and also—I could not help myself, I thought with a sinking heart, about the insurance on the Maserati. I had to explain to the officer what had happened, make it official, tell him I didn't know a Dr. Prescott.

"I'm thankful to be alive," I said. "It was all the motorcycle rider's fault."

"There was no bike rider at the scene of the accident." The Colonel crossed his arms over his broad chest, stood looking down at me.

A charmer, he was not.

"Of course not, he sped off, faster than a speeding bullet," I added, sticking to my Superman scenario.

"There was a green car, which you hit and which went off the road. The driver was killed."

My breath caught in my throat. *Oh God, oh God, the poor bastard got it, that bike rider got him. . . .* "Jesus," I said in a small, shaky voice. "I'm so sorry, I didn't know. But I did not hit him, I just saw the bike rider go at him and then it was gone . . . and so was I. There was a truck in the other lane. The driver must have seen what happened."

"There have been no reports from any truck driver. No one else saw this accident, Madame Matthews. It was just you there, and the green car with its driver. And one of you died."

I began to cry again. Somehow I could not stop. He harrumphed, passed me the box of Kleenex from the side table, poured a glass of water. My hand shook as I took it from his. Dark hair grew softly on the back of his hand, almost to the knuckles. I glanced up at him, directly into his eyes. His face was so close to mine it was almost as if we were about to kiss.

"We will talk again later," he said, rising and striding quickly to the door. He opened it, turned to look back at me. "I hope you will soon feel better, Madame Matthews."

“Oh, please, it’s Mirabella.”

He shook his head and sighed. “Madame Matthews,” he said. “This is a professional matter we are talking about. Allow me to keep it that way.”

Of course he was right, and of course I was in serious trouble.

7

The hospital found Verity and me to be none the worse for wear, despite the fact that the crash totaled the vehicle and necessitated our helicopter rescue, exciting the imagination of the media whose intrusive cameras and mikes followed us all the way home. Actually I thought Verity quite enjoyed it, lifting her chin and smiling shyly despite her bruises and two black eyes that gave her the look of a young panda, plus the over-large gray sweats that overwhelmed her. Her shoes had disappeared in the fall, as had my own, so we were barefoot as we hobbled into the ambulance to be ferried to the anonymous safety of the Villa Romantica.

I directed the driver along the coast road, then up into the hills along the winding lane, which ended at my home.

There was always something about the Villa Romantica, an air of romance. It was built in the 1930s by the beauty, singer, actress, stage personality, and mistress to a famous man, Jerusha, who needed only one name to be known throughout the globe. Many years later, even after her death, the memories and passed-down stories of those who had known her seemed to keep her alive.

It wasn't surprising then, that to me she would always seem to be there, at the villa, a half-caught glimpse but when I turned to look no one was there; a flash of red hair floating in the breeze beyond the trees, the rustle of a silk skirt . . . a mirage, I told myself, a trick of the light. Or could it be Jerusha's spirit still roamed free, restless, unable to leave the beloved home she had built and then lost? Was Jerusha unable to leave "love" behind? Never to move on? I was soon to find out.

There were no other buildings beyond the Romantica, only huge bushes of pink-blooming oleander, and the hill dotted with olive trees, and higher still almond trees which, when in blossom, scented the entire area so you felt you were breathing nature itself. Now, though, in the summer months, old-fashioned roses drooped their heavy heads and fields of lavender drifted to the horizon, while lemons and oranges hung from branches that looked too small to bear their weight. And always in sight through branches and tree trunks and the bushes, was the sea. Blue-green today.

I loved the sea so much because, unlike the garden, it gave a constantly changing image, almost hour by hour, sometimes white-tipped with surf, sometimes dark and green, often gray, but more often blue.

"Here we are." I indicated the sharp left, though

in fact there was nowhere else to go because as I said, this is where the road ended. Indeed there we were. At the Villa Romantica. My home, for better, for worse, just like in marriage. And like a new bride, I was in love.

I shall never forget Aunt Jolly. I still couldn't believe that she'd left me her beloved home. Somehow she had known I would love it too, that we were the right fit. All I had to do now was to find out why she had died so violently.

But first, what to do with the runaway waif who had become my responsibility? Sure as hell nobody else was about to pick her up from the lowly place she had fallen and take care of her. And if ever a woman looked in need of putting back together it was this one.

"Come on, hon," I said as the ambulance driver opened the door and I edged across the seat. "This is where we live."

"Jerusha's house," she said, astonishing me. She was still perched on the edge of the seat in the ambulance, seemingly stunned as she stared at the house. "There was a murder here."

"Perhaps," I said briskly. "Come on, girl, let's get on with it." And I took her hand and gave it a tug.

She swung her legs out the door, long pretty legs, I noticed, though a bit beat-up from the accident. She managed with what seemed a great effort to stand up, wobbling, so I worried whether she had been right to leave the hospital.

"She's okay," the driver said. I knew he was an expert because they'd seen everything. "Just a bit shook up. Give her a cup of coffee and she'll be fine."

"A martini is more like it," I said, putting my arm around her waist and walking her to the front door thinking longingly of a tall, cold drink and a comfy sofa.

When my houseman, Alfred, opened the door, the shocked expression on his middle-aged, usually bland face with its high, bald forehead and shaggy gray brows that met in the middle in a concerned frown, made me understand just what a sight the pair of us were.

"Madame," he exclaimed, rushing down the three wide steps to help me while the nice driver assisted Verity.

"Alfred, this is my friend Verity. We'll put her in the peony room, I think." Of course I meant the room with the original peony-print wallpaper, faded with age to a nice pale pink.

"Quite right, Madame, it's cheerful," he said, inspecting Verity closely. "And she looks as though she needs cheering up a bit."

English understatement as always from Alfred. Good servants know their profession and they should never be underrated. It's a job in which they rightly take pride, as does a good waiter.

But Verity stood still, seemingly rooted to the

top step, peering through the wide double doors fashioned from a rare oak felled in a thunderstorm when the villa was built, and with a large heart-shaped brass door-knocker, indicating, it was said, Jerusha's welcome to her guests. I wished the guests had all felt the same way about their beautiful and generous hostess, Jerusha. Obviously some had not. It puzzled me as to exactly why this was, and I was determined to find out the truth. But truth is elusive when it comes to the past; everyone has their own story and with the passing of time even those become distorted.

We walked into the hall and Verity said, surprising me again, "Jerusha was a friend of my grandmother. I remember seeing her photo on the table next to the sofa in Gran's boudoir. I always picked it up to look at it because she was so lovely, in a long flowing dress that swept to one side in a train. Glamorous, I suppose she was, though to a child she was simply beautiful. How I wished I could be like her, I remember saying that to Gran and her telling me with a sad look on her face that I should not wish any such thing. She wouldn't tell me why but she removed the photo, put it away somewhere I suppose because I never saw it again. And of course I never asked why."

"Well, now you know," I said. "Jerusha was a killer. Rotten to the core. Seduced men, they said, simply because she could." Verity stared at me, bug-eyed, and I took pity on her. "Of course, those were only rumors, there are always tales about a woman as lovely and famous as that. You've only to look at some of today's stars, hounded by the press, false stories made up about their goings-on."

"But that's so unfair."

I shook my head, smiling at Verity's naivety. "Hon," I said, "that's life. Anyhow," I added, remembering our own recent dice with death, "I've always wanted to find out the truth, and now you are here to help me. Your grandmother knew Jerusha; she must have told you stories about her."

Verity looked doubtful. "None that I remember, just her name, and that maybe she killed someone, and about the villa. There was a picture of it, you see. Gran took it herself when she stayed here. You know the kind where all the house-guests are assembled in front of the house, like in a school photo. And now I remember, the king stayed here with Jerusha, when he was still king, before he abdicated and became one of us."

"Well, not exactly," I said. "Even though Edward VIII was downgraded to a duke he was not 'one of us.' But he was said to have an eye for a pretty woman. Plus he was known to be an entertaining guest so I'm sure Jerusha would have loved him."

We both turned our heads, hearing the roar of a car's engine and the spurt of gravel as it pulled to an abrupt stop. A reckless driver, I thought. We heard footsteps approaching on the path, then a man appeared at the doorway, silhouetted against the sun so we could not make out who exactly he was, though I was certain it was no one I knew.

I met him on the stoop, annoyed at his impertinence. "Who are you? And what do you mean by walking in here like you own the place?" My anger showed in my tone of voice.

His coldness showed in his, sending a chill through my bones.

"I might," Chad Prescott said.

He stepped forward so I could see his face: lean, handsome, lightly tanned, an outdoorsman's face—sporty, horses, fishing; things like that. I felt myself melt.

It was the doctor. Ohh, I thought. Another charmer.

8

I dragged my eyes away, looking down at the parquet floor but not seeing it. In the short time available I had managed to take in the floppy blond hair, the network of lines around his eyes, blue eyes in fact, much like my own, as well as the stubble on that firm chin, and a nice-looking underlip, full and sweet enough for a bite. But what was I thinking? This man, this doctor, had just claimed he owned my villa. I should want to smack him across his too-good-looking face. But I'm not the smacking kind, I'm a giver not a taker, a softie at heart, and I do have a heart though at the moment it seems to have stopped. Taken a break. I hope it begins to beat again soon, I'd quite like to breathe.

There! I was breathing after all. And smiling at this outrageous man who had just put claims on my villa. Aunt Jolly's villa, that was. And before that, Jerusha's.

My shoulder hurt, bruised in the crash, and I put up a hand as though to protect it from his gaze, but he was not even looking at me. He was looking at the villa, assessing its value I'd bet.

"So who are you anyway?" I put enough frost in my voice to kill any nice summer day.

He did not so much as glance around, so intent was he in taking in what he claimed was his property. “Name’s Chad Prescott.” He did not offer his hand, though, silly me, I did. Good manners can be the ruination of you; someone once told me that. It had to have been a man.

“Though you have not asked, my name is Mirabella Matthews.” I waited for a response, the oh really, of course I know your books. It did not come.

Verity came and stood tall beside me. “And I am Verity.” She did not mention her second name, obviously still confused as to which one it was, the single or the married. Not that it mattered.

Aunt Jolly had an old sausage dog that still lived here, along with a Siamese cat and a bright yellow canary that sang. The dog walked cautiously toward the doctor, stretching its long neck to sniff his sandaled feet. He ignored it.

“I did not invite you onto my property,” I said, choking back my anger. “And you should at least acknowledge the dog. He lives here, this is his home.”

“No, it’s not,” he said. And with that he walked past me and through the already open door.

Mouth agape, I caught the faint tang of briarwood cologne as he passed, a warm male aroma. What was wrong with me? This guy was talking about Aunt Jolly’s house, *my* house, as though it was his, walking into it like he owned it and I was caught up in his scent.

"You have no right to walk into my house."

I hurried after him, the dog slinking at my heels. The Siamese was absent and the canary had disappeared from its open cage. I didn't blame them. The vibes were not good.

He turned and for the first time really looked at me, as though he saw me and not as though I were some insignificant servant, here to do his bidding.

"You must understand," he said. His voice was low and even and rather attractive if truth be known. "You must understand that whatever you have been told, whatever you believe or think, you did not inherit this house. It was deeded to me prior to her death by Madame Jolly Matthews."

He'd called her Jolly. Only her friends and family, small though it was, namely me, ever did that. My aunt's proper name was Juliet, though she claimed no one but her mother had ever used it.

"Well, then," I said, considering my words carefully before I voiced them, because this was a situation I recognized was fraught with sudden danger. "Well, then, Mr. . . . ?" I paused, waiting for him to remind me his name was Chad Prescott though I remembered it perfectly well. But he did not remind me, he simply stood there, arms folded now across his chest, all manly-man in a white polo shirt and pale pink bathing shorts, though had you asked me earlier how a guy in pink shorts could look masculine I would have laughed in your face.

"I'll have my attorney send you the appropriate documents," he said, turning and speaking over his shoulder, dropping his card on the hall table as he left. "I shall expect you to be gone by next week. Please leave everything as you found it."

"The dog and the cat and the bird as well?" I was steaming with the heat of sudden anger. And, I admit it, fear. Because what if he was right and the villa did belong to him? I would regret having sold my little flat in London and all dreams of sunny South of France would be just dreams again.

"Take the animals," he called back. "I do not want them around."

I yelled back, "This is my house, mister, and there's nothing you can do about it."

"Yes, there is," he said and he sounded so calm, so collected, while I had fallen to pieces. I feared he was right.

"Of course the villa is yours," my attorney, James Arnold Long, said in his usual calm, controlled, nothing-will-ever-get-to-him voice that I'm sure he uses on all his usually upset and irate clients. After all, he's the one who has to sort out their problems; they can't have him getting upset and irate as well.

"He claims he has papers to prove Aunt Jolly—he calls her that—gave him the villa."

"And when did she supposedly do this?"

I could just imagine old-lawyer-Long, with his half-specs sliding down his nose, flipping through the papers on his desk, probably doing at least two things at once as I knew he usually did, instead of concentrating on my problem, which was now a major problem.

"I mean, he's a doctor, a surgeon, he has documents," I said, sounding feeble and feminine and a bit lost. Actually, a lot lost. I was in love with a villa. It was mine.

"Did he give the documents to you, or at least copies?"

"Well, no. . . . But he seemed very sure of himself and his position as owner."

"Give me his phone number and his e-mail address," Long said. "I'll take care of him." The lawyer's voice was firm, determined; he knew his rights, that was his job, after all. "Now you just go about your business, your life, as normal, let us take care of Dr. Prescott."

I clicked off the phone and went and sat on the terrace, for once not seeing the beautiful view in front of me. I was too in my own head, even when the Siamese jumped onto my lap and settled down as though she now owned me. The dog sat panting at my feet, big brown eyes fixed anxiously on my face, no doubt taking in my worried expression.

Verity was staring at me too, all indignant. "What was that about? What does he mean, it's his villa?"

She looked so skinny and bedraggled, ready to stamp her foot in the good old-fashioned classic manner of outrage. I shrugged, assuming a nonchalance I did not feel.

"The lawyer tells me it's all nonsense. Of course the villa is mine. He'll sort out this Dr. Chad Prescott." I grinned at her. "What d'ya think, in his pink shorts?"

Verity sighed. "Cute," she said. "Like all the bad boys."

I had to admit she was right.

9
The Colonel

Rufus Barrada, or the Colonel, as he was always referred to because of his ten years of service in the French army prior to joining the gendarmes, had seen too many road accidents to be sympathetic. He'd been a happily married man for seven years when his wife was killed. She was walking from their home, an old farmhouse that had been in his family for two centuries, to the Saturday village market, striding along the side of the road when she was struck by a tourist RV and knocked into a rocky ditch.

Agnes, her name was, but the Colonel always only called her *mon amour*, and she called him *mon choux*, though never in public, of course. Theirs was a passionate relationship, nurtured over the years, and he was bereft without her. Time, as it usually does, eventually papered over the cracks of despair until it resembled some form of acceptance, though never forgotten.

Their children, the twin girls named Marie-Laure and Marie-Helene for their grandmothers, were now six years old, Laure with long pigtails, blond like her mother, Helene exactly like her father with his thick dark hair that sprouted every which way, falling into her eyes mostly so she seemed to peer at you shyly, which in fact she was not at all.

Laure was the shy one, usually walking behind her sister, head down, clutching her bookbag over one shoulder, small gold-rimmed glasses half hiding her blue eyes. Helene always looked out for her sister though.

The Colonel was to pick them up from school and because of the interviews with the Matthews woman he was late. He spotted them sitting on a low wall outside the schoolhouse, each with an elbow on her knee, chin clasped in hand, eyes blank with the lethargy of the long wait.

He pulled up next to them, apologizing, got out, opened the door, and watched while they climbed in. He fastened their seat belts, double-checked everything, and said, "Okay, girls, we're off to get ice cream."

The Colonel drove off with them chattering away about the school day. He was a family man at heart despite his formal demeanor, his position, his uniform, and his reputation for toughness, which came from a hatred of criminals and anyone against the law. He was a "true" man, in his heart.

He was not happy with the supposed "accident" in the canyon. The body of the man driving the green car had been identified as that of Josephus Raus, a Russian, in the country without a visa, yet who purportedly worked for a well-known property developer by the name of Bruce Bergen—whose passport was Italian but whose birthplace was Belarus, and who was commonly known as "the Boss."

All in all, it looked messy to the Colonel, and now those two women had almost lost their lives. It puzzled him as to why they should be so targeted. What could they have done to inspire such revenge? If in fact it was revenge. It might be unrequited love—after all, they were two fine-looking women. Or some other reason he had yet to find out. It looked like a big job to him. Less time with his girls, and more time finding out what the two women were up to at the Villa Romantica. You never knew.

10

Mirabella

My new home lies on the narrow coastal strip near Antibes, a town with two personalities, the old and the new.

New Antibes has a smart seafront promenade where artists sit in front of easels painting portraits of tourists and local landscapes, or rather, "waterscapes," since the Mediterranean is ever-present. Bars and cafés compete for those same tourists' attention, their terraces shaded from the sun by colorful awnings and where lounging around is the order of the day.

The cafés and bars are always crowded of an evening, when a cool glass of wine or a chilled beer is necessary while watching the passing parade of suntanned beauties in short dresses. Not to mention the rich and sometimes good-looking owners of the grand boats moored in the harbor, boats that cost a fortune and that can also be rented for a small fortune. Tanned, shirtless young men work constantly keeping those boats immaculate, swabbing decks, shining teak, and polishing brass. Chefs from the boats browse the local market in the early morning, seeking out the freshest goods: mushrooms picked at dawn in a field inland; melons grown near Aix-en-Provence; the tiniest and sweetest wild strawberries, the *fraises des bois* of the region. And of course, the sea bass and grouper and red mullet fished before daylight to be grilled to perfection and scattered with herbs and a little garlic and the good olive oil.

Farther out to sea is a specially constructed jetty, where giant white cruise liners moor, being too large for the harbor itself. And in back of the port, narrow cobbled streets are strung with washing from tall house to tall house and tiny shop fronts display minuscule bikinis and T-shirts with the town's name, so when you return home you'll remember you were there, and perhaps remember how it felt, and how it smelled. You'll remember the fruits too, displayed in wooden crates outside those small stores, and the lavender sold in tight bunches, picked from the lower reaches of the Alpes-Maritimes, on the peaks of which, sometimes even in summer, a snowcap might be glimpsed.

Hot new boutiques with good prices are next to jewelry stores, the cheaper ones with local handmade earrings and bracelets, the expensive ones offering diamond necklaces. The ice cream shop with popular pale-green pistachio is next to the upmarket shoe store whose custom-made flat sandals everyone seems to wear to traverse the bumpy cobblestones, while expensive chiffon evening gowns compete for attention with the skimpy white shorts and South of France T-shirts.

Flowers are everywhere, bunches of jasmine and red roses tied with ribbons. Hair bands and bathing suits hang on hooks on the sidewalks outside the shops. There are straw hats on shelves with a little mirror to check out your look and sexy lingerie shops with lacy thongs and demi-bras guaranteed to lift and shape and look adorable in every color from red to black, lavender and coral and rosy pink.

And then there's the Grimaldi Palace where Monaco's royalty still live, and the Old Town, the place the "real" people live, and where they shop at the small grocery stores with salamis hanging overhead and tall glass jars of fresh made-that-morning pasta standing by the door. You can also buy the homemade sauce for that pasta, and fresh garlic to add flavor, and the juicy tomatoes to serve with cheeses made with milk from local goats that eat only grass. You can buy chickens from the outdoor grill where they rotate until crisp and golden and whose smell makes the mouth water, and whose fat and juices cook the small potatoes underneath. There are field-fresh lettuces, green and pink and red-edged, to be served crisp and cold with a vinaigrette made from local oil and vinegar the farmer's wife has been selling at the market for years.

All of it is there, all to hand, all ready to be

eaten, or to be worn, or to slip your feet into, or to decorate your tanned arms and neck, or perfume your body. The South of France is a sensual experience and one never to be forgotten.

When I first came here, it was as though I suddenly came to life. My London body, kept wrapped in coats and scarves and with a sweater more often than not even in summer months, changed in days to a body clad in sweet little T-shirts in pretty colors, my newly brown legs displayed in those white shorts, my fiery red hair held back by a jeweled band, my lips painted pink. I had come home. I had come to life.

One day out of hospital, I was definitely a new woman. First, I needed transportation. Aunt Jolly's small SEAT was uninspiring; I wanted air and life and speed. What else but a Harley? Turquoise blue, of course. I had read somewhere about a woman with a turquoise-blue Harley and had admired her guts. Now that woman was me.

"But you can't get turquoise," Verity said. "I mean, let's face it, you're too old."

"I'm forty-two. Exactly the right age." I did compromise, but not on the color. A turquoise Harley "scooter" was what I ended up with, almost a Vespa but much cuter. It suited me because parking was tough in this town and a scooter was easier to slot into those tight spaces between cars.

I took Verity to shop for necessities. Of course she had nothing other than what she'd left with, and anything I had been able to lend her that fit, which wasn't much. She was a fast shopper and in no time we had bags of stuff draped over the handlebars as we scooted back to the Villa Romantica.

I was glad Verity had shown up in my life. It was so good to have a girlfriend. I was glad to be home at the Villa Romantica.

11

The Colonel

Later, in Antibes, the Colonel was downing a second espresso at the café opposite the hair-dresser's when he spotted the man walking quickly, head down, carrying a large flat bag, which the Colonel recognized as the kind used for architectural drawings. No surprise there. He knew the man, another Russian who worked for the Boss, who was known to be involved in plans to build a condominium on a plot of land near the seafront. Now everybody knew that the Boss did not own that land, it belonged to Jolly Matthews, recently deceased by means more foul than fair.

The Colonel had looked into her death, of course. It was in his domain and a knife in the back could in no way be construed as a normal age-related demise. The poor old girl had gotten herself killed, and as the saying goes, he'd bet it was for money. And now the Boss was acting like he had claims and could go right ahead with his building plans.

The Colonel happened to know that Aunt Jolly, as she had been known to everyone in the neighborhood—where she had been well-liked—had left her estate to the niece who had almost come to her end crashing a Maserati into the canyon. Again by means foul rather than fair. The Colonel now believed she had been pushed off that road. It didn't take more than half a brain to figure out who would gain from these deaths. And he was looking at the man that worked for him.

He drained his coffee, placed some change under the saucer, and hurried after the Russian.

He was forty-five years old; the Colonel knew that because he had studied the dossier when it became clear the Boss was trying to muscle in on Matthews's land. In fact more than one person had put claimers on it. There was also her neighbor, Chad Prescott, who had a document, purportedly signed by Jolly Matthews to that effect. Trouble was brewing and the Boss was certain to be involved in it.

The Colonel followed the Russian at a slow pace, lingering behind other walkers, trying to look insignificant though it was difficult. Despite not being a tall man, the Colonel was hard to miss with his rugged stance, his wide shoulders, and large head jutting forward as though aways late and impatient to get wherever it was he was going. Now, however, the Russian seemed unaware of him and the Colonel followed him down the alley leading from the main square, where small boutiques of the classier kind advertised handbags and smart shoes and lingerie in their windows.

The Russian stopped to glance at the lingerie—pretty stuff, sexy in red, a touch racy for this town but the tourists loved it. And so it seemed, did the Russian because he pushed open the door and went inside.

The Colonel stood, doing his best to look as though he were simply viewing the pricey lace chemises, blushing slightly in embarrassment. Why couldn't the Russian simply have stopped off at the mini-market or the pharmacy? Still, out he came, clutching a gold-and-white-striped bag by its gold rope handles. Whatever he'd bought had cost a pretty penny, the Colonel was sure of that. He wondered who the gift was destined for.

He did not have to wonder for long. He followed the Russian to the parking area, stopping to watch as he waved at the woman behind the wheel of a large white RV. The Colonel quickly made a note of the number on the plate and the fact that it was a British vehicle. He also noted that the woman was attractive, in her thirties, with long blond hair hanging straight to her shoulders, a butcher-boy cap planted over it, a white spaghetti-strap top, and an armload of clanking bracelets.

The Russian got in, gave her a long kiss, then gave her the bag. She dived greedily into it, pulling out a mass of lace and ribbons that seemed to delight her because she kissed him again, lingeringly, as if promising a reward later. And then she switched on the engine and screeched out of the lot before the Colonel could make a move.

Interesting, he thought, rechecking the number on the plate, which he had punched into his iPhone. He'd soon find out who that was, and what the Russian was up to.

12

Verity

Verity thought it was weird how fate took over and simply put you on a path, quite different from the one you'd expected to follow, meaning for her an angry divorce—a fight over money and a house, the stinging loss of love that had meant so much to her and so little to him. His name was Rancho.

"Like, *Rancho*?" she'd exclaimed, disbelieving, when he introduced himself at, of all places, a local horse event.

He was the most exotic creature she had ever met: Argentinian, he said, sitting astride a glossy little polo pony with too-thin ankles that did not look strong enough to carry his weight, yet which careened up and down the field in a whirlwind of hooves and clumps of turned-up sod, while he leaned dangerously from the saddle whacking at a minute ball with a mallet, which is what she found out they call the stick they hit the ball with in polo, a game that had never previously interested her. And boy, he did it well. And my, he looked good doing it.

It took only two months for there to be a wedding of sorts; not the floating-down-the-aisle event Verity had somehow always imagined in her future, but a runaway register-office affair in London, with only the cleaning lady and a passing delivery man for witnesses. As weddings go, it was about as anonymous as you can get. And after the first few hectic nights, all sex and wine, and sex and food, and sex and long walks in St. James Park, which was right next to the Ritz where they were staying—on her credit card as she later found out—she realized she bored him. Especially after he escorted her to her bank and asked her to withdraw her savings, which she did, then passed over to him. A couple of thousand was all, because she was not the trust-fund baby he'd believed. It was her birthday money from over the years—it added up by the time you got to your midtwenties, which is when godparents started to give up on you, thinking you were old enough to take care of yourself. And she was, just about, until she married him. Finally, she just bolted. Took off like the young polo ponies he loved more than her. In her rush to get out, to never see him again, she'd stupidly left whatever was in the bank, and her jewelry.

And now what? She had just survived a hair-raising, death-defying ride to a temporary stopover in a place she had never been before yet somehow knew, with a woman she did not know, and a future that was indecipherable from where she was sitting, gazing awestruck at the pink-stucco villa and the gardens with the low-clipped hedges enclosing flower beds heavy with the scent of jasmine, far better than any manufactured perfume. And the sky an endless blue. And a maniac on a Ducati Monster somewhere out there who had tried to kill them. Or tried to kill the woman whose car it was, whose house this was.

She turned to look at her. "Who the hell are you, really, anyway?" she asked. "And why do you wear those silly crochet gloves?"

Mirabella

Though I was not about to tell Verity, there is, of course, a valid reason I wear the gloves, crochet in summer, or in colder months, very soft, supple leather ones in various colors, sometimes even red because what the hell, if I have to wear them, why not make them gorgeous? And you are right, the crochet gloves are not gorgeous but they are cool on these warm days in the South of France. As I said, a neighbor makes them for me. She's in her early nineties now and can barely see the crochet hook and the fine cotton she fashions them from, but she says cheerfully it's all instinct by now anyway. "No need to look, my fingers just keep on doing it," she explains, making me laugh. So of course I have a handy stack of them in my new home, in all colors and weights of thread, even cashmere, stashed in the third drawer of the bedroom chest on top of a pile of old love letters I still have not had the heart to get rid of. I've always believed that when love walks out then so should the memento mori—the now-dead love letters and the small, once-sweetly-thought-of gifts, the withered roses and old memories—but when it came time, I could never do it. I simply took them with me. Still, as I said, I was mostly instrumental in having the lovers leave. I was never cruel or even unkind. "Listen babe," I'd say. "I reckon it's time to move on. We had such fun, didn't we?"

This was not always greeted with smiling acceptance, as you can imagine. Quite a lot of bad words were flung my way, along with the withered bunches of roses, but I kept my head, and my heart, and tried to move on without too much hurt going down between us, the feuding parties, the ex-lovers, the thank-God-never-marrieds. And I never, in my entire life, ever took another woman's husband; not that the opportunity did not present itself, but I had enough responsibility keeping my own life together without taking on somebody else's problem. And they were problems better kept away from.

So, now, here I am, forty-two years old and the new owner of this gorgeous villa overlooking the Mediterranean, bluer, as I said, than my eyes on a good day, and gray as the wind on a day when the mistral blows everything to bits. And also, to my surprise, "mother hen" you might call me, to a small canary bird, yellower than twenty-carat gold, named Sing.

Now, I've never been one for pets, never been one for owning a big house either, and certainly never owner of a Siamese cat like the one called Ming that seems to think it owns this villa and which has blue eyes and cream fur and chocolate-brown ear tips and tail, and on whose head the yellow canary perches to sing its song. To complete this nutty inherited household is the long rust-brown dog, obviously some remote relation of a dachshund with a lot of beagle thrown in, and that answers to the name of JonJon or to a piercing whistle. Now, never having learned the art as Lauren Bacall so succinctly put it in that old movie, of just putting your lips together and blowing, I bought a small silver whistle that hangs around my neck on a blue cord and nearly strangles me when I forget about it, but is useful for summoning JonJon, who I've refused to call by that ridiculous name and is now known as Sossy. Because he's a "saucy little bugger," you see. The word is the only one that fits his mercurial temperament. Oh, but he makes me laugh, and when the canary sings, she makes me smile, and when the cat slinks under my feet and gives me an affectionate little head-butt, I realize how empty my life was before them, and how fortunate I am to have inherited this small family, along with the big house. If it was the wonderful Jerusha that first brought the ancestors of these small creatures home to the Villa Romantica, then I owe her more than I can say.

Jerusha. Her name conjures up fantasies, images, scandals, love stories, and tragedy, though most of it has been hidden, or buried long ago. Now that I own her house, I shall make it my business to find out more about the fabled musical artist, singer, dancer, actress, and sex-symbol who captured Paris in the thirties, and who disappeared, forever it seemed, only a few years later. That is, after the death of her lover and his new mistress. Who knows, perhaps I should amend that and say "one" of his mistresses.

What was Jerusha's life really like? Did she love the man? Was he her only lover? What happened to the children she was said to have fostered, even adopted? Were they simply whisked away when Jerusha's world came tumbling down, and only the small animals, her pets, left to console her?

Jerusha is a mystery that belongs to the Villa Romantica, and now, therefore, to me, shared with my young guest, Verity.

I'm sitting on the terrace, smoking a forbidden cigarette, forbidden by myself I might say, when

I hear a footstep behind me. An arm snakes around and the cigarette is whisked from my lips before I can even protest.

"Filthy habit," Verity said, dropping into the cushioned sofa opposite. "And it'll kill you in the end."

"Like poison, you mean?"

She threw me a you-know-what-I-mean glance, then stubbed out the cigarette in the yellow ceramic ashtray labeled PASTIS, stolen in a moment of great daring from a cheap boulevard café in Marseilles. I treasured that ashtray and my own bit of daring and gave her a frown to show my displeasure.

"So. What about you, now?" I said coldly. "I see the tears are finished. Are you all set to go back to that bastard you ran away from? Give it one more go, the way all good girls do?"

She said, "I'm no good girl. I'm staying here with you." And then she burst into tears again.

I should have kept my mouth shut.

13

It seems now that not only am I stuck with a clutter of animals—well, that is, two and a bird—but also a young and miserable runaway because in my heart I cannot get myself to ask her to leave, tell her to go find a hotel room, to get on with her life and not wallow in the sentiment of a terrible marriage to an oaf who treated her like dirt, and what's more, who stole all her money. Even if it was only two thousand, it was two thou more than she has right now, you can bet on that. Plus her jewels, which I hope were not old family stuff, inherited, and probably now destined for the pawn shop, never to be seen again. You can always buy new ones when you get the money back—earn it or whatever, the way Jerusha had, until her world fell completely apart much like young Verity, who had better quit her moaning, or else.

Oh God, how can I be so unkind? Is there anything more painful than a broken heart? Not when you are going through it, I remember that now.

"My dear," I said in my kindly old aunt voice. (I mean she is so young and I am, though I hate to admit it, now "in my forties," but this is the role I seem to have been cast in at the moment.) "My dear, you have to trust me."

"Why?" She gave me a long, weepy, upward look from reddened eyes. "I mean, why do I have to trust you? I trusted him and look what happened."

"Yes, well, of course, he is a man. It's different between us women."

She stared at me. The sobbing stopped. At least I had silenced her.

We were sitting in the car, a newly rented Fiat, in place of the dead Maserati, and she was staring at the Villa Romantica like it was Dracula's castle and I was maybe the vampire himself.

"Why did you bring me here?"

"Oh, for God's sake." I managed to keep the snarl from my voice, but not the impatience. "This is my house, usually called a villa here in the South of France. I inherited it and now it's my home. My new home," I added, with a pang of longing for my small just-sold London flat where I had been happy enough, if lonely, for a few years.

"Who gave it to you?" she demanded, suspicion written all over her tear-mottled, though pretty face.

"Who the hell cares, it's where you'll spend the night, if you're lucky and behave yourself better. If not, I promise I'll pack you off back to that husband who stole all your money and dumped you."

“I didn’t have much to be dumped for.” She looked wistfully at me. “I’m ashamed to be dumped for only a couple of thousand, I mean he could have done better than that, couldn’t he?”

Filled with sudden pity, I flung an arm around her shoulders and hugged her closer. “Listen, girl, men can behave like bastards sometimes, but that doesn’t mean all of them are. Nor does it have anything in the least bit to do with you, or who you are. He was just a scoundrel, a shamless cheat and men like him usually get what they deserve in the end. I’m only sorry you won’t be there to give him a good punch in the nose.”

“I won’t?”

Sounding as firm as I could and as though I believed what I said, I answered, “Of course not. He’ll try it again with some other woman and she’ll punch him where it hurts and probably see that he ends up in jail.”

“Ohh,” she began to wail again, tears streaming.

“What now?” I was exasperated. What the fuck was I doing in this situation anyway?

“I’ll be married to a jailbird,” she sobbed. “Me. A jailbird’s wife.”

“No, you won’t. You’ll divorce him. Trust me, I’ll see to that, in fact I’ll get onto it right away. Shouldn’t be surprised if we got it annulled, under the circumstances.”

To my surprise, she cheered up immediately

and began to look around and take in her whereabouts.

"But how lovely this is." She wiped off her sunglasses, which had become misted with tears, and stuck them back up on top of her head. Apparently this was where she usually wore them, unlike the rest of us who use them to protect our eyes from the sun. Youth, I decided from my forties' vantage point, was not too smart.

The cat made a sudden appearance, leaping into the car and onto my lap with a howl of delight. It's so nice, if sometimes noisy, to be loved by a Siamese. She gave me her usual head-butt and I kissed her ears and Verity leaned over to touch her.

"So soft," she said admiringly. "So beautiful."

And then the canary flew up onto the cat's head and perched there, tilting back its own tiny head and singing with pure joy. And the dog, not to be outdone in the greetings department, scrabbled its claws on the car door, no doubt scratching the paint, but who the hell cares when love is involved. These were mine, my loves, they shared my life, they gave me a life.

"How I envy you," young Verity said. All tears were gone and she was shaking her long golden hair loose and smiling and petting the dog. Then she really looked at the villa and said, "This is Jerusha's place."

14

Of course Chad Prescott did not own the villa. It was Aunt Jolly's and, as her heir, obviously now mine, though it was named for all the romantic qualities I do not possess. How otherwise have I managed to marry three men then have them leave me? Had I left them, it would be one thing; but for *three* to leave *me,* is quite another. The implication is, and as I know everybody believes, that there must be something wrong with me—either I'm tight with my money, or it's the sex. They say it's always one or the other.

In fact it was neither; the husbands simply bored me, and I suspect I bored them. The first was too young, too full of sexual confidence and unable to admit his inexperience—my fault really, I should have recognized he was not mature enough. The second was after my money and when he found out that—at that time—there was none, he departed. The third was the kind of guy who needed to be looked after: he wanted a caregiver not a wife.

"What the hell?" I said to friends. "All I wanted was someone to share a bottle of wine with, watch the sunset together, have dinner. I didn't bargain for getting up in the morning, looking at him in his tiny whities and hairy thighs, demanding coffee and a cooked breakfast. A girl has her standards and a cooked breakfast does not take early morning priority over good sex. At least it should not."

I'm not surprised they dumped me, though. I tried others, found I was more comfortable alone, living in my London flat, writing the exotic fictional lives readers imagined were my own, and there were times I wished they were. Now here I am, the "esteemed author," a suddenly independent woman, a rich bitch with a villa, thanks to Aunt Jolly, who I first met when I was around three or four years old.

The meeting took place in what was then Harrods' Tea Room, and I remember dropping a chocolate éclair down the front of my velvet-collared little princess coat that was still buttoned to the neck practically choking me, because my mother wanted me to look like a well-brought-up child to impress the rich aunt.

As I remember it, there were no other children in Harrods' Tea Room so I never had anyone to compare it with, but it seemed to me, young as I was, that there was something wrong with being so uncomfortably dressed just to eat a cream cake, and that's why I deliberately dropped it down that hated coat that I could remember to this day choking me. *And* it was pink. I was definitely not a pink child.

But now I own a pink villa. Somehow, it was

right for the early twentieth-century stucco house, four-square except where a wing stuck out at the back, supposedly built for servants' quarters, now converted into posh guest rooms complete with cool white-tiled bathrooms with strong rain-head showers for those coming from the beach and needing to get the sand off.

I certainly did not want sand trekked into what was now my grand room. I'm calling it the "grand room" because it's several smaller rooms knocked into one and now covers the entire front of the villa, with floor-to-ceiling glass doors that slide into each other, opening it up to the pale terra-cotta-tiled terrace running the entire length of the house, wide enough for hammocks and cushioned couches and coffee tables. Plus there is an outdoor dining area that seats twenty with the locally made rush-seat chairs I love but which guests complain snag their skirts, leaving them with little pulled threads on their rear ends when they stand up to leave.

The rooms on the upper floor have their own individual balconies, just big enough for a breakfast table and chairs and a couple of loungers, striped green or coral. Deep blue awnings protect breakfasters from the sun, and a long narrow dark-blue tiled pool, bluer than my eyes, glimmers in the summer heat. Clusters of bougainvillea in fuchsia and scarlet, purple and pink, even one in a salmony-orange, soften the walls and the terrace, trailing along the pathway and down the wooden steps leading to the beach, where you have to step carefully over a clutter of pebbles before reaching the small crescent of sand and the perfect pale sea, which in summer is always just cool enough to refresh and exactly warm enough not to cause a bather to flinch.

The villa was built in the 1930s by a love-struck English gentleman for his mistress, the famed singer, Jerusha, whose flaming red hair was exactly the same color as my own. I know that because I've seen her pictures. And I've also heard that the singer's flamboyant performances sent sexual ripples through her audiences, both male and female, the men wanting her, the women wanting to be like her.

The singer's villa remains almost exactly as it was when she lived here. It's more subdued than her reputed stage persona, a cool, casual hide-away in summer, and a refuge in winter warmed by log fires in huge limestone fireplaces she purchased from torn-down chateaus that were no longer affordable. Pale paneling in a limed wood encloses the dining room with its enormous glass table supported down the center by a quartet of rampant lions, which means everybody can get their legs under quite comfortably. There are high-backed chairs in a faded brocade, built for ease over long leisurely dinners, always accompanied by local wines grown on the hills glimpsed from the balconies; wines that flowed like the conver-sation and the music.

The Villa Romantica still lives up to its original name, with spacious bedroom suites and over-sized beds piled so high with pillows you need a little flight of Victorian wooden steps to climb into their white-duvet comfort. Then you can lie back and admire your own personal view of the sea.

The bathrooms have fireplaces too, where fires were always lit in winter, with the scent of lavender burning sweetly. I've equipped them with the kind of thin, rough, Egyptian cotton towels I so prefer to those soft fluffy ones that never seem to dry you properly. The soap is made right down the coast: Marseilles soap it's called and it has a green freshness to it that leaves you feeling extra clean. Of course there is always lotion, local stuff also made from olive oil I think, and powder from Paris, Chanel naturally, my favorite, plus a small selection of scents—perfumes as they are called today: Roger & Gallet for the men, Chanel or Dior for the women, as well as fresh little cotton slippers, the kind you just slide your feet into, and those cosy, huggable, white terry-cloth robes in an assortment of sizes because you never know exactly. A bottle of Perrier waits on the night table with a selection of current magazines, *The New Yorker* a particular favorite I've noticed, and a choice of books—

biographies always disappear with the guests and have to be replaced. Odd, how curious people are about other people's lives.

Anyway, this is the villa to which I brought Verity, my new and unknown guest. Despite the fact she mentioned Jerusha and a murder, I doubted she really knew much about it. Or about Jerusha, its famous, or rather notorious, original owner, and the frightening and outrageous events that took place here, years ago.

Suddenly nostalgic, I opened the door and went into Aunt Jolly's room.

It had the best view of the sea and I remembered she always slept with her windows open, saying the sound of it lulled her to sleep. Rest in peace, Aunt Jolly, I thought. Sleeping the sleep of the angels now. I tried not to allow the memory of how she died, violently and all alone, to intrude on my good thoughts of her.

A painting hung over the night table beside the bed, half hidden by a large copper lamp with a parchment shade. I walked over and took a closer look. It was small, twelve-by-fifteen perhaps and so grayishly insignificant I might never have bothered to more than glance at it, but since it was the only form of decoration in my aunt's room, I assumed it had meant something special to her. It was a view of what I recognized as the River Thames on a windy day, choppy waves heading toward the bank, London skyline in the background. And the signature. J. M. W. Turner.

I looked closer. Could it be *the* J. M. W. Turner? Surely there could not be two artists of that era with that name. Was this a real treasure, hidden from the world in my dear aunt's bedroom all these years? Where could she have gotten it? Was it a gift, or had she seen it in a gallery and fallen in love? I looked at it again. It was still grayish and insignificant, definitely difficult to fall in love with. It had to have been a gift. And an expensive one at that. Somebody had cared.

It hung on a nail hammered into the wall like any commercial piece of store-bought rubbish. Perhaps it was only a copy after all. Yet even to my untrained eye there was something about it, the freedom of the brushstrokes, the luminous quality of the threatening sky, a spirit-of-place captured forever in paint.

I sank onto the bed, onto the white duvet, taking it in. Which is no doubt what the artist intended you to do—draw you into this scene, take you there with him. I wondered how many nights, alone in this room, alone in her bed, had Aunt Jolly gazed at it, unable to sleep, seeing it by lamplight, even candlelight, thinking about the past and her unknown future.

The frame, though, was out of keeping, gold and ornately carved, too elaborate for such a personal landscape. I turned it over to see who the framer was. Thick card covered the back, peeling at the edges. I pried it off and to my surprise, found a pale blue sealed envelope.

For my descendants was written in deep blue ink in a bold hand that was definitely not Aunt Jolly's.

I stared, fascinated by it. Well, I thought, I don't know who you are, but I'm thinking perhaps I might be a descendant. After all, we have Aunt Jolly in common, though it appears she never opened your letter. Maybe she didn't need to. Maybe she already knew what it said.

I fell back against the pillows, eyes closed, the envelope clutched to my chest, undecided. Did I have the right to read a letter not meant specifically for me?

A sudden breeze rustled the curtains, slid softly across my cheek, over my closed lids. A faint scent filtered into the room, sweet as summer grasses and damask roses.

I sat up, still clutching the letter. The scent was gone and the breeze had disappeared as suddenly as it had come.

I looked at the envelope. I knew I could not open it here, in this room. I must take it with me, go somewhere that did not hold memories and secrets, or else leave it for some other time when I felt freer—safer.

Yet curiosity held me captive. I told myself that later I would find out who had written it, who had sealed this envelope, who had decided to spill her secrets. It had to be a woman; this was not the act of a man. Men would have spoken about what they felt, shared their affairs, their indifference, or their love.

I smoothed down the duvet, plumped up the pillows, took the painting and the blue envelope, and walked from the room, closing the door firmly behind me, shutting out, I believed, the spirit-of-place, or the person that inhabited it still.

15

The second attempt on my life, after the car crash, came that night.

My bedroom was, of course, once Jerusha's. I doubted it looked much different than when she'd occupied it: the same wide bed, certainly big enough for two, with the lavishly rose brocade–padded headboard that still bore a faint dent where her famous red hair had rested against it. No doubt she had bound it up for the night in a chignon, and no doubt with glamorous tendrils curling softly over her forehead and cheeks because, even defeated, Jerusha would have retained the remnants of her spirit and her beauty.

I stuck a tack into the plaster wall and hung the painting next to the bed, which I'd piled with fine, white-cotton pillows, plus a small square one made from satin that I always used under my face to prevent wrinkles. I don't know yet whether this works but I'd been assured from whomever I bought it that it would. I live in hope.

The night was warm, muggy in fact, hinting of a storm, the faint rumbles of which had echoed all evening long, though the sky remained a clear deep blue. Probably just a storm over the sea somewhere, I'd thought, paying it no heed, until later when I was awakened, I thought, by the clatter of hard rain against the open french doors and the sudden surge of cool air on my body, clad only in my usual short blue satin nightshirt.

I always wear these nightshirts, alone or with someone, in any country hot or cold. Once I make up my mind about something, that is it: a nightshirt, a house, a man. As well as a cat, a dog, and a songbird. All of whom now share this room with me and one of whom, the dog, was growling softly, up and alert, claws digging into my calf through the Italian six-hundred-thread-count sheet. Trust me, the Villa Romantica lacked for nothing, especially if it was expensive. And now I saw it certainly did not lack for men.

I lay stiff as a board, unable to move a finger to save myself as he stepped from my balcony and through those open french doors. I was alone in the house. Panic shivered up and down my suddenly icy spine. Then I remembered young Verity was sleeping in the next room, though Alfred was far away in his own cottage near the entrance, where the gatekeeper had lived with his wife and family in Jerusha's day.

The cat yowled, leaped off my chest, and fled under the bed. The canary remained silent in its cage, which was draped with a black silk cloth to remind the bird it was in fact nighttime and not singing time. The damn creature would sing at the drop of a hat.

I remained frozen to my spot, but it appeared it was not me the intruder was interested in. I felt

his eyes on me though, as he stood by the windows, no doubt checking if I was awake, and which I had already determined it was better not to be. Unless he came at me with a knife or a weapon, in which case I would bloody well fight for my life. But then anger fizzled suddenly out of nowhere, rage, in fact, and I lost my cool. I sprang upright.

"Who the fuck are you and what are you doing in my house?" I yelled, sending the dog into a frenzy of yaps as it ran under the bed. The cat had already fled, and the canary bird, thinking morning had come early, began to sing. I could have strangled it.

He turned to look at me. I looked back at him. Over six feet tall, a black ski mask hiding his face, wide shoulders under whatever black long-sleeved garment he was wearing, dark sneakers, and a shiny steel gun, which was currently pointed at my chest.

"Jesus," I mumbled, in a voice so strangled with fear I wondered where it came from. "Take whatever you want. Please. Then just go. I won't do anything, say anything, I won't even call the gendarmes, the FBI, anyone."

He approached the bed and stood over me, the gun still aimed at my chest. I wished I were under the bed with the cat. The cat gave a cautious meow. The intruder put out a hand and touched it gently.

A *gentle* man with a lethal weapon? I did not know what to make of this though I did know how frightened I was. I could not even think of how to escape, how to get myself off that bed, across the room, and through that door where I could call for help. But call who? No one was here. Of course, there was Verity, no doubt sleeping the sleep of the gods, exhausted by her misadventures, as I was myself. Or at least I had been until my night visitor appeared.

I struggled upward against Jerusha's padded rose brocade headboard, thinking as I did so that if he shot me here it would ruin that poor woman's lovely bed. Her history would go with it, there'd maybe be a mention in the tabloids of the "once owned by then-famous-celebrity Jerusha." Not much of a legacy. I believed she deserved better and I suddenly decided to try to give that to her.

I leaped from the bed in a move never to be repeated in my entire life no matter how often I went to the gym. Fear definitely lends strength. I was on him before he knew it, scrabbling at his chest, my thumbs searching for his eyes, the dog nipping at his ankles, the cat slowly stalking around him, looking, I knew, for an opening suitable for claws. My defenders. My little family.

I didn't realize I was yelling until the door was

flung open and I glimpsed Verity standing there in an old T-shirt and skimpy shorts, golden hair straggling over her face. She peered through the strands, taking in the crime scene.

"Ohh . . ." she exclaimed, a hand flying to her mouth. And then she screamed.

Verity was a good screamer. It echoed off the walls, out the open french doors into the quiet night gardens, bouncing back just as the storm broke. Lightning illuminated us like a stage set: the two half-dressed women; the man with the shiny steel gun and a ski mask over his head; the small animals arranged before him, one growling, one hissing. I might have laughed it was so funny, except I was scared as hell. And the canary awakened by the storm-light kept on singing.

16

Before I could move, the man was gone, through the open french doors.

"Fine, I'll call the cops," I managed to say between claps of thunder. Then I remembered I was in France. I didn't know the French equivalent of 911. "Ohh," I stammered. . . . Verity understood at once.

"Call the neighbor," she yelled, wrenching her hair back from a face parchment-pale under the soft light of my bedside lamp.

"What neighbor?" I could not think who she meant, I knew no one.

"That man, Chad, he lives next door."

I understood she meant the doctor, Chad Prescott, who'd helped me after my accident and owned the land contiguous with mine. He was my only neighbor. I did not like him, he was gruff, abrupt, good medically I'm sure, but no charmer, and he wanted my land. He certainly did not like me and now I was supposed to ask for his help?

"Jesus, Mirabella, there's a guy with a gun in the house," Verity snarled. "Give me the phone." She grabbed the handset and Chad's card from the night table where I'd left it, quickly thumbed the number, and handed me the phone.

He answered on the second ring. I heard him say, "Yes?" He did not sound a bit surprised or even puzzled at being awoken in the middle of the night; his voice was light, expectant.

"It's me," I said (even as the thought crept through my head, it should have been, "It is I"). "Your neighbor," I added.

"Ms. Matthews? I assume this is something important?"

You couldn't shake this fella, he didn't even sound interested in hearing my answer. But then I said, "There was a man in the house, in my room . . . he had a gun. . . ."

There was a short pause, a tiny flicker of time. "Are you alright?"

"Yup. Just scared."

"Did you call the cops?"

I shook my head though of course he couldn't see me. Verity came and slumped on the bed next to me. She swept her hair to one side, clutching it in a sideways ponytail. I'll bet she was wondering what the hell she was doing here in this mad-house; she might have been better off with the cheating husband than with a potential killer running around with a gun.

The cat jumped up on the bed and went and sat on her lap. The canary sang, and the dog, panting as though from a run around the woods, reclined against my knee and I choked back my tears, not wanting Verity to see my fear.

"I don't know the emergency number here in France," I said to Chad Prescott, sounding, I knew, as foolish as I felt, all helpless woman appealing to the strong male.

He said, "I'll be right over."

I told Verity to get dressed; we couldn't have strangers and possibly policemen gaping at us in our night attire, such as it was. We both slipped on jeans and T-shirts, mine emblazoned with the logo *CLUB 55 SAINT-TROPEZ*—hers with *GRATEFUL DEAD FINAL CONCERT*. Just in time.

The doorbell chimed a loud ear-blistering rendition of "La Marseillaise." I'd have to change that, get something more soothing, though I'd still keep it French, of course. Hurrying to answer the door I asked myself how my mind could fill with such trivia when I had just almost lost my life? Was it a safeguard, so I wouldn't feel threatened? Afraid? But hell, I *was* afraid, I was shaking in my flip-flops I was so afraid.

Chad Prescott pushed into the hall and grabbed me by the shoulders. "Are you alright?"

His firm hands held me up since my knees were definitely wobbly.

"Yes," I said as calmly as I could manage. Then I spoiled it all by bursting into tears.

He did not, thank God, put his arms around me and tell me I was okay, it was all going to be alright. In fact he said it very much was not alright. An intruder with a weapon meant business.

"What was he after? Do you know?"

His eyes searched mine, a deep narrow blue, or was it brown? Too dark to tell, and when I thought about it he was about the same height and build as my would-be attacker.

"It might have been *you,*" I said. "*You* could have come into my room with a gun and tried to kill me. *You* want my villa." I nailed him with my glare.

"Don't be ridiculous." He turned on his heel and made for the door. "I can see you're alright. I'll leave you for the cops to deal with."

The whine of sirens could be heard rapidly approaching. In seconds blue lights were flashing outside the window.

The three cops didn't knock, they just strode in. One grabbed Chad by his collar, pinning him against the wall. A second went and stood in front of him, gun in hand. It was like a scene in news broadcasts I'd seen on TV. The gun was a Glock. I'd heard the name, and once you've seen one, it's easy to recognize. Whatever, it was lethal looking and I had no doubt it was loaded.

I asked myself how this could have happened. My peaceful villa, Jerusha's home, Aunt Jolly's legacy, the Siamese cat—still on the bed along with the sausage mutt with the soulful eyes, while the damned canary that, despite being covered for the night, now would not shut up. And Verity, whose screams still rattled in my head, and the next-door neighbor who'd obviously bitten off more than he could chew merely by coming to our aid. Even if he did behave like a shit once he got here.

"Leave him alone," I said to the cop who was holding Chad Prescott, speaking my just-sufficiently-decent French so I thought he might get my message. He ignored me. Perhaps I hadn't said it right. I tried again in English.

"Leave him," a male voice said in French from behind me.

At least they understood *him*.

"*Bon soir*," I said to the newcomer, trying a smile. He ignored me and stepped up to Chad, standing so close in front of him they must have breathed the same tiny bit of air. He thrust his face even closer.

"What are you doing here?" he barked at Chad.

It was a true bark, a fast, authoritative, questioning tone that let you know he meant business. Chad threw back his head, out of breath's way I guessed, and said nothing. The look of contempt on his face struggled with anger.

"No, no, it's alright, he's not the intruder," I told the cop quickly. "He only came to help us."

I grabbed Verity by her cold hand and dragged her forward so they could see who we were, understand what two lone women had just gone through: a masked man in their house in the middle of the night, with a gun.

I spilled out the story in English. The cops stared at me like I was a crazy woman.

"Perhaps it would be better if we started at the beginning," the officer in charge said, also in English.

I knew that voice; I knew that man. He was the Colonel. The stocky, bearded, uniformed gendarme with the piercing eyes that I'd met after the accident. He was the one who had questioned me, made notes about the small green car, the anonymous Ducati. The cop who, as far as I knew, had not yet come up with any answers. I heard him sigh.

"It's you again," he said in a resigned I-might-have-known-it voice.

I remembered we had not gotten along; after all I had just been in a terrible accident, been helicoptered out of the canyon, lost my beautiful blue Maserati, almost lost my life. And Verity's. Somebody had tried to kill me then, and this . . . this *Colonel* . . . had acted like it was my fault. So now I did it again. I burst into tears. Me, who never cries, never, ever, at least only at weddings, and that's probably because they are not my own.

I heard Verity telling him there had been a man in my room, that she had heard me scream, and that he'd escaped through the french doors.

"We have him," the Colonel said, indicating the now-handcuffed Chad Prescott, who we could see outside on the steps, about to be bundled into the cop car, blue lights blazing like in a true crime scene. I almost smiled through my tears; I thought that would show the bastard who'd claimed he owned this villa. Let him try to take it away from me now, when he was inside a jail cell. Then I remembered, he had come to my aid.

"He's my neighbor," I called loudly so the officers outside would hear. "He came to help me. He is not the intruder, that man had a gun, he was wearing black, he got away through the doors. . . ."

"No one was seen outside, Madame . . . ?" The Colonel gave me a questioning glance.

I could tell that, like I had done with Chad Prescott, he was pretending he could not remember my name. Maybe it was true and he couldn't. After all, I was not that memorable, except for my red hair.

"It's Mirabella Matthews," I said and gave him a sharp look that let him know I knew he knew. He gave me what I assumed was a smile back, a mere lifting of the lips. I took another deeper look at him. Medium height, stocky, rumpled dark hair, an impression of strength, maybe a little dangerous. Of course that could be because of the stubble; a whiskery chin always lends itself to a look of masculinity, a not-quite-had-time-to-shower-and-shave, just-left-my-bed look. I quite liked it, actually. My imagination could take off on a look like that.

"Madame Matthews." He was not in a joking, lighthearted, flirty mood. He was deadly serious, and with reason. "This is the second time you have been in mortal danger." He gave me another long look from his flinty, dark eyes—gray, I think, unusual anyway. "You seem to attract trouble."

He was being mean and I knew it; still he was attractive in an offbeat way. Another of the "bad boys" was how Verity would have described him. You just knew *he* would be trouble. And right now he intended to give *me* that trouble, though I had done nothing wrong, only summoned his professional aid.

"I can't help it if someone pushed me off the road and someone else came into my room with a gun," I managed to say, albeit tearfully.

"You don't seem to understand," he said almost pityingly. "Someone seems determined to kill you. And what I want is for you to tell me why."

I was suddenly back to the frightened woman I had been before he rescued me. Well, not exactly *rescued,* but saved me anyway. That man in my room would not, I was sure, have simply gone away. Had the cops not announced their arrival, sirens and lights blazing, I might have been a dead woman, bullet through the chest from that silver gun, the Siamese and the sausage dog sitting helplessly at my head, the canary singing a mournful anthem to my passing.

"I'm scared," I admitted. "I don't know any reason why someone should want to kill me. I've never done anyone any harm. I don't even know many people here. I inherited the Villa Romantica from my aunt, I don't even know much about it. . . ."

"Do you know about Jerusha?"

I was silenced by his surprising question.

"Jerusha?" he repeated. "The woman who first owned the villa. The woman for whom it was built."

"I . . . well, I've heard of her, of course. I knew this was her place."

"Her lover built it for her. It was the most expensive villa on the coast at that time. The grounds alone were several hectares of land. There was a lavish lifestyle, famous guests, many servants."

"I had heard," I said, though in truth I did not really know the whole story, it had all happened so long ago. "Surely nobody really cares about all that anymore."

He was silent for a while, then he said, "Perhaps," as he got to his feet. "I shall leave two men on duty tonight. You will be safe. Tomorrow, I suggest you get yourself some able-bodied help. For security purposes."

“*Bodyguards,* you mean?” I couldn’t believe it. I needed security? “But why?”

“That is a question only you can answer, Madame. But I might suggest you look into your past, into everybody’s past, to find out. Meanwhile, get that security.”

And the Colonel turned and left me, mouth agape, wondering what it was all about.

Part II

Jerusha
1930s

17
Mirabella

Much later, as dawn was lifting the sky, I sat on my bed, alone again, with the envelope containing a letter written by Jerusha. I was holding a piece of history in my hand, meant only to be read by her descendants, or those that remembered her, or at least remembered more than the scandal, the disaster she was involved in, the events that had brought her and her entire world down, and after which she simply disappeared. No one knew and, as time passed, no one even cared where she had gone.

But before that, and perhaps what led up to it, was her early story written here in her own hand, of a girl born to beauty and poverty, a combination that spelled disaster. Life did not offer much to a girl in those circumstances, a girl that looked like that, other than to go to the stage. It was 1926. "Theatre" was what she was destined for, at least that's what her mother told her when she took her by the hand, aged thirteen, on the train to Paris to "seek her fortune." And the fame that assuredly would come with it.

The letter was written in the distinctive violet ink Jerusha preferred, and began with the words, *This is my story.*

Jerusha

You will have read other tales, different versions, of what I am about to say, but as the woman to whom all this happened, only I know the truth. I shall tell it to you now, in the hope it will be remembered, that I will not be judged forever for what happened. I have lived my life extravagantly, I admit it, but I also lived it honorably, or at least within the standards I considered honorable, showing compassion to those who needed a shoulder to cry on, giving material help to those who came to me in need, caring with all my heart for those young ones, the children I took into my life, who shared my life, who were my life.

I was born in a village near the town of Sarlat in the Dordogne region, a land spiked with young vines that over the years would become producers of the good wines of Bordeaux, but which were then still a work in progress. No vintner, no farmer, no field worker was making money. Poverty claimed our lives, kept us hand-to-mouth for decades.

I attended school, as was usual, until I was twelve years old. I learned to read and write but not much else. Too tall for my age, too much hair always unkempt, too long and too red, scraped back with a bit of string. There was no money even for ribbons from the tinkers that sold door-to-door. They did not bother so much as knocking on our door. It was a one-bedroom cottage, built a century or so before, as a stable. There were no foundations and it listed to one side, its black-and-white timbers were cracked, the door lintel sloped, the door itself hung off rusted hinges, and a bead curtain always rattling in the wind. Nothing kept out the bitter chill of winter, the rains of spring, the heat of summer. I knew nothing different. I never complained, though I would have liked a ribbon. I thought it would have made me like the other girls, the ones that ignored me, gathering together in a giggling clump, whispering behind their hands as I stood silently across the school-yard. It was only a small stretch of beaten-down earth, unpaved and weedy and where the few tufts of grass hid bugs so small you never saw them but that bit your ankles, leaving ferocious red welts that lasted for weeks.

I wore my faded blue smock, my wrinkled once-white stockings, and clumsy black shoes with broken heels. They had belonged first to a neighbor girl, then to her sister, and had finally been passed pityingly on to me, who stuffed them with rags and bits of paper to keep out the wet and keep them on my narrow feet.

Later, when I was a success and told this story about myself, I claimed I did not care. All I knew was that I loved my mother, and she loved me. My mother told me I was destined for better things than life in this village where those other girls, the ones that had mocked me, would themselves end as beaten-down housewives, with too many children, and probably with a drunk for a husband struggling to provide a roof over their heads, because work was scarce and young love long since lost.

You, the stranger reading this now, will know, or at least you can find out, who I became. Who Jerusha used to be, that is, because now I am no one. I barely remember myself the extravagant, joyous, carefree life I led, that began with my introduction, still clutching my mother's hand, a too-young thirteen, innocent in the ways of the world and with no idea that a body could be used for sexual purposes, or that men would want my body, or that later I should find fulfillment, pleasure, even find "myself" in giving that pleasure to my lovers. Never a husband, though. Unlike my school friends who married for a house, I paid to keep my own roof over my head, kept my closets filled with couture dresses, evening gowns that sparkled the way I had imagined them in my dark little house, while now I had crystal chandeliers to light every corner. I had new friends to share this with me, friends that enjoyed my success, who cared about me for who I was, the same girl I had always been, the naive, too-extravagant "beauty" who all her life, when she looked in the mirror never saw that beauty, only the poor child with the broken shoes and her uncombed, too-red hair tied back with a piece of string.

That is, until the day Maman brushed out the tangles, washed and ironed my blue smock, hitched up the too-long stockings bleached back to whiteness in an ammonia-smelling cauldron, and who purchased new shoes with the little money she'd hidden from the man who was my father. He had never married her and came only at night, usually Friday when he had been paid and gotten drunk and wanted her, and later would not remember where his money had gone. Maman did though. It was in the black leather satchel with my borrowed schoolbooks.

Choosing a day when my father was gone to work in a faraway area, Maman cleaned me up, tied back my hair with a black ribbon she'd bought specially from the tinker, smoothed me up and down, and tied the newly polished shoes that shone like coal on top. She walked with me to the train station and bought two one-way tickets to Paris, where she told me I was going to be a star on the stage.

I believed her, of course. Who else could have taken me out of that village, dressed me up, fixed my hair, my shoes, so I could get to go on the stage? Me, who had never so much as seen a real stage, only the traveling circus in its small drafty tent with the dancers in their tatty finery, and the clowns that ran through the aisles tripping over their enormous shoes and making the children laugh. Was I, I wondered, clutching Maman's hand, about to become one of those dancing girls? Would I get to wear a sparkly tunic like theirs? Would I wear ostrich plumes in my hair that nodded with every step I took? Could I even dance?

It turned out it didn't matter if I could dance or sing. All I had to do was stand there, in the glare of the stage lights, in tights and silver shoes with high heels and a sequined tunic, my immature breasts covered with a fold of tulle, and smile at the unseen audience, who loved me.

18

Mirabella

I put down Jerusha's letter, more of a diary I thought, suddenly ashamed of intruding on another woman's personal life, on her thoughts and emotions. Diaries were not meant for other eyes: they were the writer's inner thoughts, wishes, memories, expressions of their fears and pleasures. I had no right to know Jerusha's.

I stuffed the thin pages back in the blue envelope. It was too small and I was afraid of crumpling them. Jerusha had written so carefully, she had put them in this envelope herself, never knowing who might read them. Yet, surely she had realized that one day, maybe long after she was gone, somebody would. Why else would she have told her story, especially after all the notoriety, when she had been accused of murdering her lover? Yet I could not bring myself to intrude on her thoughts now.

Restless, I went outside into the garden, pacing the path that led to the pebbly little beach. To my right was the dual driveway that serviced both villas, mine and my neighbor's, the oh so uncharming Dr. Chad Prescott, whose pink shorts I recalled too vividly for a woman who supposedly hated him. Well, disliked him, anyway, though he was undoubtedly good-looking and he had played a part in saving my life. At least in helping to fix me up after the accident, plus rushing to my aid and saving me from the villain with the gun, who later, even the Colonel had not been able to find, let alone identify. Had I even so much as thanked Chad for that? I could not remember, and taking the path that led to his villa, I decided to do so now.

Despite the early hour, I found him outside his triple-size garage hosing down a British racing green Jaguar convertible—which means it seats two in front and with a squeeze, two in the tiny space in back, a myth I've never gone for. However, the thought was irrelevant since I did not believe this man would ever put any passengers in the back, maybe not even in front. It was obvious from his intent expression and the way he stroked his hand lovingly over the surface that this car was his toy and he was not a boy that shared.

"How about taking me for a ride?" I said, putting him on the spot and startling him at the same time. He had not heard me approach, he was so intent on what he was doing. I liked that: a man who can concentrate that hard would be good at whatever he did. I'd heard he was a brilliant surgeon but I'd bet he would have been a great car mechanic in another life.

I watched as with an effort he brought himself back to the moment from wherever he had been lost. He took me in, feet planted firmly on his side of the drive, cute denim shorts a bit shorter than they should have been, long legs brown from the beach and early morning swims and late-afternoon cocktails on terraces, red hair floating out in an uncontainable cloud that perhaps I should have tied back with a bit of string, like Jerusha. And a white tee that, against my better judgement, I had bought secondhand—what they now call "vintage" in the local market—the one with the Rolling Stones' tongue and lip logo.

Bad move, I thought now, seeing him eyeing it with a condescending frown. I folded my arms over my breasts. I'd also forgotten to put on a bra—well, not forgotten, I'd chosen not to because I hadn't anticipated seeing anyone this morning. I'd decided to visit him only moments ago.

He put down the chamois cloth with which he'd been polishing the car and folded his own arms. "Feeling better, I presume?" he said, brows raised in inquiry.

"I was kind of hoping that *you* were feeling better," I said honestly. "I couldn't have known—I mean I didn't realize the cops—the Colonel—would think you were . . ."

"That I was the suspect? And why should he not? I was the man in your home and that's why you'd called them."

He hitched up his shorts, pale blue this time, I noticed. The man went for pastels. We stared at each other. I thought he was definitely cute. I had no idea what he thought about me in my unlovely tee with my messy red hair and too-short shorts that were meant for nobody's eyes but my own.

To my surprise, he walked the few steps over to where I was standing. He stopped in front of me. I was five-nine in my flip-flops but he was way taller. He bent his head, and put his face close to my uplifted one.

"I don't know whether you realize it, but you are in a frightening situation. You have come close to death two times recently. Shouldn't you be asking yourself why? Who wants you out of the way?" He shrugged. "Seems logical to me."

"To the Colonel too. He said exactly the same thing, but you see I don't know anyone here, or almost no one. I only ever came to visit my Aunt Jolly and she was hardly the social runabout, though she did give some good dinner parties. She was the old-fashioned sort, liked a proper sit-down dinner, white linen cloth, silver, crystal . . ."

"Finger bowls."

I met his eyes. "Not quite that far."

"So," he said. "Who was the half-naked young blonde, the one screaming her head off last night?"

"The one that got you arrested?"

He gave me a long look that said not to even mention that.

"The Colonel apologized later," he said.

"That was Verity. I picked her up on the Paris-to-Nice train. She was running away from her husband. Not only did he cheat on her, he stole all her money.

"All of it?"

"Well, all she had was a couple of thou, but he took that, and the jewelry. She had nothing, literally the clothes on her back and a tiny duffle with a few photos, her hairbrush, and some underthings. I don't know how far she imagined she could get on that, but fortunately I took her in. I've sent her into town now to pick up some more suitable clothes, at least jeans and a couple of good shirts, a frock or two in case of a party."

"You are having a party?"

"I'm not, but I heard the gossip that my neighbor on the other side from you is giving a monster bash tomorrow night to which half the monied world around here is invited. Of course, he's Mr. Money himself, so few will turn down an invite to the Villa Mara. You'll have heard of Bruce Bergen?"

"I've heard him called the Boss."

I nodded. I was still clutching my arms across my unfettered bosom, fearing a jiggle. "That's what everybody—including, I believe, himself—calls him. I see him sometimes, on the café terrace in town, always with a tall glass of lemonade. It's the kind of thing you notice when most everyone else is sipping rosé wine."

"He's hard to miss, a man that tall, and built like a champion wrestler."

"He's Russian," I said, as though that explained it.

I eyed Chad Prescott up and down, considering. "You might care to accompany me," I said in my most formal voice so he did not think I was coming on to him and asking for a date. "It'll be the party of the year, no expense spared, no celebrity left out." I spread out my arms, felt my boobs jiggle, wished I had not, and saw him politely avert his eyes. "Of course, it's up to you, you might not like that kind of thing."

"I don't."

"Oh."

We stared at each other.

"For you, I will make an exception," he said, still looking into my eyes. His were blue. I could see into them so clearly I caught my own reflection. It almost made my heart stop, or at least that's what it felt like, and I have not felt like that in a month of Sundays, as the saying goes. In truth, much longer than that. Well, except when I'd first met him.

"I'd better come with you to protect you," he said, looking all serious, a furrow creasing his brow, eyes squinching intently. "You do realize somebody means you harm? I know you joked about it when the Colonel suggested body-guards, but I'm telling you now, that's what you need."

"Somebody at my back, you mean."

"Try the front as well," he said. "Bullets are not choosy."

I refused to believe he was serious. "I'm just a woman who inherited a beautiful villa, a few hectares of land, a small fortune. I write novels about stuff like this. I mean, it doesn't happen in real life. At least not to people like me."

He was still giving me that long look that was sending shivers down my spine. "Cute," Verity had called him. And she was right, but there was more to him than that. This was a man who knew his role in life, who gave of himself. He was not just another member of a summer South of France playboy society. He was the real thing, and I was lucky to have met him, to have been rescued by him, even though it meant he'd spent a night in the local jail.

"I hope the Colonel fed you properly, in the clink," I said.

"Pizza, half bottle of red. Not bad, these local French jails, when you know the proprietor, so to speak."

"So to speak," I agreed.

"Look, I'm serious about you." He stepped forward and took my gloved hands in both of his, gripping so hard I almost yelled out.

I gasped, half in pain, half in wonder. What could he mean by "serious"?

"There's a danger here, something is wrong, somebody has it in for you."

"That's what the Colonel said."

"I believe he's right. Ask yourself, Mirabella, what's wrong? Who wants what you have?"

I loved the way he said my name, pronouncing each syllable so precisely it almost sounded like a woman other than me.

I thought for a second, had no answer, and I told him so. He was still holding my hands in his.

"Then we shall have to find out."

"Wait I minute." I snatched my hands away. "I said it before and I'll say it again now. You are the one that wants something from me. You want my land."

"*My* land," he said with equal firmness. "Remember I have the letter from Aunt Jolly in which she gave it to me."

"An old woman like that, she could not think clearly, she did not know what she was doing."

"I wonder," he said, looking as though he was thinking hard. "I wonder if she did it to try to keep you out of danger."

I stared blankly back at him. "I don't know what you're talking about."

"Is it true or not true that since you inherited the property there have been attacks on your life?"

I thought about it again. "True," I admitted. "But

that could be a mere coincidence. Somebody made a mistake on the corniche road, and some cat burglar thought I'd have jewels, wanted my pearls."

"You've seen too many movies. There are no cat burglars anymore. Everything's done by computer, shifting stuff from vaults, from bank accounts. No one's risking life and limb for a pearl necklace now."

"That's just as well, since the only one I have is fake. I'll wear it to the Boss's party."

He nodded and turned to walk away. "Hope you'll wear some clothes too," he called over his shoulder. "I'll pick you up. And Verity, of course."

"Are we going in the British racing green Jag?" I yelled after him.

He turned, standing there looking very Greek godlike with his floppy blond hair, his lean body, his friggin' pastel shorts, and white polo.

"Of course," he called back. "Can't let the parking valets down, amongst all the Bentleys and Rolls-Royces, can we?"

19

The Boss

Sitting at his usual terrace table, third row back, closest to the building, at his favored seafront café, the Boss added more ice to the tall glass of lemonade. He stirred a lemon segment into it with a long spoon and took a first sip, assessing its acidity. He liked it best when it hit his throat in a sharp rush that a lesser man, or one less experienced in the ways of lemon, might have choked on. It was one of the many small ways he tested himself, though some were tougher, like, for instance, the knife, honed to the thinnest of points that he would hold to his own throat while watching himself in the bathroom mirror. The slightest move, a blink, a tremor, or God forbid, a sneeze would have done him in. He enjoyed that feeling. Danger was a dangerous game: living on the edge, feeling every moment.

He also enjoyed playing that game with other people, real-live people whose death he could enjoy with no danger to himself. Of course when he said "people" he meant girls, young women, teens—older too, though forty or thereabouts was his limit. He preferred the tight body of youth to the overblown tumultuous flesh of the older woman. Like, for instance, the young blonde racing across the street, dodging traffic with a cheeky wave and a big smile as cars screeched around her, making for the very café where he sat, sipping his lemonade.

Folding his arms across his massive chest, the Boss leaned back in his chair—the extra-large one the café kept specially for him—enjoying the sight. Medium-tall, slender, with long legs shown off to perfection in short white shorts that also showed off her pert butt, and a black tank top with, thank God, no insignia inscribed across it. Instead he could take note of her small high breasts, bouncing attractively as she skipped through the traffic, noticed, of course, by every man in the café, as well as by the irate drivers. She stopped suddenly in the middle of the road. Cars screeched to a halt, windows were lowered, angry shouts made her shake her head and point down at the small sausage dog tangled in its lead around her own ankle.

"Sorry," she mouthed. "So sorry, oh dear. Oh, gosh darn it, Sossy, get a move on, won't you?" And the dog miraculously untangled itself and shot forward, jerking her off her sneakered feet and onto the sidewalk fronting the café.

The Boss admired her as she stood for a minute, a hand on her hip, dog lead wrapped securely around her wrist, surveying the crowded terrace. There were no free tables, there never were in the early evening, when everyone stopped for an aperitif, though inside the place was empty. He saw her mouth the word *shit,* almost thought he caught a hint of a stamp of her foot, but no, surely not. . . . Whatever, it was an opportunity sent from heaven.

"Mademoiselle . . ." He waved, caught her eye. "There's a free chair here, if you don't mind sharing. I'll be leaving soon anyway, then you can have it all to yourself, and your little dog, of course. Looks like a sweetheart," he added, though he was obviously not referring to the dog.

Verity heaved a sigh of relief. "You are so kind to offer, I mean, you don't know me or anything and sharing is such a . . . well, *intimate* . . . thing, isn't it? Especially with a stranger."

"My pleasure," he said as the waiter appeared out of nowhere to adjust the chair, set down napkins, a coaster for her, a bottle of Perrier, chilled glasses. He noticed there was no ring on her finger; not married then, or engaged, a free spirit perhaps. Or there was a divorce. Either way, it was good.

"You can't imagine how grateful I am," Verity rattled on, exhausted from chasing the dog around the back streets. She had already stuffed it in the car and had simply turned to get something when it took off. "You'd never think a small dog like this could move so fast," she said, finally managing a smile and remembering her manners. "Thank you so much, Mr. . . . ?"

"Bergen." He held out a large hand that almost swallowed hers as she took it. "Around here they call me the Boss."

"Wow. You must really be somebody. I myself go by the name of Verity. I am currently choosing to forget my last name, until a more appropriate time."

The name Verity rang like a clarion call through his brain. He leaned back in his chair, the cane creaking under his bulk, arms crossed, hands flat against his chest, and eyelids half lowered as he took her in. He was looking at the young woman whose death in the car accident he had ordered, for no good reason other than she was Mirabella Matthews's friend and companion. Her bad luck, his good fortune.

He allowed a small worried frown to cross his face. "I'm sorry, I didn't mean to pry, to intrude . . . I simply wanted to make your acquaintance."

She was smiling at him, sipping the icy Perrier, burping softly on the bubbles. The dog nudged her foot and she took a couple of ice cubes, put them in the saucer meant for the waiter's tip, and set it on the ground. The dog licked, took a step back, looked up at her, and growled.

"There's thanks for you," he said, patting its golden-brown head. It growled again.

"Okay Sossy, I'll get you the real thing," she

said, but with the flick of a hand he beat her to it. A waiter appeared with a bowl of water for the dog who proceeded to splash it lavishly all over Verity's sneakers as he lapped.

"Good dog," she said happily.

A second waiter appeared bearing a tray with duck pâté, St. Aubin cheese, black and green olives, and chunks of sliced baguette.

"Oh, and lucky us," Verity said, even more happily. "In fact, just what I felt like."

"Surprising how I guessed," he said, laughing.

Looking up at him, she said, "Well, now we've introduced ourselves, can I ask what brings you to the South of France, Mr. Boss?"

"Please, just 'Boss.' And to answer your question, I have a place here, a villa up in the hills. I come here often. In fact it's my favorite home."

Verity's eyes widened, she was impressed. "So, exactly how many homes do you have?"

He smiled. He liked her innocent smart-ass attitude, but chose to ignore her question. "And what are you doing in this part of the world, then, Miss Verity?"

"Running away from my cheating husband." As always Verity wished she'd thought before she'd spoken. It had just slipped out. She bit her lip, staring down at the dog who'd flopped, limp as a rag in the heat, between her feet. "Sorry, I shouldn't have told you that. No need to go into my problems, spoil your nice holiday."

"You are certainly not doing that. In fact, Verity, you have made my day." He took a long drink of his lemonade, signaled the waiter for more ice. It's not often I get to meet a pretty girl."

Verity gave him a skeptical upward glance that meant she certainly did not believe that. "Take another look around this terrace, Mr. Boss," she said with a smile. "There's dozens of them, most hoping to meet Mr. Right, and that he's rich."

The Boss laughed, he was enjoying her. He reached out and tucked a stray strand of corn-blond hair away from her face where it was in danger of dipping into the glass of Perrier. "I certainly qualify for one of those conditions," he said. "Not boasting, mind you, but I'm a property developer down here, and it's a rich man's world, in case you had not noticed."

"I had noticed. My friend, the one I'm staying with, Mirabella Matthews, inherited a wonderful old villa from her late aunt."

"You must mean Aunt Jolly."

Verity stared at him, astonished. "You *knew* Aunt Jolly?"

"Everyone knew her. She was here, on and off, for many years, quite old when she passed, I believe. And left it all to a niece she barely knew."

It had not occurred to Verity to question how well Mirabella had known her aunt; all she'd heard was the Harrods story with the throat-choking velvet-collared princess coat and the dropped cream bun. She took a gulp of her Perrier. "Very generous of her, I'd say."

"Or foolish. It depends on how you look at it."

She sat up straighter in her faux-wicker chair. His tone was cold, dismissive. "Well, Mirabella looks upon it as a stroke of good fortune. And my good fortune was to meet her on the train coming down here."

"Running from the cheating husband?"

She nodded, sighing. "You'd be surprised how many more cheaters there are than charmers."

"Then we must hope that next time you find a charmer," he said with a sudden smile of such warmth that Verity was indeed charmed.

"Hopefully," she said. Then, getting quickly to her feet and unwinding the dog lead from the table leg, she said, "I must be on my way. So nice to have met you Mr. . . . er . . ."

"Boss," he said.

She glanced suspiciously at him, as though he might be laughing at her. No, he was nice. She liked him. "Y'know what, Boss?" she said. "*You* are one of the charmers."

"I hope that means you'll come to the party I'm giving tomorrow night. My villa, the one you can see from here, the Villa Mara. You make a right off the up-road, can't miss it. Eight. Black tie."

"How very James Bond," Verity said. She had

not enjoyed herself with a man so much in years. "I'll be there."

"Oh, and bring your friend, Mirabella. After all, we are close neighbors."

"Yeah, sort of like Chad Prescott." She tugged the dog's lead, edging from the table.

"Sort of," the Boss agreed. He knew Chad Prescott.

20

The night of the party, the Villa Mara, on top of its own hill overlooking the Mediterranean, could surely have been seen from outer space, illuminated so extravagantly, so spectacularly, that every rosebush was defined in soft pink, every tree under-lit so its branches spiked into the dark blueness of a sky that seemed also to have been lit by the monied hand of the host.

The Boss had inspected everything an hour before his party was to start; checked the all-so-important lighting, the premier necessity for atmosphere, he'd always found. He'd seen that the tables were properly draped in simple white linen in classic style; that the white-cushioned chairs had golden chiffon bows tied around their backs; that the seventy-foot turquoise pool glittered like a jewel in the twilight; that crystal gleamed and silver shone and the bar was big enough to accommodate every guest, and stocked everything any guest could possibly want. Including, of course, Roederer Cristal Rouge. He believed it was every woman's favorite champagne. Nothing like a slender flute of pink to elevate her sense of well-being, while at the same time possibly loosening her morals.

He was alone now, before the guests arrived, in

the anonymous square concrete bunker directly on the seafront he called his own place, and where no one else was permitted access—without, that is, a direct personal invitation from the Boss himself. Which meant those invited were there on spurious business of an illegal and possibly lethal kind.

He was sitting in his big leather chair in front of the screen that showed the entirety of his villa: every room, every part of the grounds, almost every blade of grass and grain of sand, even the waves hitting the beach. He knew he could never become careless, take his life for granted. Enemies and danger always lurked, always would for a man in his position who had earned his wealth by eliminating anyone that stood in his way. Somehow they seemed to end up losing their businesses, their homes, their wives, their reason for living, and even occasionally, their lives. He had never tried to count how many enemies he'd had but it no longer mattered. He had come out the winner; whomever had opposed him remained at the bottom of the heap. A few he had permitted to continue running their lives just for appearance's sake, building here and there, usually on the Costa del Sol where things were easier.

Outside, the waiters waited, and a quartet played softly, the pianist plucking jazzy chords that suited the quiet moment before the guests arrived.

The Boss adjusted his black silk bow tie in the mirror, thinking that as he had grown financially and therefore was more powerful, last-resort measures against rivals or enemies were rarely used. Those days were over; he was a sterling member of the community, a philanthropist who gave lavishly to causes that would get him publicity, make him known as a "good" man to those who counted in that world he craved and yet to which, despite his lavish charity, he still did not belong. It was, he thought—still looking in the mirror at his reflected self that gave no clue as to his true self—as though he was permanently locked out of the world he considered paradise. He and Orpheus. Good company, he supposed.

But it was the women he was really thinking about, those elegant creatures who would soon enter his door in their couture gowns, jewels gleaming at slender throats, with coiffures that had taken hours to construct, simple as they looked; in tall heels that lengthened their legs even though the shoes were killing them; silks gleaming, tulle fluttering, chiffon flowing soft over their bodies, hiding their secret selves. Some of them he knew could be bought for the price of a jeweled necklace, or a few weeks' pampered vacation on a yacht in the Aegean; for a dinner on his arm at Paris's best restaurant where she would be treated like the goddess she might suddenly have imagined she had become. Until reality was forced upon her and she found she was lucky to leave with her life intact, if not her body.

The Boss enjoyed violence, he enjoyed the knife against the throat, the threat. For him, sex was aways better with a threat, he had found that out long ago. And besides, afterward, money took care of everything.

But with these new women, the writer, Aunt Jolly's heir, who was the new owner of the Villa Romantica and its land, the place where he'd planned to build his fourteen-story condos and make more than just a few millions over a short period of time, plus her silly little blond friend who was overeager to be liked and who he had charmed at the café; now *there* was a challenge. A challenge he would face tonight, with the help of the Russian, of course, though that bastard had not lived up to his promises. Still, in lieu of anyone better, he was being given a second chance. The Matthews woman, whose name he must remember was Mirabella, would be taken out this time. No mistakes could be made. And the little blond darling? Well, perhaps another role could be found for her, for a short time, anyway.

21

Chad Prescott

Chad left his house at two minutes to eight. Precisely at eight, he parked the Jag convertible in front of the Villa Romantica, slung his long legs out the door, and strode up the shallow front steps. He was greeted by the small brown dachshund, which, it seemed, liked to show its teeth to visitors. Chad did not fancy having a piece of his tuxedo trouser leg torn off right now. God knows he wore it rarely enough but it had served him well over the years and he was not yet ready to buy a new one.

"Good dog," he said, not meaning it, but the dog seemed to take it the right way and backed off, tail wagging, snarl gone.

The door stood open. Moths and other small night creatures fluttered around the lamps that stood on each side of the hall, and which Chad recognized as being from the deco period; their square black shades had surely never been changed since they were bought. A pair of malachite-topped tables, the likes of which would not be made today, were set on narrow gilded legs with lion feet, surely dated from the turn of the century. Rugs were flung carelessly across the marble floor, each a beauty of Eastern workman-ship, in silk or the finest wool, their colors faded into a harmonious blur. A pair of love seats in a muted green brocade that brought to mind the first pale leaves of spring, faced each other across the hall, framed in gilded wood that also brought to mind a great deal of expense.

Nothing was cheap in Aunt Jolly's house, which, of course, Chad remembered from the several visits he had made to take tea with her. Which is how Aunt Jolly had described it in her invitations.

Please come and take tea with me at four this afternoon, was exactly what she'd written, and he had come here and drank the Earl Grey she'd poured from a silver pot, refilling it from a matching pot of water set over a small burner to keep it hot. Aunt Jolly was old school, and she respected the past. Chad was deeply troubled by Aunt Jolly's violent death. And especially by the fact that the so-called Colonel had so far done nothing about finding the perpetrator.

He stood on the front steps, looking into the hallway, remembering the old woman who had cared for this villa, who had known all its secrets, had known all the people from the past, and who'd told him she wanted him to have it. "After I am gone," she had said.

Of course Chad had protested that it was not right, said what about her family? But she had reiterated, "I have reason to believe it would not be safe for my niece to inherit the villa. There are people out there, developers they call themselves, who would ruin this place, ruin this whole countryside, all for money. Whereas a man like you, Doctor, can take care of yourself, take care of things."

Naturally he had asked what Aunt Jolly meant, and her answer, in the precise high voice that matched her precisely attired person, was that no doubt he would find out, and anyhow the niece had her own life, her own place in the world.

"As do I." He recalled his reply, now.

"Indeed." She'd handed him a Wedgwood cup and saucer, offering a plate of Garibaldi biscuits. English to the core, he'd thought, eyeing those biscuits.

"You are a man who knows how to look after himself," she said. "You have faced enemies in jungles and remote villages, in outposts of countries most of us never go to. You have the instinct to protect yourself from danger. My niece, Mirabella—Lord knows how she got that name, her mother was on the stage—well, Mirabella does not have a single self-protective instinct in her entire body. Though she writes about it, of course. Detective stuff, you know."

Chad did know. In fact, surprisingly, he'd read a couple of them, alone in the lamplight on his sofa, far from the jungle villages, glass of wine in hand, a smile on his face. He'd always guessed who'd done it—of course, but that wasn't her point; it was *how* and *why* he had done it. Chad appreciated that.

Having tea with Aunt Jolly, he'd eyed his hostess over the edge of the cup, seeing beyond her age to the beauty she had surely been. She was in her seventies then but her face was unlined, no sag to her neck and definitely no plastic surgery. Simply good genes. Beauty never disappeared, it simply grew softer with time.

"I want you to have this." She'd handed him a piece of blue writing paper torn from a pad. "I put everything in here, so there'll be no problem. Mirabella gets my money, but you get the land that runs contiguous with yours. And the villa of course. On condition it is kept exactly the way it is now. I love this place, it's always meant 'home' to me. And family. I'd like to think it will always be the same because you own the land next to it, you are the only one I feel I can trust to do this. I believe you care about it, just the way I do."

At this point she had put on her spectacles and eyed him keenly for a long moment. He'd shifted under her glare, not knowing what to say, how to accept such a responsibility.

"Don't worry," she'd said. "All I want is for Mirabella to be safe. I don't want her to go Jerusha's way."

"Jerusha?"

"Jerusha was her great aunt. And a murderer, you know."

He stared back at her, stunned.

"Oh, don't worry, it was a long time ago. Back in the thirties. Killed her lover, shot him, or so they said. I don't believe it was ever proved. Still, it ruined Jerusha, ruined her career. She was a star, y'know, musicals, a singer, dancer, a great beauty. So they say."

Aunt Jolly took a photo in a silver frame from the side table. "This is Jerusha."

The picture was of a tall, rounded woman, her long red braid tumbling over shoulders bared in a low-cut evening dress, one foot in a silvery slipper peeping from the ruffled hem, a slender arm resting along the back of a silk chair, a cluster of lily of the valley in her hand. Her eyes looked into the camera confidently, Chad thought almost challengingly, as though she had to meet life and cameras dead-on.

Aunt Jolly said, "Jerusha was a woman who fought to get where she was, Dr. Prescott, and she was enjoying the fruits of her labors. Until she met the man who caused her downfall." She took his empty cup. "More tea?"

"Thank you. And it's *Chad,* please."

"Well, with women, it's usually one of two things that get them in the end. The first is money, lack of it, or working out how to get it. The second is a man. Personally I've always thought the man should be placed first. My cousin, Mirabella's mother, had other ideas, which is why she got herself into trouble, and hence, years later, the reason for Mirabella. Who, it seems from all I hear, and the little I know of her, is a very smart cookie." She smiled. "I do so like that expression, 'smart cookie.' Do have another Garibaldi, Dr. Chad."

"Just Chad." He took the cookie though he did not want it.

She put the plate back on the tray and got to her feet. "It has been nice seeing you, Dr. Chad. I have a feeling in my bones we shall not meet again."

Now, standing on the steps of the Villa Romantica, gazing into the hallway, Chad remembered the old lady who had met her end so violently here. He wanted to know why.

22

Mirabella

I'm looking at myself in the long mirror, dressed for the Boss's party, all snazzy in long aqua chiffon, cut low on the bosom and narrow on the hip, flaring out just sufficiently at the hem to make walking possible, though not probable. This dress, and the heels I'm wearing to accompany it, strappy gold five-inch sandals in fact, are definitely not meant for walking. In an outfit like this I might make it from a limo into a New York restaurant, but it's doubtful I'll make it into the front seat of that low-slung Jag. That is after squashing Verity into the back, though of course Verity is less disabled by her outfit, which consists, as far as I can make out, of a swathe of white silk hitched high on her right thigh, low to the knee on the left, with a strapless silvery bustier that clutches her small breasts in a lover's grip, sending them spilling nicely over the top.

I smoothed my silver gloves, put on the sapphire ring. Verity was standing next to me. "Is that really what you're going to wear?"

"That's it." I took the aggressor role before she could get onto me, as I knew she was going to, about being a bit more daring.

"At your age you should be flaunting it a bit. Shorter is almost always better. Wait, though, I have an idea."

She dashed out of my room and returned moments later, brandishing a pair of scissors.

I held out a hand to ward her off. "What are you, girl, mad? This is an expensive dress, bought specially for the occasion, and I am a woman in my forties who knows her style and is sticking to it."

"But you have great legs." She stopped in front of me, twirling the scissors around three fingers. "We women must always understand what our assets are and make the most of them. That way men won't notice our shortcomings. Like for instance your hair," she added, eyeing her scissors once again.

"Jesus, girl, you *are* mad." I retreated farther, hands up to my newly styled hair. I had taken a couple of hours out of my busy schedule and submitted myself to the ministrations of the hairdresser in the town square, a young man who did everybody of note in the area. Nobody went to the posh salons when they were on vacation in the South of France and dipping in and out of the sea or the pool all day. Waste of money.\ Even for that upmarket event the Boss's party promised to be.

"Put those scissors down," I ordered. Thankfully, Verity obeyed.

"But it's so stiff," she complained. "Your lovely red hair, sprayed to within an inch of its beautiful life. Wait, I'll take care of it, I'll set it free." She grabbed a brush, shoved me into the chair in front of the mirror, and attacked my mane vigorously.

"Tilt your head forward," she commanded. I obeyed.

"Up now, toss your hair back, shake your head."

I did so.

"There, take a look at that," she said proudly.

I looked, and looked again. I twisted my head to the left, to the right, shook my hair out again. It shone, a burnished red-gold cloud of waves in a way it never had before.

"How do you know how to do all this?" I asked, amazed.

Verity shrugged. "All girls know. I just don't know what to do about the dress without lopping off a chunk. But since you're not about to allow me to do that, we'll just have to divert attention."

She studied me again, more closely. "I know. A necklace. Something big, dramatic."

"Don't have one," I said firmly. I did not want a chunk of gold choking me. I just wanted to get this over with, torture-by-outfit was not making me a happy girl. But then I remembered the pearls, the ones Aunt Jolly had given me a few years ago when I was visiting the villa. I was more into bikinis than jewelry, but she had hung that heavy rope of pearls around my neck where it fell to just below my breasts.

I kept them in the wall-safe hidden behind a row of sweaters in the closet. Of course, all my sweaters were black; I never was one for change. I hadn't checked recently but I hoped the pearls were still there.

I opened the safe and breathed a sigh of relief. There they were, wrapped in the same piece of crumpled tissue, exactly the way she'd handed them to me. I held them up to show Verity.

She actually jumped up and down and clapped her hands together. "OMG! Perfect!"

She let them slide through her fingers as she put them over my head. "Like silk," she said reverently.

I rearranged them so they sat nicely on the base of my neck and fell more prettily across my chest, ending exactly between the curve of my breasts, which themselves looked much improved with the added gleam of a pearl or two. "They can't be real, of course," I said. "Cultured, I believe the word is; probably grown in Japanese oysters or mussels or something seaweedy like that."

Verity lifted the pearls, inspecting them intently. Had she had a jeweler's loupe I might have thought she was a professional.

"Wrong," she said. "My mom had pearls like

this. She sold them when we were broke. They brought in enough to pay off the mortgage for a few years 'til my dad went broke again and they lost the house anyway. I always wished she'd kept them. They would have been my only inheritance. My parents went and got themselves killed—a holiday helicopter jaunt in Majorca, and there was nothing left. And then my husband who'd mistakenly thought he'd married big, not only cheated on me but then he stole the rest of my money. And that's when I met you."

Suddenly tearful, she put her arms around me and I gave her a hug.

"Don't worry, sweetie," I whispered in the ear closest to me. "You know I'll always look after you, real pearls or not."

She wiped a tear with a finger, leaving a streak of purplish mascara. "I'm alright," she said. "And your Aunt Jolly not only left you her villa and whatever money she had, she also left you a fortune, right here, around your neck."

Of course I did not believe it. How could I? To me they were simply a string of creamy, evenly matched pearls that surely would never come up to the standard of the late Queen Mary who'd draped herself with multiple strands of the best until she looked like a decorated doll. Plus she'd added a few diamonds of extra-large size. The story also went that she had had a shifty hand in removing anything she fancied from the homes of friends or her hosts, to the point where things were hidden before her arrival. A kleptomaniac queen was a nice touch, I had always thought.

But what if Verity were correct and these pearls were the real thing? I hefted them in my hand: weighty, smooth, properly strung with tiny knots in the silk between each bead.

I said, "Well, anyway, I'm wearing them tonight. Aunt Jolly would have liked to see me in them. I expect that's why she gave them to me."

I had a sudden thought. "I wonder if these were what the thief was after when he came into my room. Maybe he didn't want to get rid of *me*. He simply wanted the pearls. He was a cat burglar after all."

I saw Verity's skeptical expression, but right then the doorbell played "La Marseillaise." Chad Prescott awaited us.

Cinderella would go to the ball.

23

Chad Prescott

At the Boss's villa, the first team of red-jacketed valet parkers was already racing back from the long-distance lot, while the second team picked up guests in golf carts so they did not have to wait in the long line of traffic.

"This must be some party," Chad said to Mirabella, in the convertible's passenger seat, her long dress hitched up over her knees, a swathe of chiffon keeping her hair intact in the breeze, old-movie-star style. Still, Chad thought, what hair was visible looked as though it had been tamed with a proper brush and comb instead of the usual flaring red mass spiraling from her head as though she'd been electric-shocked. Well, maybe not quite that bad, but definitely out of control.

"What did you expect from the local billionaire?" Mirabella said. "A dinner for twenty? Port and cheese afterward for the gents? Ladies retire to the withdrawing room to powder their noses?"

Sort of like that." He threw her a grin, which he knew she knew meant he didn't mean it.

"There he is, our host, the Boss himself, out

on the steps to greet us," Verity said. She was squashed in the Jag's tiny back space meant for nothing more than a weekend bag and maybe a dog or two, knees under her chin, valiantly holding down her short skirt.

"So he is," Mirabella noticed. "I'd forgotten how good-looking he is," she added. The Boss was smart, even chic, in a dinner jacket that slid over his broad shoulders as though it was made for them, which of course it was. The Boss would not stoop to ready-to-wear; he was way beyond that. Just take a look at his villa, a palace. Lights gleaming from every window, gardens lit so every blossom showed its petals, even the sea was prettily floodlit to show its cresting white waves. Tall, black-lacquered tubs were placed on the steps leading to the open front door, each with a flowering syringa bush whose lilac scent permeated the night air. Music filtered from the terraces along with the sound of laughter, the clink of ice in glasses.

The Boss spotted them and came quickly over, holding out his arms to help lift Verity from the tight backseat. "Welcome to my party."

She quickly tugged down her white silk skirt, which unfortunately had creased on the short journey.

But the Boss's eyes were not on Verity's skirt right now. They had moved on to Mirabella. His prey was here, on his turf.

Chad went to help Mirabella, but the Boss was there first, already holding open the door, eyes checking her head to toe.

"I remember your aunt wearing those pearls," the Boss said as he walked with her up the steps.

"Is that right?" She was surprised because to her knowledge Aunt Jolly had rarely worn the pearls. "Well, now they are mine," she added, patting them against her chest.

"Those and the Villa Romantica," he said. "My, aren't you the lucky girl."

Mirabella gave him a quick sideways look. Could he be laughing at her? "I am a lucky girl to have had an aunt like Jolly Matthews. We didn't see each other often, but there was always a connection."

"Which I assume is why she left you her property."

She gave him another sideways glance, but he was looking away from her. She thought surely they would not be going to get into this "sell me your land" business at the party.

"Chad." The Boss had moved on and was shaking Prescott's hand. "I think you will find everything you need, and whatever drink you want, it's available. Pink champagne, of course, as always. And my chefs have prepared a veritable banquet. They do so love the opportunity to show off their talents."

Mounting the steps, Chad thought he caught a glimpse out of the corner of his eye, behind the line of waiting valet parkers, of a man he recognized. The next minute he was gone. Now Chad remembered who he was. He'd seen him on the café terrace. He was the man known as "the Russian."

24

Mirabella

This is the grandest party I have ever attended. My life as a writer is by its nature solitary, except for those spurts in between books when I escape into what I call "the real world" and take myself off to places like Paris or Venice, where I gorge on historic beauty, and where I prefer to be alone. Other places, for more intimate reasons, I travel with the man of the moment, though lately, no one special enough to last the course all the way to the altar. I recently contemplated getting engaged, but he changed his mind before I could. So there it was, three down, all escapees from my clutches, and maybe more to go. Not many though, are as attractive as Chad Prescott, even though I consider him a shit and full of himself. Still, he is good-looking and a good doctor, I'll have to give him that. And now, he is my escort for the party of the year.

Never doubt the allure of a man in a tuxedo; there's just something about that crisp black-and-white look, or maybe it's simply seeing a man wearing a jacket in this era of casual dressing that can make a girl's heart flutter.

He put a hand under my elbow as we walked up the steps and into the Villa Mara. The Boss, our beaming host, was already holding Verity's hand firmly in his own. She threw back her head in a laugh and I wondered what he was saying that was so amusing. I was uneasy. She was so unworldly. She had already been taken by one man, and this one was rich and powerful, a dangerous combination to any young woman.

The Villa Mara looked like the Acropolis with double-height white columns supporting an upper verandah, lined with zebra-striped pots of flowering jasmine. A long terrace fronted onto a vast lawn clipped to within an inch of its life by the dozen gardeners our host employed and who, I'd heard, replaced every flower every week so they were only ever seen at the height of their perfection. Looking at his garden I understood that this billionaire knew what he liked and what he wanted, and knew how to get it. Money speaks, no doubt about it. But when it spoke like this, then I was the beneficiary of his perfect dreams.

"Mirabella," the Boss called. He was alone and looked around for Verity, saw her propped on a high stool at the long bar, smiling as she was given a glass of pink champagne. I doubted she realized her skirt had hitched up to the top of her thighs. I nudged Chad, indicating what was up.

He nodded good evening to our host then departed quickly in Verity's direction.

The Boss followed Chad's progress, taking in Verity and the skirt and the champagne. "No need to worry," he said confidently. "She is so young. My staff will keep an eye on her."

"Not that young that she can behave badly," I answered. I was a little upset with Verity. No woman, young or not, should drink too much.

My host took the seat next to me. We were suddenly alone, except, that is, for the shadowy shapes of two men in the background. Bodyguards, of course.

"What do you think?" I leaned closer so he could hear me over the music—dancing was well under way, heels already coming off, jackets soon too, I'd bet.

"Think about what?" The Boss signaled a waiter from the darkness to top-up my glass, and I let him. I knew good champagne when I tasted it. And I liked it. One and a half glasses. I was keeping count, as Verity was not and I knew a girl must. I was also watching Chad, who was now sitting next to Verity.

I caught her dismayed look, then her cheeky grin as she attempted to pull down the white skirt. She slid off her stool, patted Chad on the arm, said something to him, then wandered off in the direction of the house. She stopped momentarily to slip off her silvery sandals, then sauntered on her way, swinging them by their straps. I'd almost bet she was humming along as she went. I recalled the desperate, crying young woman on the train, her story about the cheater; the stolen money, such as it was; the runaway girl not knowing where she was going or how to get there or what she was going to do when she did. My little Verity was definitely coming into her own.

Chad returned, frowning as he took another look after her. "She told me she was okay," he said. "And I told her that, as a doctor, I thought she should not have any more champagne. And she told me that champagne never did any girl any harm."

"She should have been grateful for your medical attention," I said with a smile. He was so handsome, so man-of-the-world and famous doctor all rolled into one, for this night anyway before he took on his other persona, back in some jungle village fixing little kids' faces so they might have regular lives.

The Boss, who was still sitting on my other side, said, "Well, how are you enjoying my little party, Doctor? Different from your usual surroundings I'll bet."

I looked at them, pleased. For the first time in my life I was with the two most attractive men in the room. I preened myself metaphorically and took another discreet sip of the pink champagne.

Perfectly iced, perfectly chosen. Nothing escaped the attention of the man of a different world from mine and Chad's.

I noticed the two guards who had been watching discreetly had disappeared. They must believe their boss was safe with us.

"Mirabella." The Boss smiled, the kind of intimate smile meant just for me. The man knew how to charm and, what the heck, he was attractive, with that tall, dark, intense look of his. Besides, it was a good opportunity to make Chad Prescott jealous, perhaps make him take a second glance and maybe think I was okay in my floaty aqua gown that showed off my curves, and the pearls that showed off my breasts. And my hair in a red cloud that was expertly made-up-by-Verity. I didn't look so bad, even if I did say so myself.

"May I have the pleasure of this dance?" the Boss said. And this time it was my hand he took as he escorted me to the parquet dance floor that had been specially installed over the lawn. He slid his arm around my back and I slid against his starched shirt front, breasts crushed, hair flying. It was, I told myself, very nice.

25

Sometime later, Chad and I were hovering over the buffet tables, pretty in linen cloths with crystal bowls and silver platters with tiny softshell crabs, sweet shrimp fresh from the bay, grilled red snapper, and hot potato pancakes.

Fettucini was piled with morsels of lobster. The french fries were scattered with herbs and cheese, and slow-roasted pork was sliced to order and soft as butter and twice as fragrant. All the elegant, thin women who lived on salads tucked in, saving room for the desserts, a pyramid of chocolate and cream profiteroles.

He had put on the great all-American barbecue when everybody had expected something fancier, and I saw he was very much enjoying the astonished looks on his guests' faces when they inspected the serving tables, trimmed with orange and yellow unscented marigolds and purple pansies and other common or garden flowers, not the expected orchids and roses flown in from South America. First came the looks of shock. Then the frowns of worry that all was not correct, then the murmurs of delight as compliments came his way. Somehow, it all just worked.

Of course his guests were used to the best, that's why they were here. Many of them the Boss did not even know; his party planner had a list of accessible people who were always up for freebie top-drawer events, and who looked good and had the right clothes to qualify.

"But how wonderful," I said as Chad and I inspected the lavish spread. "And how beautiful it all looks, so simple and pretty, like a real back garden on the Fourth of July."

The Boss smiled at me, pleased at the compliment, but Chad was not looking at the buffet.

"Will you excuse me for a moment?" he said. "I need to check something."

I wondered what it was he needed to check so urgently. Then I remembered he was keeping an eye out for Verity.

I excused myself and edged through the perfumed crowd, aware that the women were eyeing me. They'd seen me talking to the Boss; he was the prime catch and any one of them—the unaccompanied ones anyway and probably some of the married ones too—would like to catch that "catch."

I caught up to Chad as he was coming back from the house.

"She's not there," he said shortly.

"But I could swear I saw her go in."

"And so did I."

"I mean, I just thought, well, a bathroom break, you know. . . ."

"She's not in the bathroom. Not in any bathroom. There's staff everywhere, guarding the doors to all the rooms so nobody can make off with the silver, I guess. They all claim not to have seen any woman of her description. I even checked with the one in charge of the ladies' room, who threw me out and said I had no right to be in there. Well, of course I didn't, but she had not seen Verity either. What worries me, Mirabella, is that we both know she'd had too much to drink and that she went into the house. And now everybody is saying she did not. What the fuck is going on?"

He glared at me like it was my fault; that deep penetrating look that earlier I had taken as interest, or lust, or love at first sight, something along those lines. Obviously this was not the case.

"Nothing could have happened to her," I said. "I mean, look at this place, there's enough armed guards to stop a tank attack. And a girl doesn't just get lost at a grand party like this."

"Well, it seems this girl has gone missing at this grand party, and I'm going to ask the man in charge about it."

I grabbed his arm. "You think something has happened to Verity? But why *should* anything happen to her?"

He shook his head. "Mirabella, your own Aunt Jolly was murdered, almost next door, in your Villa Romantica, and you are asking why I am worried that Verity disappeared from the party? I come from a different world. I see danger behind me, in front of me, over my head, everywhere I go. I've learned to trust my gut when I feel something's wrong and that's probably why I'm alive today. And trust me when I say something is wrong here."

I thought of Aunt Jolly's still-unexplained and violent death, of my lovely, unworldly aunt, who in fact was so like Verity in her nature they might have been related. Aunt Jolly had been killed. A violent attacker was still on the loose. The Colonel, who I could see across the yard, smart in what must be some kind of dress uniform and attractive as all get-out and didn't he know it, was chatting up a group of women who seemed attached to his every word. Even he had failed to find the killer.

Beyond the magic circle of light around the villa, the hills loomed dark. Not a light shone past our enchanted surroundings. The sheer blackness was foreboding and I shivered. Anybody might be out there, watching.

I saw Chad prowling the edges of the party crowd. The music played on, ice tinkled in glasses, laughter rang out, chatter and gossip, women admiring each other's dresses, stilettos dangling from their hands, bare feet cool on the grass. Everything looked normal.

I hurried across the lawn to where the Colonel

stood in his merry group of admirers, grabbed his arm, and said, "I need you."

The women glanced at each other, smiling at my forwardness, my deliberate cutting out of anyone else. *"Bitch,"* I heard someone mutter as with my hand still on his arm, I dragged him to a quieter place, beyond the reach of the music and the banter and the drinkers.

"It's Verity," I said. "Verity, you remember?"

He nodded. "How could I forget?"

Of course, he had been one of the first there, in the canyon, after the accident. "She's gone," I said. "Disappeared. Just went into the house and then . . . gone."

"I imagine she went to the restroom." The Colonel spoke mildly, at the same time removing my hand from his coat sleeve.

"You don't understand." I was panicking now. "*Verity is not here.* Chad went looking for her. She's nowhere to be found. We saw her go into the house half an hour ago. She never came out."

"But we are in the garden at the back of the house," the Colonel explained, exasperated. He obviously thought women like me got endlessly into trouble. "Does it not occur to you she might have left of her own accord by the front door, which I assume is the way she came in?"

"And does it not occur to you that my aunt was murdered almost next door, by person or persons as yet unknown? Is it that there's a curse on the

Villa Romantica, Colonel? Do you believe in mumbo jumbo like that? Well, I can tell you, I for one, do not. Unless Chad is able to find her, we have to believe somebody took Verity, some madman . . ."

The Colonel put a calming hand on my shoulder. "You are jumping to ridiculous conclusions. Why would anybody want to 'take' Verity as you put it? She's simply a guest, and I'm betting she'd had a little too much to drink and decided bed was the place for her. Someone would have driven her home."

"How can you say that? How can you just stand there and not do *something?*"

The Colonel's eyes were suddenly unsmiling. "Tell me why you think anything should have happened to her."

I stared back at him, wondering why I should. But Chad was uneasy too; he'd felt something was wrong.

"Gut instinct," I said.

Our eyes linked for a second. "I've always been a believer in that." The Colonel took my hand in its silver crochet glove, with the large sapphire on the right middle finger. His hand was warm, strong, comforting.

"Let's go find her," he said.

26
The Boss

At the edge of the party crowd the Boss observed the sudden whispering, the hands across mouths as the story of the missing girl spread from woman to woman. The men seemed unconcerned, still busy with men-talk: golf and boats, cars and the stock market. So, Verity's disappearance had been noted. Time now for him to take over, to become the crusader, the man intent on finding the lost girl, the man who would become her savior. Even if ultimately it did prove too late to find her alive.

The fact was, it had not been Verity that had been his original target. It was the elusive Mirabella, who had escaped twice already, and now another time. Of course Verity was a lovely substitute. Such a nice young woman, still a girl really, all blond bounciness and wide smile and those amazing round boobs that were unmissable—her greatest asset in fact, and one he appreciated. He was about to let her know that. The thought of the sharp point of his knife between Verity's breasts excited him and he stepped quickly behind the bar to hide the evidence. He was a well-endowed man, as many women had told him. Which was fine, in the right place at the right time. In public it was not correct and he would be taken as a pervert.

"Pervert." An odd word for a state of mind, of body, that to him was acceptable. How else would a man enjoy himself if not for a few perversions? There were women that catered to his brand of sexuality; the dominatrix in London was a favorite, as was the Russian housewife in his old hometown of Minsk, where it had all started. She had known instinctively what he liked, the whip, the knife, the threat, the danger. The knife edge of danger was what he called it, with a knowing smile. God, how he enjoyed it. The only thing he enjoyed more was money.

A quick sprinkling of Rohypnol had disappeared in Verity's third glass of champagne, sufficient to send her wobbling away, into the arms of his handlers who'd caught her before she made it to the bathroom.

He'd watched from the library door, heard her quick cry of surprise when they came from behind; saw one throw an arm around her neck, the other lift her feet off the ground, then both run with her out through the sliding glass doors, into the darkness.

Now, Verity was safely ensconced in his concrete bunker, its design based on the ones Hitler had built at the old Nazi fortifications along the Normandy coast in France. This one was equally impenetrable. Nobody could get in there without a special key, but before that they needed to know where the door was, and where that special key was kept.

To the naked eye, just walking past, there seemed to be no entrance. It was cleverly hidden beneath the swathe of miniature-leaved ivy that softened the bleak appearance of the concrete cube. No windows looked out from it. The only person with access was himself. All the Boss's perversions, all his black thoughts, all his murderous past was enshrined in there, in videos, recordings, writings, on computer. A narcissist supreme, he kept a record of his doings. It did not make attractive reading, or viewing.

He stood at the window in the main house, which was open to the terrace and the gardens, taking note of his guests, seeing Chad still wandering around looking for Verity.

Others were busily chatting, drinking champagne, eating. Mirabella stood next to the Colonel, her eyes fixed on him, one hand worriedly to her face. The large sapphire ring she wore over her silvery glove glinted in the light. Of course the Boss knew why Mirabella wore those gloves. There was little he did not know about every one of the guests in his house right this minute. And that included the Colonel, who was far too attractive to be a cop. Women doted on him, despite his meager salary and lack of possessions and the two kids he had to bring up, alone. Still, he was not smart enough in these circumstances to pose a threat to the Boss, whereas the doctor was. The doctor was a man used to jungle tactics, who knew to look for the unexpected. And in this case the unexpected was Aunt Jolly.

The Boss had noticed Mirabella was wearing Aunt Jolly's pearls. They were probably the only jewelry of value she owned, apart from the sapphire ring, of course, both of which had once upon a long time ago belonged to the gorgeous Jerusha. He doubted Mirabella was aware of that; she only knew that the ring and the pearls came from her aunt. Along with the villa, and the painting, both of which the Boss desired. He needed the property for the immense amount of money to be made developing it; and he wanted the painting because of its history. In fact, he lusted after that painting.

He was a man without a past, not one he could speak of anyway, and he had almost succeeded in putting it out of his mind. The future was all he'd ever thought about since he was a boy in Minsk lopping down trees, his hands cracked from the bitter cold, bleeding as he worked. He'd sworn then to get out, to leave it behind, never to tell anyone where he came from; never to remember a single emotion, except the urge for revenge against the world. And the need to kill. The knife yielded ultimate power, and he liked to use it on women. Verity was to be his next "guest," as he liked to call his victims.

He had thought about the act of killing many times before he'd enacted the role of murderer. To kill was easy enough; to dispose of the victim's body and also any evidence that might lead back to him was less easy. Still, he had perfected it. He was simply the stranger, passing through town, dressed like any workingman, a cap over his head, a knife in his pocket. He had studied the art, as he called it, of the famous Yorkshire Ripper, as well as the predecessor, Jack the Ripper, who to this day had never been traced, though speculation abounded.

Their tactics had been the same. A woman unknown to them. An area they did not inhabit. A method of getting in and out without exciting notice, like an autoroute stopover, where often the little runaway girls might be found, begging a lift, with promises. That was his beginning. He had quickly moved on to much more sophisticated venues and classier women. And he'd never been traced as being in the area, even the city where these murders took place. There was nothing to match the thrill of it.

Clever, of course. Having money made it easier. But this was the first time he had flirted with danger in exactly this way, on his home ground. What, he wondered, had made him do it?

Well, first, he'd wanted Mirabella out of the

way so he'd have access to her land. Then he had an overpowering urge for Verity that he could not deny, which was why he had to hide in back of the bar so his excitement would not be noticed. Also, Verity was available. But she was in his way. And biggest and most important was ego; he knew that by instigating a search, offering a great reward, talking publicly on TV and radio about his sorrow that one of his young guests had disappeared, by vowing to find her, to find who was responsible, he would become a national hero.

Right now, though, Verity was sprawled on the narrow bed in the concrete bunker, in the space behind the sitting area, divided by a wall with a large-screen TV from his office. She had been bound and gagged. The two Lithuanians who had carried out his instructions were paid and gone, exactly the same way the failed killer on the Ducati had left immediately after sending Mirabella and this stupid girl over the edge into the canyon. Money talked.

She would not escape this time.

27

Mirabella

I'm standing alone near the wooden steps leading down the small cliff to the beach, exactly where I'd stood ten minutes ago, and probably ten minutes before that. The waves have picked up as the tide turned and are now splashing noisily on the pebbles, then flowing back again. Endlessly. Forever.

I refuse to believe Verity is lost in the sea. I cannot. I will not allow it. I saved her from herself on the train and there's an old saying that when you save a person you are responsible for them forever. You become the keeper of their soul.

I can see Chad silhouetted against the waves, striding back toward me. I know he fears she has drowned. And in my darkest place, I begin to fear it too.

My once-lovely aqua chiffon dress is plastered against my body with the wind that's gotten up and the spray carried on it. I feel Aunt Jolly's pearls, cool against my breasts. I put up a hand to touch them, wishing the aunt who gave them to me could be here to help me now. And also Jerusha, the enigma whose life I was so determined to explore, to find the truth about whether she had committed a terrible crime of passion or if someone had framed her. The story that she had found her lover with another woman and in a jealous rage had shot him did not ring true. Her lover adored her, and the woman was a stranger who'd followed her home, spied on her, envied Jerusha's success, her beauty, her home. And her love.

It was not in her character, and "character," as murder psychologists tell us, is where the truth lies. You are who you are.

All I know is if she were here now, she would help. I have a gut feeling about Jerusha, as strong as my gut feeling that Verity is here, somewhere. I will not give up hope.

Chad came to the top of the steps and stood next to me. He put a hand on my shoulder and I pushed the pearls to one side so I might feel his warmth, the strength I needed. I turned to him and tripped awkwardly. I put out my hands to save myself but fell onto the grass, which was cold and damp. The sea sounded suddenly louder. Chad hauled me back up. He stroked away the strands of hair sticking to my face where tears were now running. I hitched my dress back over my bosom, smoothed my damp skirt. Oddly, I was still holding onto my sandals. I held them up to show him, managing a half smile. "Thanks. I'm sorry, I always seem to be crying."

"That's okay, cry if you need to. Lord knows

it's a relief sometimes, just to get all that emotion out of you. And listen, the Boss has men out searching for Verity. Nobody is sure she went into the sea, nobody remembers anything other than seeing her go into the house. She could turn up anywhere."

He was doing his best to sound convincing but I wasn't buying it. It was a good try though and I wanted him to think I felt better because of it.

I slipped my hand into his and we walked back to the house, still festively lit for the party. The black hills loomed beyond, a dark forested backdrop. A killer might be hiding out there, peeking through the windows, watching the privileged enjoying the rich man's bounty.

How the Boss had managed to keep Verity's disappearance a secret from everyone I did not know, but his party was going right on; wine was still being poured, chefs were still sizzling things on their barbecues, lanterns glowed and moths and night creatures still batted their wings against them, the small ruffles of noise competing with the laughter and the tinkling of ice. All the normal things when nothing was normal anymore.

I took my hand from Chad's and looked at my ruined silver mesh gloves, stuck with black earth and flower petals and grit. Yet my sapphire still glowed.

"Thank God," I said. "I should have hated to

lose Aunt Jolly's ring. She treasured it because it came from Jerusha."

Chad took my gloved hands in both of his. "One day I want to ask you about your hands, and what happened," he said. "But now is not the time. We have to find Verity. She can't have gotten far. I think maybe she was a little tipsy, I saw her stumble as she walked to the house. Mirabella, let me ask you, what do you really know about Verity? Is there anyone she told you about who might wish to harm her?"

I shook my head, tears spilling. Some women I know look glamorous when they cry, but not me. Red eyes are not becoming.

"Only the rotten husband," I said. "The cheater. I told you all he wanted was money. He took what little she had. She left him, never to be heard from again. Until Verity files divorce papers, that is. I expect he'll have plenty to say about what a bad wife she was. Little Verity who's so innocent she makes me feel like a woman of the world. How could anyone wish to harm her? *Why?* I ask you."

He made no answer and we walked in silence up the rise to the party. A passing waiter stopped to offer a tray of martinis. Chad snagged a couple and put one in my hand.

"Drink," he said. "You have to get yourself together."

The Colonel came striding toward us, head

poked forward in his usual urgent manner, though his face was grim.

"My men have searched this stretch of the beach," he said, taking a silk handkerchief from his breast pocket and mopping his brow. "Nothing. No discarded clothing as if she had gone skinny dipping . . . ." He glanced apologetically my way as if I might be offended by the very suggestion. "It has been known, at parties like this, at beach houses."

"Of course," Chad said.

I knew the Colonel had noticed my skirt clinging to my legs, and my tear-dampened face and windblown hair. "I need to go home," I said. Aunt Jolly's villa, *my* villa, suddenly seemed a haven of safety. I suddenly realized that of course it would be the place to which Verity would return. If she were free to do so.

Chad went to look for the Boss, to tell him we were leaving, but was unable to find him. He left a message with the head waiter, offering apologies and saying he would return and help in the search.

Guilt washed over me. "I *should* stay," I said, shivering, as I thought of Verity in that dark sea, the waves closing over her head. But Chad insisted on taking me home.

He drove fast, swinging the convertible sharply into my driveway. The villa was in complete darkness. Obviously, I had forgotten to leave the outside lights on, though I thought I remembered leaving a lamp on indoors.

He got out and hurried to open my door, taking my hands to help me. There was something so reassuring about him, he made me feel safe, even when the worst had happened.

"It hasn't, you know," he said, knowing from my face what I was thinking. "I've learned," he added, "that things are not always what they seem. Whatever has happened to Verity, we'll find her and I promise I'll find out why." He bent his head and kissed my hand, the one with the sapphire. "We can't let Aunt Jolly down."

Chad turned on the outside lights, and insisted on coming into the house with me. The dog came running, and the cat sat on the stairs watching us.

Chad turned on the lamps and said, "There must have been a power outage. It happens quite often around here. Probably the Boss's illuminations overloaded the system."

Still, just to be sure, he walked through the rooms, checking there were no villains hiding under beds, no robbers prying open the safe, no killers in black masks. Like last time.

I had treated that incident almost as a joke, a prank, a mistaken identity by a unskilled thief who'd thought I had something more worth stealing than Aunt Jolly's ring and her pearls, though nowadays I believe thieves go more for laptops and electronic devices. My laptop however, still sat on my desk, untouched by any human hand other than my own.

Eyes still checking, Chad said, “I’m calling the Colonel, telling him to get some men up here instead of uselessly combing that beach, where they’ll never find Verity anyway.”

“Why do you think that?”

“She was last seen entering the Boss’s house. No one saw her come out. The beach was well-lit so the guests could wander at will. There was even a bar down there, sandwiches for the taking. The Boss thought of everything.”

He was right, and the Boss was certainly not a man to miss a beat. In fact if anyone had seen Verity it would have been him.

“I saw him watching her,” I remembered. “I thought he had his eye on her, fancied her . . . you know.”

“Pity yours wasn’t a keener eye,” Chad said. “Then we might know more about where she went.”

He was already on his mobile calling the Colonel. “I’ll be right there,” I heard him say as he turned back to me.

“I’m not the domesticated type or I’d offer to make you a cup of tea,” he said. “But I suggest you at least get out of that wet dress, take a hot shower, and get into your pj’s. I’ll be back in half an hour to check on you. I’ll bring tea from the

Boss's party. After all, he's thought of everything else—he must have thought of that too."

I watched him drive away. The house was suddenly silent. The animals had gone into the kitchen. Even the moths had given up beating their frail wings against the lights. No small creatures rustled in the undergrowth; no sweet voice called me, saying, *It's Verity, I'm home, Mirabella, I'm back . . .*

I switched off the lamp in the hall and walked to my room, pausing outside the closed door that led to Jerusha's boudoir, the lovely woman whose home I had somehow inherited, with all its beauty and its tragedy. Yet Aunt Jolly had been happy here, and look what happened to her.

I walked into the room, turning the lamps on, closing the heavy cream linen curtains, shutting out the darkness, and any eyes that might be watching. The wind had dropped. As I turned from the window I thought I heard a noise outside. I stood perfectly still, ears straining. No. All was quiet. I told myself I was foolish, imagining things because of Verity's disappearance. Nobody had come to any harm, Chad and the Colonel would find her, they had promised.

But there it was again. The rustle of leaves underfoot.

I froze, a hand clutched to my chest. Then, as always when I was afraid, anger rushed through my veins in a sudden heat. If this was a robber he would not get any of Aunt Jolly's treasures, never, however many times he tried. . . .

But I also remembered my other near-misses, in the canyon, in my bed. I realized it might not be the treasures they were after. I was suddenly afraid it could be me.

28

Chad Prescott

Chad stood on the strip of grass at the edge of the cliff overlooking the beach. It could hardy be called a cliff, more of a steep rise, a climb up from the shore easily doable by any active person in appropriate footwear, sneakers or work boots, but certainly never in dainty female evening sandals, which was what every woman was wearing at the party tonight. Those that had not taken them off, that is, when their heels sank into the grass, and who'd sought firmer ground on the paved terraces. Whatever, everyone had been in plain sight, and that included Verity, right up until the moment she'd wandered into the house, through the door that still stood wide open, though now there were no men in black T-shirts standing guard.

Farther along the beach, above the tide line and away from the lights, he made out the shape of a building—square, boxy almost. No lights shone from it. No men guarded it.

He stood for a while, watching. Nobody came out. Nobody went in. Which made him wonder exactly what it might be. A generator room, perhaps? But no, that was well away from the house, the monstrosity called the Villa Mara, which the Boss called "home" and from where a DJ was now blasting hot dance music the party crowd found hard to resist.

Undecided, he wondered whether to go back to the villa, check every room one more time for Verity, but somehow he knew he would not find Verity there.

He slithered down the slope to the pebbly beach. It was much darker and he waited for his eyes to adjust. The square building was about a hundred yards away. He might have thought it was a storage unit, a place for garden equipment and the like, but this was on a prime bit of shore, worth many dollars per square meter. Not even a billionaire, especially a sharp and successful property developer like the Boss, would squander such top real estate on a garden shed. This had to be important. More, it had to be of great importance to the Boss himself.

He walked silently, the way he'd learned in the jungle, no sound of a footfall or a twig snapping, his dark jacket held closed over his white shirt, head down. He had spent half a lifetime under these circumstances; knew exactly what to do, how to make himself invisible, how to stalk a prey, how to find his way in uncharted territory. This Mediterranean garden was easy.

Now he could see the building close up. There were no windows, not even the old arrow slits of medieval times. This was a modern building, and it was windowless for a purpose. Either the Boss did not want anyone to see in, or he did not want anyone to see out.

A faint noise came from behind. Chad flattened himself against the trunk of a jacaranda tree whose purple blossoms fluttered onto his head. He wanted desperately to sneeze.

A man came hurrying along the gravel path leading to the bunker. It was dark but from his height and his bulk, Chad recognized the Boss. Keys clanked as he walked past, so close Chad could hear his breathing, rapid breaths, as though he'd been running. He stopped in front of the bunker, keys rattling in his hand. He pressed a button and a swathe of ivy-clad wall slid magically to one side, revealing a steel door. The Boss inserted his key, stepped through the door into darkness, and the ivy-covered wall slid back into place, as though the door had never been.

Chad waited a few minutes to see whether the Boss might be coming back. When he realized he was not, he ran silently to where he'd seen the door. He grappled with the ivy but could not get it to move. For all intents and purposes the door did not exist.

Chad wondered if the Boss could be holding Verity captive there. But why would he? He was a well-known philanthropist, a man of the world, businessman supreme. The Boss could call the shots, have almost any woman he wanted; many women at his own party tonight would have been only too delighted to share his bed, share his fame, his glamour and his money. Yet if there was one thing Chad had learned it was that appearances could be deceptive. Money did not make a man. A man was where he was born, how he was raised. In the end that was what he was.

The door to the bunker was suddenly flung open. Chad slid deeper into the darkness of the trees. The Boss strode out. He slammed the door and locked it behind him, and again the door disappeared behind the ivy. He was no longer wearing his tuxedo. He had changed into a black turtleneck, running pants, and sneakers. As Chad watched, he strode down the slope to the beach and began to jog in the direction of the villa.

For a second Chad wondered if he had gotten him all wrong; could the Boss still be intent on his search for Verity? Was he so concerned he needed to have looser clothing so he could check the farther reaches of the shore, the wilder parts of the extensive gardens himself, though a dozen men had already checked? Yet this was the Boss's own house, Verity was his guest; she was his responsibility and perhaps he was now taking that responsibility seriously.

From the grassy rise Chad saw the Boss swing up from the beach, then up the steps to the Villa

Mara. Chad followed, stopping when he rounded the corner of the villa and saw the assembled video and TV cameras, the pressmen already taking quick shots of the Boss standing there in his special searching-for-the-lost-young-woman outfit.

Unsmiling, the Boss looked into the cameras directed at him. He held up a hand. "I know you are all here for a good reason. Our sole purpose is to find the missing young woman. You will need her name for your reports. She is Verity Real and she was—she is—a guest of Madame Mirabella Matthews at the Villa Romantica."

"Jolly Matthews's old place," someone said, catching a quick picture as the Boss glanced his way.

"Exactly. Mirabella is the late Jolly Matthews's second cousin. She inherited the property and has recently come to stay, bringing with her, her friend, Verity. Both were guests at my party tonight. The Colonel, who you all know, of course, is now organizing the search so I'm sure you will excuse me. I'll just let everyone get on with their work."

He paused, one hand held up in front of him. "One more thing. I am heartbroken that this event has taken place on my property. I feel somehow responsible. I should like to make it known that I am offering a reward for Verity's return. I am speaking to you all, and possibly to someone here that might have taken her from us. That reward is one million dollars."

A stunned gasp fluttered through the crowd.

"Of course," he said, holding up his hand again to stop the buzz of comments. "It is not nearly enough to pay for a life. This young woman is here somewhere. We must save her, we must earn that reward."

He stepped back out of the lights and made his way down the steps, jogging back along the gravel path to the bunker.

From his place in the shadows, Chad watched him go. It was, he thought, the performance of a lifetime. Either the Boss was a born actor, or he was for real.

29

Mirabella

Later, I was back in my bedroom at the Villa Romantica, still hoping Verity would come through the door, when again I thought I heard someone outside.

I clutched a hand to my chest, holding my breath, afraid any small sound might tell an intruder I was there. Yet if he were an expert intruder obviously he would already know that, and also know I was alone.

So where was my dog? Why had Sossy not rushed barking to my side to alert me? Had the Siamese simply gone back to beautifying herself, licking her paws, washing her velvet ears? And what about that friggin' canary? Wasn't it supposed to sing? Tell me the way it told the coal miners in those underground tunnels that there was danger around? Even Chad, who'd gone to get me something as simple as a cup of tea was not here when I needed him.

The cream linen curtains billowed inward in a sudden wind. Somebody must have opened the window. I froze, expecting to see a pair of feet, a shadowy figure.

A small art deco lamp sat on the side table. It

had a straight copper base etched with a pattern of wavy lines, topped with a bronze parchment shade.

I picked it up. It was heavier than I'd thought and I almost dropped it. That would have taken care of my foot . . . and what would the Colonel have thought when he found my dead body with one smashed foot? That my killer was a fetishist of some kind? *What* killer?

I was a fool, I was acting crazy. I told myself to settle down, get ahold of myself, get a grip. . . . A calm came over me, a sudden resolve. I would not go gently into this night . . . I was a fighter and whoever it was, I would fight.

I wished I were properly dressed though. In my girly butterfly-printed pj's I felt vulnerable. I needed my jeans, my shoes on, to be ready for running. The big empty hallway was in complete darkness.

I had no choice. It was now or never. A swift turn of my hand and the door opened without a sound. No one was there. I slid through the crack. With my back to the wall, I edged, like a cat, along the side of the villa.

Minutes passed, how many I could not tell. All I knew was the too-loud noise of my own breathing, the feel of the damp of the grass under my bare feet, the prickle of a thorn from a rosebush that smelled sweetly in the dark. And then the muted roar of a car's engine.

I slid to the ground, flattening myself so my outline would not show under the glare of its headlights. Dazzled, I peered into the night, saw a convertible. . . . *Oh dear God, thank you, thank you*. . . . It was Chad. And he was carrying a paper cup that I'd bet contained tea.

30

A short while later, I sat on the edge of the bed, hands still shaking as I sipped the tea that by this time was cold.

Chad said, "I have to get back to the Villa Mara."

"I'm coming with you." I got up and made for the closet where I knew my jeans would be on the floor, exactly where I'd stepped out of them.

Uncaring of modesty, I simply turned my back, pulled off the pajama bottoms, and tugged on the jeans. Somehow I knew Chad had turned his back too. Ever the gent, I supposed, though I kind of wished he'd sneaked a peek, shown some interest in the feminine side of me, and not merely the detective/novel writer who was no good at real life detecting and had not so much as a clue as to where her lovely friend had gone.

"She must be somewhere at the party," I said, desperate now because I felt in my bones it was possible someone had really harmed Verity.

He held me by the shoulders. Tea slopped all over my jeans. He said, "I'm going alone. You must stay here where you will be safe."

"Look what you've done." I dabbed at the wet spot. "Good thing it's not hot."

"Get back into bed. I'm better off without you."

I knew it wasn't true.

The fireworks that delighted the partiers crashed through the silence. Rockets whizzed, Catherine wheels whirred, red-and-blue lights flickered over our faces, mine anxious, his stony.

I thought of the Colonel, of how he'd helped me search the house for Verity, how he'd helped the Boss summon men to aid them, of the Boss calling the chief of police to the area. The Colonel had held my hand as we walked through the Villa Mara, told me not to worry, he would find her. . . .

I sat looking up at Chad. With him and the Colonel and the Boss all looking for my friend, I was in good hands. Yet I had to be there. I had to know. I walked out into the hall.

Chad was right behind me, a hand on my shoulder again, a gesture of comfort now.

"Don't worry," he said. "It's going to be alright."

This time I did not know whether I believed him.

The Russian

The young Russian, all in black, with a long white apron tied around his middle and knotted in front, French waiter–style, hovered with his tray of martinis on the edge of the party crowd. He circulated, restocking every now and then from the bar. He had no fear of being asked why he wasn't one of the usual waiters. Staff had been imported for this event, so nobody knew who anybody was. Anyone at all, he thought with a grim smile, could have infiltrated the Boss's party. Anyone at all might have slipped a little something into a woman's drink. And anyone had. Namely himself, at the orders of the Boss, of course, who could never be seen to get his hands dirty. Plus he paid well. Extra well, sometimes, when extra things were asked for and received.

He'd taken care of business. No "funny business," mind you. Just done as he'd been asked: drugged the girl, got her into the bunker. What the Boss did with her after that had nothing to do with him.

Duty done, the Russian liked to say to himself, metaphorically washing his hands of whatever nefarious business he had just completed, by request, of course. For himself, he did not care. What he did care about was the money, and now that the Boss was in so deep, he'd decided it was time he collected more. "Enough is never enough," was the Boss's own motto. Now it was to become the Russian's.

He stood in back of the bar, unobserved. People were watching the fireworks shooting through the night in starbursts and shimmers. The party sounded like a battlefield.

He noticed that the doctor was back, and with Mirabella, who stood out amongst the party-goers in jeans and what looked like a pajama top.

He stamped out the cigarette and waited to see what would go down now that the doc and the girlfriend were here. He looked around but the Boss had disappeared. Seemed like a friggin' disappearing act tonight; everybody was doing it.

He took the crushed pack of Marlboros from his back pocket, shook one out, and with a hand cupped over his old Zippo, lit up again. In his waiter's apron, he fit into the scene perfectly. Nobody would suspect a guy who'd been offering them drinks from a tray all night. That straight-up Colonel, smart-ass that he was, would be looking for a proper kidnapper, a robber with a swag-bag over his shoulder—or else a girl over his shoulder. Easy enough; she hadn't weighed much. Too skinny for his taste, though obviously not the Boss's.

Well, his work was done. Payment would, as usual, be deposited in his bank account, anonymously of course. He'd work for the rest of the evening, serve them drinks, act normal. And see what happened next.

31
The Colonel

Holding Mirabella's gloved hand in his, the Colonel had to admit he did not have his entire mind on her supposedly missing friend. He was enjoying holding her hand, though he did wonder about the gloves; some sort of affectation he guessed, or perhaps it was just that her nails were the wrong color for her dress, or any one of a number of feminine reasons. Women were a mystery in themselves, and now this one was insisting her friend had disappeared.

The Colonel had been to many a grand party; he knew that drink—or too much of it anyhow—could loosen morals just a little bit; that a young woman might find herself in an inappropriate situation, sometimes even dangerous. He hoped this was not the case with Verity, though he doubted that at such an elegant event anything like that could have taken place. The Boss had his own security, his men were everywhere, or had been earlier, though he saw none of them around right this minute. Still, they were under the Boss's orders and would do as he asked.

"I'm so worried about her," Mirabella was saying as they walked through the party crowd to the strip of darkness around the edge, where all light ended.

The Colonel did not let go of her hand. "I think she might have had a little too much to drink. It happens at parties, especially when the champagne is flowing. Trust me, nothing could have happened to her."

"Not *here,* you mean?" Mirabella stopped. She turned to look at him and took his other hand in hers.

Like a lover would, the Colonel found himself thinking. He caught a hint of her scent on the soft breeze that later would become a strong wind. He knew that because he'd heard the weather forecast. He hoped it would not be strong enough to take down any of the beautiful tents covering the buffets and the bars erected on the terraces and along the beach.

He was a man faithful to the memory of the woman he'd loved above all others. This was the first time she had not come foremost in his thoughts. Mirabella's scent, her warm gloved hand in his, even the giant sapphire ring that cut into him when he gripped tighter, made him want to hold onto her.

Mirabella threw him a quick upward glance, a practiced look to be sure, because obviously he wasn't the first attractive man she'd flirted with, and even under dire circumstances, she was still a flirt at heart.

"You *will* find her for me, Colonel," she said, resting her head for a moment against his shoulder.

"I promise," he said. And he meant it.

32

Mirabella

I was back in my room, alone. Again. The story of my life. The Colonel had gone with Chad to search for my friend. *Oh God, oh God, let her be alright.* Selfish me, I was thinking only of how *I* was affected, when my poor darling lovely Verity was gone. *Please oh please come home. . . .*

It's odd, how I think of the Villa Romantica as home now. It had been home to my aunt, and before her to Jerusha, the woman who'd built it, who had poured her love, her happiness, her very soul into it, only to be forced to leave.

I decided that I needed air. I went out and walked a short way along the beach. And then I saw the Boss.

He was standing by an odd, square, dark building. In his black turtleneck and pants he almost blended into the background. The man who had everything looked very much alone. Wasn't great wealth said to make you lonely, afraid of friendship because of who might want something from you, who might want to get their hands on your money, to invest in their scheme, or buy a diamond necklace? I thought about going over to talk to him, but he walked quickly away and disappeared.

Chad had told me he didn't think the Boss was a man who would accept scandal without fighting back. In his opinion the offer of a million dollars to find Verity was the Boss's grand gesture, meant to divert attention, even suspicion, from him and any of his guests. He was not about to allow himself to be publicly tainted by that image. Women did not go missing at his villa.

I reached for the coolness of my pearls against my skin, and realized they were gone. I thought quickly back to my movements, remembered when I had tripped and almost fallen, and Chad had hauled me back onto my feet. They must have slipped off then. They were so long, they could easily have gotten lost. They were probably right there now, on the grass in front of the Boss's villa.

I'd promised Chad I would behave myself and stay in my own villa but I wanted my pearls. And I wanted to speak with Chad. I immediately tried his mobile but got no answer. Not that I'd expected one; of course he would have turned it off. Nothing like an earsplitting blast of music on your cell phone to alert anyone to your presence, a bit like "La Marseillaise" on my own doorbell. Got to get that changed. A snatch of

Beethoven perhaps, like that which was now soaring loudly over the sea from massive speakers, accompanying the fireworks.

I suddenly realized I was all alone. No one even knew I was here. No one knew where Verity had gone either. Scared, I ran back to my villa, shut the door, and locked it. And then I heard the sound outside the open window.

I refused to be afraid of shadows. I strode to that window, snatched back the cream linen curtain and . . . nothing. Simply a curtain blowing in the breeze from an open window was all it had been. Only thing is, I had not left that window open.

Somebody *had* been out there. Someone had been here in my room. Maybe he'd waited for Chad to leave, for the noise of the fireworks to cover my screams. Somebody wanted to kill me, I'd felt it before, now I knew it was true.

But why? I was no threat to anybody. I was merely a writer of detective novels, I didn't know about real crime, or real criminals. Mine were simply characters I invented and therefore over whom I had complete control. I had no control over whoever it was that had taken my Verity, and who now was after me.

I wished desperately that Chad would come back.

Angry with myself for being afraid, I tugged

my jeans back on, buttoned the pajama top, and tied my sneakers. I would go look for Chad. For Verity. For the Colonel. The Boss. Anyone at all. Just someone to help me.

33
The Boss

The Boss thought the timing was perfect. The fireworks would end in approximately five minutes, when the music would change from Beethoven to a Chopin piano etude, soft and sentimental, stopping guests in their tracks as they whispered about the missing girl. Very few of them had left the party, all wanting to know what was going to happen, and about the million-dollar reward. Now he was about to show them.

He had never been a man that sought the limelight. Out of necessity because of his business practices and his sexual desires, both of which sailed a little too close to the wind, he had kept his private life private. Now though, he saw an opportunity to become a man to be reckoned with, a man whose name would be on everybody's lips. He was about to save Verity's life. The allure of becoming a hero won out over his desire to torture and kill Verity. That would come later.

He had dismissed the black-T-shirted guards, sent them around to the front of the villa to keep an eye on any departing guests. "See if anything's up," he'd said. "See if Verity's come back." He'd even mentioned it to the Colonel, who was parading around like he was the star of this show, looking solemn and concerned, speaking on the phone to the chief of police, asking for even more men than the half dozen already sent to help in the search. The Boss allowed no one back here, though. They were told this area was off-limits. This was his home, his private place. The Colonel respected that.

Back at the bunker, he pressed the electronic button that slid the section of wall with the ivy to one side. He took his key from the niche and opened the door.

The place was in semi darkness, only one lamp lit. The giant TV screen that took up almost the whole wall was on, though the sound was muted. It was showing an old Katharine Hepburn and Spencer Tracy movie. To any unsuspecting visitor, all would look normal. Unless, that is, they stepped behind that large TV screen and into his world.

He'd had this room designed by a Hollywood movie decorator, telling him he was going to use it for a TV program. The walls were covered in padded black silk, studded with inch-thick bullet-shaped silver nuggets. The ceiling was black too, but when he pressed the remote it slid back to reveal a smoky mirror, edged all around with a thin strip of lights. The custom-made bed looked simple enough, though extra large. The sheet covering it was a deep burgundy and it was piled with long pillows, where right now Verity's blond head rested.

She was, of course, still "asleep."

He stood for a while, watching her. Her complete vulnerability gave him a thrill. He could do anything he wanted, touch her, feel her warmth, smell her secret woman scent. . . . But he wanted none of that. He had decided that now Verity was to be used for a different purpose. Her role would be amplified.

He checked the monitors that showed the grounds immediately outside the bunker. The shadows were deep and for a second he thought he saw a movement under the jacaranda tree. He pressed the pause button, stared hard at that area. The wind had gotten up and all the trees were bending under it. He saw no one there.

He decided that the wind was not a bad thing, since it would hide any noise he'd make when he carried Verity down to the beach. First though he had to prepare her. After all, she was going to be on camera tonight, so the better she looked—or perhaps the worse—the better for him.

He walked over to take another look, stood for a minute assessing her again, then slid his arms under her and lifted her off the bed. He was shocked by how cold she felt. Had he left her too long? Was it too late? She couldn't just die on him now, not yet, at least not until he had "saved" her. He must warm her up, get her into a hot bath. . . .

She was unexpectedly heavy. He put her down, took her by the feet, and dragged her across the marble floor. Her dress ruffled up. Her panties were white satin, edged with black lace. He thought she looked like a dumb young bride on her wedding night, except this was not going to be the marriage culmination that would have been expected.

She seemed to be getting heavier by the minute as he lifted her over the step at the edge of the tub and slid her legs into the hot water.

Startled, he heard her sigh. Could the drug be wearing off? God knows she'd been given enough to take care of her for the entire night, but still she was reacting.

He stood over her, waiting to see what would happen. Her eyelids fluttered and for a second it seemed she was looking at him, then she slid away again. Her head thunked on the marble step. Jesus. He did not want any marks on her; she must appear intact, unharmed, except by the tide from where, as the valiant rescuer, he would pull her. He had better hurry.

He left her lying on the floor and went to the cupboard where he kept the stretcher. He returned, knelt beside her, lifted her shoulders, and got the stretcher under them. Then he lifted her body and her legs onto it. He jacked up the lever, the wheels emerged, and the stretcher rose up off the ground. Now he was in business.

He went back to look at the bank of TVs showing the exterior of the bunker. Lights still glared from the house where he knew the Colonel would be doing his job of grilling his guests, while his half-dozen men combed the grounds. Nobody would come here though. He was safe.

He rechecked Verity on the stretcher. He didn't want her to slide off at the crucial moment. She looked so pretty, just a girl sleeping, long blond hair mussed, cheap diamante earrings glittering. She was all his to show the world.

The secret door leading directly onto the beach opened at his command. He pushed the stretcher through, cursing as her arm slid off and scraped along the floor. Now she would have bruises and he did not want that. Still, it could be assumed she had been bruised when she was swept against the rocks in the sea.

There was no light where he was walking but he knew the path, knew every step of the way, he'd traversed it so often. Pushing the stretcher in front of him, he walked steadily down the slope to the beach. Once there, he got her—with some effort because she was dead weight now—off the stretcher and lay her down on the sand. Then he folded the stretcher and carried it back to the house where he returned it to the cupboard.

It took only minutes yet he knew anything might happen in only minutes. But nothing had. She was still lying there, eyes closed, bruised arms spread wide, exactly as he'd left her. Now, though, was the time for the main event. The rescue.

He hefted Verity over his shoulder and stumbled through the soft sand to the firmer part of the beach where the tide came in. He lay his burden down and watched the sea sweep over her. He caught a murmur as she moved her head to one side. She was good and wet and the time was right.

He hefted her in his arms, not over the shoulder this time, because she was meant to look like the maiden in distress and he was her valiant savior. Our hero.

Carrying her, he staggered back down the beach along the tide line and into the brightly lit area where his guests still mingled, drinks still in hand, worried looks on their faces. The Colonel was there, and Mirabella and that bastard Chad.

"I found her," he gasped, staggering as he ran with her in his arms. "I think she drowned."

34
Chad Prescott

On the beach, Chad raced toward what looked to him very much like a dead woman. She lay immobile, her jaw slack, eyes rolled back in her head. From experience he feared there was little he could do for her.

He knelt on the sand and felt for her pulse, felt it flutter under his fingers. Immediately he turned her over onto her chest, placed his hands firmly on her back, and pressed with all his might. Again. And again. Water trickled from her mouth. Then she coughed. A small thing but it meant she was returning to the land of the living. Just. He kept on pressing. A big cough. Then she vomited seawater and he knew she would live.

Standing next to him, the Boss said, "If I were a praying man, I would be praying."

"Then become one," Chad said abruptly. "Pray, for fuck's sake. Just pray she doesn't die."

"Not at my party," the Boss said. "I wouldn't allow it."

Shooting him a disbelieving look, Chad saw from his expression the Boss meant it.

Over his shoulder he saw Mirabella, a hand

clutched to her throat, a look of horror on her face.

"Tell me she'll be alright," Mirabella begged.

He rolled back Verity's eyelids, noted the dilated pupils, knew she had been drugged. He recalled how she'd appeared drunk at the party, how she'd stumbled as she walked into the house, after which nobody had seen her again. Until now, unconscious in the incoming tide with the waves breaking over her.

"I have to get her to the hospital." He reached into his pocket for his mobile, to call them. "I'll drive her there myself, it'll be quicker than waiting for an ambulance."

"Wait." The Boss held up a hand, palm out, to stop him. "We'll use my helicopter. I'll call the pilot now. He can be here in five minutes."

Chad nodded. It was pretty amazing that not only had the Boss rescued the half-drowned girl from the sea, now he was about to save her life a second time, by helicopter. It seemed there was nothing the Boss could not do.

The Boss stared down at the immobile girl, then suddenly covered his eyes with his hands. "Oh God," he murmured. "How could this happen? At my party? What will my guests think?"

He turned to the Colonel who was also on his phone. "You have to find the culprit. Somebody did this to her, put drugs in her drink the way

I've heard men do in cheap bars. There's something they use to make young women unaware of their actions, then they take them home and rape them. I can't have someone doing things like that, here, in my home."

Though the Boss did not actually say it, looking at him, larger than life and twice as rich, the Colonel half-expected expected him to say, "Do you know who I am?"

"You have to find the culprit," the Boss stormed on. He was pacing now, hands clenched. Tension radiated from him. The Colonel respected his concern, his need to do something to help the young woman lying on the beach, more dead than alive. Chad was still pounding on her back. He turned her over, and gave her the kiss of life. The Colonel did not think it was going to work. How had this happened? What was she doing in the sea? Even drunk, even drugged, surely she would have recognize the difference between walking on sand and struggling through waves. It did not make sense.

"We're not after a 'culprit,' sir," he said to the Boss, who turned to look at him, eyes wide with anger. And with something else. The Colonel wondered if it could it be fear. "This was no accident," he said. "What we'll be looking for is a would-be killer."

The Boss stared back at him, silenced.

Chad attempted to lift the girl, intending to carry

her to dry land and the Boss seemed to return to his senses. "No. Wait. I have a stretcher."

They watched as he hurried back into the bunker. Chad checked Verity's pulse again. Mirabella sank onto the sand next to him.

"I promise I won't cry," she said, despite the fact that tears were already running down her cheeks, along with a great deal of blue-black mascara. "Oh, dear God, please, please, Doctor, save her."

"I'm afraid I've done all I can here."

The Boss came back from his bunker with a folded lightweight stretcher. Chad glanced at him, surprised. It was not exactly the kind of thing you kept handy. In fact he did not know anyone who had a stretcher in their home. Two burly men accompanied the Boss. Now they helped move Verity onto the stretcher and carried her to the helicopter landing pad. In minutes the six-seater Beechcraft Bonanza G36 clattered overhead. The Boss was as good as his word.

In the stretcher Verity was lifted inside and placed across the seats. Chad and the Boss climbed in behind. The two men sat in back of them.

In less than ten minutes they were at the local hospital. The Boss was already on his mobile, speaking in French. Astonished, Chad realized he was talking to the party organizers, telling them to keep the party going, ordering up more wine, more champagne, more food, louder music.

"Let them dance," Chad heard him bark in his giving-orders voice. Chad bet they would dance. They would not dare not to.

35
The Russian

The Russian found the pearls right where Mirabella had dropped them. He scooped them up, on the run, shoved them in his pocket, and kept on going until he reached the lane and his car parked beneath an overhanging tree, which conveniently hid it from passing traffic.

He threw the door of the Renault open so hard it crashed back on itself with a loud smack of metal on metal. Jesus. It sounded like a road accident. Anybody might show up now. He had the ignition turning almost before he sat down. He switched off the headlights, tense, waiting, eyes and ears straining in the darkness. No sound of following footsteps, no shouts, only the music still coming from the Boss's party, which he knew would go on until morning, when a breakfast of bacon and eggs, sausages and pancakes was to be served. God, he could use that breakfast right now, his stomach was rumbling with nerves and hunger, plus a couple too many drinks.

The Boss's rule was no drinks on the job, but fuck it, a man had to live. If caught though, a man might also die. He should know. Often enough he'd been the man who'd done that job.

That's what happened to his pal, another Russian who'd done work for the Boss. Drank and opened his mouth, until he'd shut it for him. Forever. Which is why he was about to take the Boss for a hefty chunk of money. Blackmail. Dollars in his pocket, or at least in his bank account. Maybe open a new account in Switzerland, a secret one with only a code to identify it. You didn't know the code, you didn't get access. The Swiss were good at things like that.

Only trouble was, he had missed again. Missed killing Mirabella, who he knew the Boss needed dead so he could get his hands on her land, and also that little painting, on which it seemed he'd set his heart. Who would have known the Boss even had a heart? Ah, perhaps he was just an art lover. Anyway he'd missed doing the deed, simply because the fuckin' doctor had shown up at the crucial moment. Fuckin' nearly gotten himself caught, had to slide out from behind those curtains, off into the night like a fox, well, maybe a wolf was a better description. Yeah, he liked wolf. Fanged, fierce, fearless. That was him alright.

Okay, so now he was out on the lane, dodging the young parking attendants in their red jackets running back and forth as though their lives depended on getting cars in the right spot and returning them fast for the no-doubt lavish tips. He knew all about that, he'd been there, done that, once upon a time, as he'd also been the waiter, a role he'd played again tonight. The white apron was stuffed in the backseat, along with the bow tie, an item he considered a symbol of servitude. He was no waiter, not anymore he wasn't. He'd played that role many times in his life for real. Not like now. Now it was for big money and he was off to collect it. The Boss had better be ready for him. Plus, he'd sell him the pearls. He was sure he'd want to give them back to Mirabella.

At the beach, the lights were still on everywhere. Police dogs were sniffing every bush and sand dune. The Villa Mara was lit like a friggin' birthday cake. Music still wafted into the night, people still stood around with drinks clutched in their hands, heads together, talking urgently. Wait a minute, wasn't that the Boss himself? Running down the sandy path leading to his bunker? And wait again, wasn't that Chad Prescott sneaking along behind him? Well now, that was good news. With Chad Prescott otherwise engaged, it meant Mirabella would be alone. Perhaps now he could get the deed done; kill two birds with one stone, so to speak—Mirabella for money and the string of pearls for more money. This was going to be his night. After this he could retire.

He got back in the car and reversed along the lane, waving a disparaging hand at the parking guys that got in his way and who shouted at him, like he had no right to be there. Fuck them. This was his turf.

Of course he knew the Villa Romantica. He'd done his research when the Boss had first given him the job of eliminating Aunt Jolly. Nice old woman. He had taken her by surprise and she had surprised him. Calm, she was, and in control.

"Well, now, good evening," she had said to him when he'd appeared in her room out of the blue. Not smiling, mind you, but looking him straight in the eye. She'd glanced back to the teapot she held in her hand. He knew from the pattern it was Wedgwood. Old and valuable too, he'd bet, though there wasn't much of a market for goods of that nature. Not worth pinching.

"I was just about to have a cup of tea," she continued. "I hope you'll consider joining me?"

It had thrown him completely, of course. She was supposed to panic, call out for help, even run. Old though she was he'd bet she could still run. As he watched, speechless, she took a second cup and began to fill it.

"I trust you like Earl Grey. It's my favorite, a bit lemony tasting, y'know. Refreshing," she added, with an upward glance and a smile as she offered him the cup and saucer. He noticed her hand did not so much as tremble.

He had enough sense not to accept it. Even though he was wearing gloves, the less he touched the fewer clues left behind.

"To answer an old woman would be polite," she said, putting down the cup. "Of course you'd have to take off that ridiculous mask," she added with a tinkling little laugh that annoyed the hell out of him suddenly. "Impossible to drink in one of those, I know from ski trips I made with my niece, Mirabella. I'm assuming you know of whom I speak?"

His confidence was being quickly eroded. She was treating him like a fuckin' visitor, not a masked man with a knife in his hand and eyes that glared malevolently at her. Didn't this woman understand she was about to be murdered? He'd never been in a situation like this before. It had always been get in, do the act, get out fast. Now she was offering him cups of tea for God's sake.

She turned her back to put down the teapot, and at that moment he had her. The knife slid between her old bones to the heart. He knew his anatomy. Had to, a man with his job.

She remained standing for what seemed to him an eternity, then crumpled to the floor, as though her bones simply withered and gave way. A woman like that, an old woman, it had been her strength of purpose, of character, of dignity and position that had kept her upright. Until she was dead, that is.

For the first time the Russian felt what might have been a pang of remorse. He wasn't meant to be killing old ladies. He was a wolf: fierce, feral, a street fighter.

He stared for a long moment. The urge to kneel next to her, to take her hand was almost overwhelming. In the end he simply said, "I'm sorry, ma'am." Then turned his back, left the way he'd come in, through the open french windows.

When, he wondered, would people ever learn that an open french window was an open invitation to men like him? Too late now. What was done, was done. He would go immediately and collect his king's ransom from the Boss. Plus the bonus he would demand. All remorse aside now, he considered it a job well done.

He suddenly realized there was only one problem. He'd left without the painting, which was an equal part of his commission. He glanced in the rearview mirror. People everywhere. Christ, too late to go back. He'd just have to bluff it out with the Boss. Claim there was no painting. It was already gone.

Part III

Jerusha and the Past

The Beginning

Mirabella

I spent days sitting at Verity's bedside, at first simply staring at her, sleeping or in a coma, or perhaps something worse. I was afraid for her, afraid for myself. I could not stand it and finally I succumbed and took along Jerusha's letter to read. What could be better than going back to the past to take my mind off the present day?

It began simply enough with Jerusha saying no one could imagine the love with which she'd built the Villa Romantica.

It was to be a place of refuge for me and my lover, she wrote, *but there I go, starting in the middle again when I would be better off beginning at the beginning.*

Jerusha

I was so young when I started out, I needed to lie about my age even to appear on stage. "Exactly how old are you?" producers would ask, giving me an up-and-down look as though they might be able to tell by the curve of my hips or the size of my breasts, which were small and of no help. Resisting the urge to fold my arms over my chest, to hide myself, I wished with all my might I could be the kind of statuesque woman they required to pose on stage. I wished I could at least dance or just jump crazily about, wagging real bananas around my middle like the wonderful Josephine Baker, the performer from Harlem in New York City, who had taken Paris by storm and was the main competition for any girl attempting to do the same.

Standing in the wings of yet another Paris theater, my mother lurked within earshot, "to protect" me she said, though she never told me from what I needed to be protected, and anyhow, innocence was my stock-in-trade. Not that I knew that either, but those producers, those stage people did. They recognized the real thing when they saw it and one of them, a successful director, inspecting me back and front, saw a fortune in his future.

"If you can dance, at least," he said, stepping back, chin in hand, looking consideringly at me again.

His name was Arturo Bonifacio Ramos and he was from a country called Argentina, a city called Buenos Aires. Both places might as well have been in fairyland; I'd never heard of them. I would only learn geography later in life when I finally traveled to those places, and even then I counted them as sea journeys—seven days, ten days, three weeks—whatever it took, that's that's where they were. Give me a map and ask me to put a finger on Buenos Aires right now and I might easily put a mistaken finger on Cape Town.

Geography, I might not be good at, but I was certainly good at money. Excellent in fact. Within a year I'd gone from that shy, lost young girl ripe for exploitation to a shrewd young woman who knew what she wanted and was hell-bent on getting it. You don't grow up poor and hungry, demeaned by your neighbors and schoolmates, without acquiring that simple need for . . . What? I have to think about what it's for. Not revenge. I did not need that. Just plain "to show them," I think was all I wanted. And that's exactly what I did.

It was also a year before I could call Mr. Ramos by his first name, Arturo. And of course he became my first lover. Did I want him as my lover? I certainly was not in love with him. No, what I needed was a pair of arms around me, someone holding me close, my head resting on his masculine shoulder, my heart beating against his. I had never had that, not from any man or woman. My mother was cold and ambitious, affection was not part of her life. She was not the hugger, kiss-good-night mother of my dreams and that I always swore I myself would be, if I ever had a child of my own. Then I would become that "mother," the giver not simply of life, but of love and protection, determined at all costs to save my child from harm.

The fact is, like everybody else, I had but one mother and I had to put up with her. I had to do as she said. I had to submit to having my hair washed in cold rainwater caught in the bucket under the drainpipe that ran from the gutter along the edge of the roof. Then I had to sit while she tugged a wide-toothed comb through the knots, and afterward smoothed on some kind of oil, the smell of which I could not stand. Ever after, in my life, my hair was taken care of by professionals, by my own hairdresser who treated it gently and used a drop of scented lotion, then polished it with a different kind of oil until it shone smooth against my scalp, a glossy sleek helmet that ended in a single fat braid.

That fiery red braid was to become my signature. I never bobbed my hair even when it was fashionable. Every picture painted of me, every photograph taken throughout my life, every moment in bed with a man, I wore that braid. Of course the men loved to unravel it, to spread my lavish locks across the pillow, to match it up with my lower red fuzz that intrigued them twice as much.

When I first experienced this kind of "intrigue," the gentle touch of a man's fingers, I thought this was maybe the way it felt when you died and went to heaven. My entire body soared upward until I seemed to be floating, crying out my joy, screaming for more, more, do not stop . . .

I wonder how many women know what I mean. So many I met, and with whom I tried to discuss these feelings, simply gazed at me as though I were mad. Sex was for men. Money was what women got for giving them sex. It was a hard lesson, but I learned it.

Only one woman understood, a girl I met in the dressing room backstage at the Royalty Theatre in some small French town where we were both the "chorus" and the "magician's assistants." She got sawed in half—I held up the box cut in two to prove it was real. Her name was Milan. I told her I thought it was an odd name for a girl. No odder than yours was her smart answer. At least there's a reason for mine, she added. I was born in that city.

I had no such reason. Why I was named Jerusha would be forever a mystery though it was believed my mother, still drowsy from the drugs given to help the birth, had really meant to say Josephine. She had a thing for Bonaparte, and for small men, like my father, the "small man" who rarely darkened our doors. Certainly never long enough to pay for us. Poverty was a day-to-day event.

It was obvious from a young age, three, I

believe, that I was to become a meal ticket. How can I blame her? I was odd-looking, my hair was red and impossible, my feet were large as doorstops, I was ungainly, I never had a dance lesson because we couldn't afford such a luxury, and yet her confidence that I was to become "a star" never wavered. How she accomplished it I still really do not know.

"Determination," was what she told me later. When we were still speaking, that is. "Courage" was what I would have called it. That woman never let me down, well, in a way she did, selling me off like that, or at least turning a blind eye when it happened and pocketing the money that was never called a fee, simply a man's recompense for taking my virginity. Actually, as I said before, I enjoyed it as much as he did, and as I was to do for the rest of my days. And nights.

This must make shocking reading, I know, but I promised when I started that I would tell the truth, the facts as they were, exactly what happened so the reader, whomever you might be and I shall never know, will understand how events took place that were beyond my control. It seemed I was always being "taken-care-of," as they would put it. "Looked after," as my mother said. "Exploited," as I knew it.

Anyhow, that was my first time but certainly not my last. Having discovered the delightful art of making love, "sex" as men termed it, I knew which course my life would take. And I knew if it came along with my fame on stage, the richer my lovers would be. The more famous I became, the more aristocratic they would be. I knew "stage-door Johnnys" lined up outside the wonderful Josephine Baker's theater, bearing gifts of diamond bracelets as well as armfuls of roses. I wanted that too. And succeeded before long—in fact by the age of fifteen—though I lied and claimed to be sixteen in order to get a permit to dance on stage but also so no man could be accused of taking advantage of my youth because he truthfully did not know it. Only my mother and myself knew and we both lied about it. Or rather she lied, I avoided the issue.

One night, perhaps a year later, I was in a chorus line of five girls. We were at the Folies theatre and were to follow the great Josephine. Well, not exactly *follow*. You did not "follow" a great star like her. She was wonderful, divine, sexy-black with shining limbs and naked breasts and hips that sniggled from side to side, back and forth, a bunch of bananas jiggling suggestively between her legs. God, she was good. She had the audience on their feet, applauding, yelling, whistling, begging for more.

After her, I went on with my young cast mates and did a sort of Isadora Duncan Greek dance, all floating arms and wreaths of lilies held over our heads. Except my red hair fell from its topknot and tumbled around my shoulders, and somehow my little Greek tunic slipped from one shoulder, baring one breast to the nipple, and with a tiny shake I allowed that to happen. And I was made.

36

My first true love was young, though not as young as I, and a little more experienced. He was English and had a title, which I am not going to write here because I have no wish to discredit his family's reputation. He is a well-known member of the British House of Lords, a father, even a grand-father by now, I should think. I know he lives a peaceful life, happy with a woman a little older than himself, which I know to be a good thing because, despite being so attractive and so kind and so nice, he was a man that needed boosting up in the world if he were to make anything of himself.

He showed up at the stage door at the Folies, blond hair falling over his embarrassed pink face, blue eyes searching mine as he handed me the cheap cellophane-wrapped roses I knew came from the stall on the street corner. No diamonds here, I remember thinking. But my, he is delicious.

Delicious was the proper description for him. He was almost edible in his sweetness, his geniality, his desire to please, and the love he offered. Straightforward, no holding back. "I'm in love with you," was exactly what he blurted out, and then he took a step back from me, as though I might slap his face at the impertinence.

"How very pleasant," was my ridiculous answer.

But in truth I had not expected such a direct approach. And my God, he was cute. His just-shaved chin had that sweet little haze of new beard already growing in, darker than his hair, which was fair and swept straight back from his wide forehead and had a dear little tuft at the crown, the way a small boy's sometimes does.

I handed the pathetic roses to my dresser who was standing immediately behind me with a bodyguard, a burly, strapping fellow who used to be a policeman until he got injured in a robbery, when he took a pension and came to work for me, intimidating unruly admirers. It worked quite well. At least, so far it had.

"My name is Rex," the young man said, all eagerness in his expression.

Of course I've changed his name to keep his anonymity, but he certainly was what you might expect a "Rex" to look like. A young king. And maybe, just maybe, I'm saying, he was.

Despite the cheap flowers, a chauffeured motor waited at the curb. A Delage I think, dark maroon in color and shinier than any other motor I ever saw. A crest was emblazoned—discreetly though —on the front door. Of course I was impressed.

"Will you do me the honor . . ." He stuttered slightly, stumbling over his words though his eyes told me what it was he wanted.

I said, "You would like me to have dinner with you?"

I waited for his response, which took a while to come. I smoothed my fur-trimmed satin cape over my shoulders, and waited some more. The cape was pale green, Chanel, I believe, though memory is tricky when it's the 1930s you are remembering. And me, so old now. And that's the first time I've ever admitted that. Still I recall the dress perfectly, it slinked around my body as though it loved me, fashioned from the new soft silk-jersey pioneered by Madame Chanel and that did things for a woman's "look" no fabric had ever done before. At least none I had been aware of, but then I was fairly new to money and fame and designer clothing.

He was eager, he was young, he was adorable. Of course I took pity on him.

The Delage was as luxurious inside as it was out; cushioned in cream leather, small posies in silver flasks at each side of the backseat, a burled-walnut bar built in behind the chauffeur's seat, with crystal decanters and a silver ice bucket and tongs and lemon and . . . ohh just anything you might think of in a well-stocked bar. Plus a dish of sliced, fresh, out-of-season peaches, a bowl of sweet almonds, a carafe of ice water, and about a million tiny white linen napkins all emblazoned with his crest.

Looking at my new admirer, I thought this might not be love. But on the other hand, it could be.

37

Of course there was no question a woman like myself might become the wife of an earl, an English lord, a man with a powerful family and also, I assumed, with a titled-debutante already awaiting the engagement ring and probably already having fittings for her wedding dress, which, naturally, would be of virginal white satin scattered with pearls, and with a sweetheart neckline demure enough to be approved of by the bishop yet just low enough to be admired by the male wedding guests. It would probably take place at Westminster Abbey, or the smaller St Margaret's, though they might opt for the venerable Norman stone church in the bride's village, where locals would stand outside to watch and wave to the smiling bride, who had known them all since she was a child, and who had played with them then, and who now had envy behind their smiles.

This beautiful car, the very same Delage in which I now sat, as if I owned it, queen of the day in fact, would for the wedding be driven by a uniformed chauffeur to her stately home. The entrance would be ablaze with banners and buntings and great hoops of white flowers, maybe to remind the guests that the bride was, of course, a virgin. Or if she wasn't then she had been very clever about it, and later in bed, she would have to be a whole lot cleverer. One never knows.

Whatever my speculation, I knew that bride would never be me and I accepted it. I was born who I was; I have become who I am; and right then it was enough. Enough to have this lovely young man so madly in love with me that I felt like a great lady; enough that after that first wonderful night when we entwined like two stalks of roses, scented and thorny and sweet and hard and pliant, all at the same time, my lover, Rex, as I called him, left our bed, tumbled and "smelling like a whorehouse," I said laughing, to rush out to buy me a gift. Pearls. What else would a man like that think of as a perfect gift for a woman, lady or no lady?

I was asleep, still in that same hotly perfumed bed, hugging a pillow with his scent on it, when he came back, triumphant. He commanded me to sit up. I did so, clutching the soft linen sheets modestly over my breasts because somehow, with daylight seeping through the curtains and somewhere the smell of bacon that tingled my toes I wanted it so much, and a fully dressed man looking at me with a delighted expression of one who brings a great surprise, it seemed only proper to behave modestly and not command him to get back into bed immediately, though I should have liked that. Besides, he was holding something behind his back and I knew that meant a present. And not just the street-corner roses this time, he was too eager for me to admire what he had.

He looked so young, so serious, torn between wanting to give me his surprise and worry that I might not think it as wonderful as he himself did.

"For goodness' sake, darling Rex, just give it to me," I said, laughing as I lost patience. I was a woman just woken from sleep, I wanted to bathe, brush my hair, eat that bacon with a slab of homemade bread that tasted the way bread should taste in Paris, and besides, love him though I did, I did not trust his taste.

He came and knelt at my bedside. I reached out to stroke that little tuft of blond hair that spiked up at the crown of his head despite his applications of a delightful smelling pomade, purchased in London, I knew, from a firm called Trumper.

"My love, my only love," was what he said to me as he offered me the long blue leather box, inscribed with the name of a famous Parisian jeweler who, I knew, designed for royalty.

Forgetting all about modesty in my excitement, I accepted the box and with first a long smiling glance at my young lover, I clicked it open.

It was lined in velvet, a dark violet color, across which lay a rope of evenly matched pearls in a true mouthwatering cream. Each pearl shone with a deep luster, and when I looked more carefully I saw each one was a tiny bit different, a slope to one side of the bead, another a little rounder, yet the whole absolutely perfect. The clasp was a lion's head in gold, catching a pearl ball in its open mouth.

It was perfection. More, it was a gift from a man who truly loved me. Our tears mingled as he slipped the rope of pearls over my head, smoothed them over my breasts, kissed my neck where the golden clasp lay.

"I would like to marry you," he said, his voice gentle yet strong.

Of course I knew he would, right that minute, that is, and I would have liked to marry him, but one of us had to be sensible, face facts, even at an emotional moment like this, when his declaration came with a fortune in pearls.

I allowed my mind to drift from the reality of who I was, to pretend for a few minutes that I was a real titled lady, that we lived together in his English manor house, with a cook in the kitchen and a nanny in the nursery taking care of our three children, a boy and two girls, and the two of us, ever young, ever in love . . . Dreams are like that. They can ruin reality.

I realized I was stepping on our dream when I smiled and thanked him with a million kisses for the pearls, assured him I would love him forever, when the truth, known only to myself, of course, was that I was never absolutely sure I loved him, or knew even what love was. I knew only that I cared deeply for him, that I admired him, that I loved his body, his eager youthfulness, that tuft of hair that sprang from the crown of his head. I loved his charm. But I knew it could not last.

I wore those pearls for the year we lived together, but the even greater gift he gave me was his love. And beyond that, even more of a miracle to a young woman like myself who had never known a true "home," who had never owned property, never thought to do more than pay rent for a fashionable house in Paris. He built me the Villa Romantica.

38

Of course the villa was not there yet, but we drove together to the place it would be, in that lovely Delage, chauffeur in gray uniform at the wheel, champagne chilling in the silver bucket, flowers fresh each morning in the silver vases, always lily of the valley. I remember the scent so clearly across all these years. And thank God, I also remember what young love felt like.

The Villa Romantica took a mere twelve months to build, mainly because of my insisting that I intended to occupy it in the New Year when I would hold a party in celebration—a costume party, with every guest masked, the women in feathers, the men in black silk. I had no idea what kind of omen this might represent. And why should I?

I almost fell for the inevitable Marie Antoinette costume but caught myself just in time, realizing there would be at least a dozen others in the same powdered wigs and billowing skirts. I went for the Cinderella look instead; the most charming silken rags in cream and coffee and a touch of raspberry to set off my red hair that I wore not in its usual braid but wrapped round and round my head in a great fiery swirl, studded with the sort of large diamond pins the true

Cinderella would never have seen, until she captured her prince, that is. And maybe not even then. After all, we don't really know the ending of that story, do we? Not the way you are about to know the ending of this one.

Let me tell first how wonderful my Villa Romantica looked, pale pink against a midnight blue sky, lanterns hanging from the branches of the newly planted, though mature, trees that looked as though they had been there forever.

We were to welcome in the year 1938. Peace was all around us, at least those of us who ignored the saber-rattling emanating from Germany and its raucous, hotheaded maniacal leader. All we heard was the soft dance music and the music of the sea and the nightingales, and even the cuckoos that could wreck any girl's romance remained outside the window, cuckooing like the clocks the Swiss made.

Was there any night more blissful? Just warm enough for bare shoulders; just cool enough later for a man to lend his jacket to slip over those shoulders; just elegant enough to dress in your best, the latest Paris fashion, the biggest jewels taken from bank vaults and displayed like play stones around elegant necks and on elegant arms. Myself, I wore the pearls. I also wore the new ring, the sapphire from Ceylon where all the most beautiful sapphires were mined, and sold via Amsterdam, where the most expensive and largest stones are cut by craftsmen who are artists too, so every facet catches the light and gleams, a bit of deep blue heaven.

And who was the man that gave me this precious gift?

It was not Rex, who I had unselfishly sent back to his debutante. It was Walt Matthews, known as "Iron Man" Matthews because of his daring adventures in parts of the world most of us never venture to go. He had survived not only the sinking of the then-brand-new and biggest liner ever built, the *Titanic*, but had rescued many passengers from the ship, refusing to take a place in the last small orange life raft, knowing he had no chance. Yet, survive he did in a sea so cold it froze his feet until he feared he could no longer kick or swim, then suddenly he hit the warm Gulf current. He drifted for hours until he was picked up by a passing cruiser. Such is life, or death, he said, in an emotional speech he made about his experience. He also said he never feared death again after that.

I told him later that he only survived so he could find me, and fall in love with me. I was his fate. He said he fell for my scent. Evening in Paris it was called, or in French, of course, *Soir de Paris*. It was by Bourjois and I never knew if I was more enamored of the pretty cobalt-blue bottle with the silver stopper, or the violet-lilac scent itself.

We met, not in Paris, but in London, where I had gone to visit an art exhibition and to see old friends. The exhibition was held in a gallery on Bond Street, which suited me as it meant I could at the same time take in the new fashions displayed in the shop windows, and in particular a small jewelry store called, I believe, *A La Vieille Russie*, which naturally showed beautiful items from the old Russian Court that had to be sold by émigrés desperate for money in the new country in which they were now condemned to live.

In my faulty memory, I'm trying to recall whether I went first to the art exhibition and fell in love with the man, or whether I went to the jewelry store first and fell for the sapphire. Either way, I ended up with the man and the ring, and later, a painting. And of course, the painting turned out to be the most treasured possession of my life, even more so than the Villa Romantica.

The exhibition was not an important one, simply a hundred or so artworks propped up against a stone wall, not even on tables—they were con-sidered so unimportant—brought in by would-be sellers verging on starvation and for whom a few English pounds might make the difference between a future and no future. Of course I was happy to help. I had been where they were, not so long ago.

There were also a number of more valuable

paintings on display that were not for sale. One caught my eye. There was something familiar about the location captured in that painting. I stepped back to take a second look. It was by an English artist, J. M. W. Turner. A river scene, turbulent water with white crested waves, the bank grayish-green in the rainy light that so often covers the English countryside, only emphasizing its loveliness. A small inn hovered over the river, seeming almost ready to tumble into it, with a second-floor window projecting over it, diamond paned, with deep red curtains half-hidden behind the glass. Somehow, I felt I knew that inn; knew that room with its bowed window, and the red curtains I would draw tightly to shut out the night, shutting out the world so I might be alone with the man I truly loved.

But to begin at the beginning. Our meeting was a whirlwind event, a pickup if ever there was one, in a public place in front of dozens of people. We simply stood there, eyes linked, so deep into each other with that physical impact that happens so rarely but cannot be ignored when it does. We were unaware of other people staring, amused no doubt by our obvious sexual frisson. There was no hiding it, I was smitten so hard my legs turned to jelly and my body to liquid, while he carefully held the paper program booklet over his masculinity. "Would you join me for a glass of champagne?” he asked. Of course I would. I would have joined him in bed right there and then, had he asked.

Though I was realistic where sex was concerned, emotions were quite another matter, and something I had been careful to exclude from my life. I was twenty-five years old, never married, never likely to be, not with my reputation. In fact my only offer had come from the delicious Rex, and even then I had known in my heart it was not real. He had meant well, he loved me, it was the appropriate gesture for a gentleman to make to the woman he loved. I will remember him always, for that. And for what came later, because when I needed help, he was there for me.

Anyway, before then, and in fact right there and then, I was in love with Walt “Iron Man” Matthews.

I can remember exactly what I was wearing that night: a black Chanel dress with long, tight, silk-mesh sleeves and a prim white satin collar. Black satin heels, of course, with small diamante bows on the backs, not on the front as is more usual, but then I was never one for the usual. Of course I’d had them moved there. It caused quite a lot of comment and envious female glances, I can tell you.

I wore black silk stockings with a seam up the back as was the style, tricky to keep straight but very sexy. I'm sure every man there wondered where those seams ended up.

My Iron Man certainly did. And it was all the two of us had expected of each other. Was it really love? I ask myself even now. And yes, it was. He was, in fact, the only man I ever truly loved.

We were to stay at that inn many times, in that same spacious room overlooking the river, drawing closed those red damask curtains but leaving the diamond-paned window open so we might hear the river rippling its way toward the weir, where it would fall in a great tumble of white froth into infinity, and perhaps, oblivion. It was as though that river could foretell my future.

39

One year was exactly what we had together. One perfect year that I was to remember for the rest of my life.

We spent that perfect year at the Villa Romantica, shunning the everlasting parties, sharing glasses of the local wine over dinners often cooked by myself, a talent I had not known I had, never having taken much interest in food before. But now the markets were all around, with produce grown in these local hills, milk and cheeses from local cows, flowers bunched and tied with ribbons by our local girls. And I loved every minute of it, everything about it, and I loved my man.

How wonderful it was to say that. My man.

We spent every second together, often in the spacious kitchen while I fried the breakfast bacon (usually late in the afternoon). The smell always made my mouth water. He would slice hunks off a huge crusty loaf and rub them in the bacon fat in the pan, letting them soak up the juices until just crisp enough to add bite. Coffee brewed slowly in the new drip machine, leaving me to crave it, hurrying it on while it took forever it seemed. The buttercup-yellow plates and coffee bowls were already on the table. When the coffee was finally ready, I filled those bowls almost to the brim, adding just a splash of rich, creamy milk, picking up the bowl with both hands to drink. A custom my man considered barbaric, having been brought up to use cups with handles at the table, though I suppose it was alright to drink beer in mugs without a handle. Anyhow, barbaric it might seem to a foreigner like him, but to a French woman like me, it was breakfast heaven.

I would slowly come awake with that coffee, sitting in the sunshine, the breeze just sufficiently cool to be pleasant, the cuckoos thankfully gone to their daytime rest. The small gray cat that had adopted us sprawled, paws stretched out in front of him, certain that tidbits would be tossed his way. It was a scene of such peace I could never have foretold the violence that was to come.

40

The year 1939 was upon us. It seemed like any other, spring merging into a summer of such blue-skied perfection surely winter would never return. I basked on the narrow beach, cooling my feet in water that lapped over pebbles smoothed by centuries of waves, and where Scott Fitzgerald had played out his life and love with his wild-crazy wife, Zelda. It was they who had cleared the tiny beach of its masses of seaweed and detritus to make a sweet little spot, half-hidden from the crowds, for sunbathing, for drinking rosé wine at noon, for wearing daring bathing suits and where their friends, the rich Americans, Gerald and the beautiful Sara Murphy held picnics. Sara, with her long string of pearls thrown casually back over her shoulder instead of in front, created a new fashion fad that year.

They were gone, of course, as were many Americans, heeding the warning signs and hurrying to embassies and consulates to obtain the all-important visas to Spain or Portugal that could get them out to safety and eventually home.

I never wore my pearls to the beach, but I did wear a rather daring white bathing suit. It was a thin silken fabric, ruched here and there to emphasize my curves and my waist. And of course I always wore my long hair in a braid, sometimes entwined with white ribbons, sometimes with a flower, a daisy perhaps, tucked into it. It was my style, my own fashion. I never copied anyone. I was always me. If that sounds egotistical, pretentious even, I can only say I am sorry, but it's true, I was unique.

My Iron Man, of course, was with me, though he spent much more time in the water than I ever did. I was always worried about my hair, like most women, and I hated those rubber bathing caps. He would emerge, dripping, usually carrying a shell, a conch, spiraled and cream with a pink interior that he swore looked like me. Or intimate parts of me, anyway.

It was at the end of a calm, hot day, when I noticed a woman standing at the back of the beach. She was tall, her long dark hair drifted over her shoulders in the fresh breeze that had sprung up, the way it often did of an evening. In fact, I had seen her several times, always standing in the same place, always with dark glasses, always watching. She'd made me feel uncomfortable, but I'd dismissed it; she was just a woman, taking the air, looking at the sea, as we did, because it gave us never-failing pleasure. After all, is there anything more sybaritic, more sensual than a long day spent at the beach in the shade of an umbrella, lying on a towel, gathering the sun into your body, like wine for the soul?

Now I gathered up our scattered belongings: the towels, the wet bathing suits, the books and sun creams, the tired bunches of grapes and cast-off sandals and began to walk back to the lane fronting the beach, where the villa was located. She turned her head as I approached. I threw her a friendly smile, as one does when sharing a beach, but this woman did not smile back.

Surprised, but untroubled, it was so insignificant a thing, I continued on my way, followed by my Iron Man, carrying the heavy bags. Behind me, I heard her say something. Since I was sure she was not addressing me, I simply walked on. Of course, I was not unaware of my Iron Man's attraction for women, but I was sure of him and sure of myself. I reigned, I believed, supreme in his life.

I heard his bare feet clacking across the slatted wooden walkway laid over the hot sand, and turned to smile at him, to say what a lovely day and that I had champagne cooling in the refrigerator. I did not say I also had a great surprise, a secret I was going to tell him over that delicious chilled glass, both of us cool and fresh from the shower, which was where I intended to make love to him, or he to me, or both to each other. The end of a perfect day.

I saw the polite puzzled smile on his face as the dark-haired woman confronted him. She grasped his arm and held onto it, talking all the while. I couldn't hear what she said and alarmed by her behavior, I hurried back toward them. She turned to look at me. I shall never forget that look. It was what hatred means, though why, I did not know. But I knew it was also what evil looked like.

And then I saw the gun.

It all happened in an instant, on a beach still busy with late sunbathers, swimmers, and children. I could hear their shrill happy cries, even as she lifted that gun and aimed it at me. I felt sure my heart stopped beating even before she shot. But then she swung around, held the gun to my lover's chest.

For me, the world stopped. It fell silent. Yet everything was going on as normal around us, the three of us isolated in our drama of terror.

Walt raised his arms above his head, he spoke softly to her, told her not to worry, everything was going to be alright, he would take care of her, make sure she was safe. I stood, frozen, listening to him saying these words to a mad-woman who at any moment could blast him into eternity. I thought of the child he did not know about, growing inside of me, of our love, our lives together, our perfect happiness. Terrified, I lunged for that woman, screaming my own hatred and fear at her.

She went down under me. I heard Walt yelling at me to watch out, felt his weight as he threw himself over me, heard the dull thud of the first bullet, then the second and a third. I grabbed the revolver from her, even noting as I did that it was feminine, pearl-handled, a swanky kind of gun that I might have chosen myself. In fact that Walt had chosen for me. It was my gun she held. My gun with which she had shot my man. My child she was now threatening.

She lay back, hands held out in front of her, a mocking look in her eyes as she looked at me. "Go on, then, do it, why don't you?" she said.

So I shot her.

41

It all happened so quickly. In moments everything that had been so right went wrong. I remember sinking to my knees in the sand, putting my hands under my man's head, trying to lift his face to mine with some misguided thought of breathing life back into his lifeless mouth.

A group rapidly surrounded us, silent, shocked. "She shot him," I heard someone say. "She shot the woman, then she shot him. And isn't she Jerusha? And isn't he Walter Matthews? Iron Man Matthews? Oh my God," I heard them saying, the words sounding as though they were in capital letters. And then, "Call the gendarmes immediately," they cried.

Police sirens wailed as half a dozen cars, blue lights flashing, screeched onto the beach. What seemed like a dozen uniformed men spilled out. Two of them pried me off my dead lover. Others checked the body of the woman I had shot.

"She shot him," I heard people saying. "But she shot the woman first. He'd gone to help her." Jerusha was jealous. He'd been having an affair; the woman was known in the local cafés and bars and she'd told everybody about her famous lover. Nobody believed her, until now.

Because how could Jerusha's lover want another woman? They had mocked the girl, at first. But now they saw it was true, and I had taken my revenge, the way all betrayed women did. I was, they said, a classic case.

I heard it all through a haze of grief as the gendarmes took me, unhandcuffed as a tribute to my fame and for the benefit of the photographers that clamored around as they walked me from the beach to the police car, pushing my head down to get me into the backseat, a cop sitting to either side, both smiling for those same photographers. That photograph went around the world. It was my epitaph.

I told them I was three months pregnant and was afraid I'd lose my baby, so they took me back to the Villa Romantica and summoned a doctor. It was thought the hospital was too public a place and privacy was essential if the case was not to be tainted. For when I went to court, they meant. Accused of two murders.

I was healthy. I was famous. I wasn't even a widow because we had not been married, though I'd meant to propose to him when I told him about our happy event, that was no longer so happy. I had killed my baby's father. I had no right to that baby. Iron Man Matthews had given me his heart and I had taken his life.

How does one live with such a burden on one's soul? How do you come to terms with the death of the man you loved, when you were the cause of his death? Of course, there was no way.

It was Rex, my ex-lover, my honorable man, who came to my aid, who mapped out my defense and exactly why I would never have shot any man, especially one I loved. I was not just "any woman," I remember him telling the courts. I was Jerusha. It would be impossible for any man to cheat on me. And, he added, he should know.

Stunned, the court took him at his word. They respected his courage in standing up in court, a man like him, with his background, for a woman like me, with my background. Jerusha was already a household word, and now he became one.

After it was over, I thanked him, of course, briefly, in private, in a small bleak room behind the court that smelled of stale coffee and cigarettes. The walls were institutional green, the overhead lighting harsh and unflattering, but still Rex told me I was beautiful.

"I'll never forget," he said as he kissed me first on one cheek, then the other, and then a third time, as we did in the South of France.

"That one is for memory," he said, smiling as he departed.

I shall always love him for that.

In a quick decision, a judge found me guilty of the murder of the unknown woman and of my lover. But, this was France and this was a *crime passionelle*, a "love crime," where it is believed the balance of one's mind is disturbed. Add to that, not only was my lover said to have been cheating on me, I was also carrying his child.

They were lenient. I would not die for my crime. I would not even go to jail. I would be taken to some safe place in the country where I would bear my baby in secret. It would then be taken from me and given to the sorrowing members of the father's family, to raise, in England. I would never be allowed to see my child again.

It was the cruelest punishment they could ever have thought of. No woman could ever have done this to me. This was men's justice.

She was beautiful, my tiny baby. Well, at least I thought so, but then doesn't every woman on first seeing her newborn, exclaim how beautiful she is? I named her for her beauty. Jolie. French for pretty. She was always, forever after to be known as Jolly. And I never did see her again.

I remained in France while she was to live in England with the large Matthews clan that loved her and cared for her and saw she was happy. To her, her mother was dead. Rest in peace. I know they would have told her that and I feel sure she nodded sorrowfully. I think she would have liked to have had a mother. I hope she would have liked me. I know I would have liked her.

I left the Villa Romantica and went to live in the lower mountain regions of the Luberon, where I bought a small farm, nothing more than a homestead really, a few hectares, a few animals, goats that butted me and made me laugh; a cow splotched black and white that gave me milk that I sold at market, with so much cream it would make anyone gain weight. I found a little brown dog in the window of a store with beseeching eyes that told me he was as lonely as I was. I named him Enfant, child in French, which got me some stares when I called for the child and a dog answered. The joke made me laugh at least. The gray cat who had adopted us at the villa came with me and soon acclimated himself, the way cats can, to his new surroundings. His devotion was first to his home and second to me, but I settled for that.

The canary was part of a traveling circus troupe that came through the small town. He walked across a wire singing his song while people applauded. I swear that, like myself, that bird never got over his moment of fame. He loved an audience. But I could not bear his life of servitude so I paid a small fortune, as it seemed to the owner, and took him back to his new home, where he sang every day—and sometimes nights—for my enjoyment, as well as his own.

So there we were, me and my new little family, making the best of what we had, who we were, content, happy even, in each other's company. The past, with a great effort, was put behind us.

And then the war came and changed everything.

42

The real war, the hand-to-hand fighting, the tanks, the bombing, did not come immediately to the South of France. For a while, life seemed almost normal. The market opened every morning, the fishermen delivered their catch, though admittedly now smaller since they did not venture out as far; the purveyor of fresh eggs rode her bicycle, fragile bags dangling from the handlebars, then sat sipping her usual mug of cold coffee topped up with a slug of crème de menthe, "to keep out the morning chill," as she told us, each and every morning.

At first, I kept to myself, as was my custom, but then I was sitting with my usual glass of red and a slab of St. André cheese, which I liked because of its semisoftness. It was not runny, but had just enough texture to get your knife through, to smear a little onto a piece of the excellent—baked at six A.M.—"baton," which is the same as a baguette, only thinner, which gives more crust.

"Madame Matthews?"

I glanced up at the man who had, without my leave, taken the seat opposite. I knew he could not be French. No Frenchman would have been so impolite. I chose to ignore him.

"I wish to speak to you on a matter of importance for La France." He leaned forward, gazing earnestly at me, as though making sure no one could overhear.

Now, when anyone speaks of La France, and not simply "France," you understand immediately it is important.

"You speak of my country," I said, arranging my cheese on a morsel of bread and taking a bite. "Though you are not French."

"I am speaking of what you can do for your country, Madame. And you are correct, I am English. But it is your country that I, and others like me, wish to help. And you are in a position to help all of us."

I listened carefully while he explained that he was a member of the British Intelligence Service, that they needed to connect with French people who had access to the Nazis because of who they were, and who they knew, or who they might meet at social events where gossip flowed as easily as the wine, and where many a detail of a planned raid or a troop movement or the whereabouts of important enemies might be overheard, and noted. And then passed on to the trusty intelligence officer, who recruited me right there and then, as a member.

I put on my old finery, and sometimes my old flirt face, and it was astonishing what secrets a man would let slip when he needed to boast to a woman like myself. Flattery, with those men, I discovered, got you everywhere.

At first it was not difficult. I was able to help in several cases, which I was told later resulted in lives saved, positions altered, a safer escape route taken. I played only a small part, but I helped in my own way, and I hoped some of those saved lives were because of me.

I also picked up my old self, the singer, the entertainer. I offered my services to the War Office and put together a pianist, or sometimes an accordion player for when there was no piano, as well as a guitarist, and the woman who had for many years been my dresser.

I unpacked some of my "glamour" from the trunks full of stage clothes, unearthed myself from my farm, and I went out and sang to those troops, most of whom were too young to remember who I was, but who showed their appreciation loudly with whistles and cheers. And I showed them my legs and got more whistles and cheers.

I'd had my uniform tailored in London. Not that it was a real uniform, since I belonged to no armed service. I designed it myself. A soft olive green, with with a Sam Browne belt like the Americans had, only mine had a polished gold Hermès buckle. Breast pockets with crested gold buttons; a silver flask of good brandy tucked into the hip pocket of my trousers—I only wore skirts when I was "on display," so to speak.

Trousers were much more comfortable and more discreet when walking and climbing or driving in bumpy jeeps was involved.

We jolted in an ancient jeep across the deserts of North Africa, constantly breaking down, tires too worn to cope with the blazing hot sand, sleeping in small tents at night, me always worrying about scorpions and bugs. They placed lighted candles around to keep them at bay. And if occasionally some delightful young man I had met at dinner in the officers' mess, came to ask if he might join me, who was I to say no? When this might be his last, forever, chance to hold a woman in his arms. Call it promiscuity, if you will. For me, what I offered was comfort. And the best sex he'd ever had. And in case you are interested, oh yes, I did enjoy it. But then, I always had. Remember?

Would I be wrong in saying I enjoyed that part of the war? That it took me back to who I once was? For a brief time, yet all the while I was aware that some of those boys cheering me would not return. It was a love-hate affair, at best, but I tried to do my part. Until it was over, and I returned to normal. The forgotten woman with a past.

Did I not say the war saved my life? It did more. It saved my self-respect. I did whatever I was asked. I drove ambulances to the front line to bring back the wounded, and too often, the dead, young men I had probably met the previous evening. I steeled myself to go on, told myself this was war, this is what men did to each other. And I prayed it would never happen again. Every night I prayed. And sometimes during the day-time too, when guns flared their lethal fire at us, at anyone, anywhere. It was the world gone mad.

Then, one day, when I know we all thought we could take no more, the American troops walked into Paris and we were free again. God bless you, the crowd yelled, women rushing to kiss these super men, so tall, so strong, so handsome in their uniforms and helmets, handing out candies to the eager, sweet-deprived children, and with kisses to the womenfolk.

Life returned to normal, but I would miss that world forever.

A few years later, anonymous on my farm in the Luberon valley, I received a letter from the French government, the Department of Affairs. The president, it was said, had decided to honor my war work and courage with a medal. Unfortunately the president himself could not pin this emblem on my shoulder since he was away, but I would receive it in the mail.

And I did. I took it out of its velvet box, stroked its blue, white, and red grosgrain ribbon, kissed the small golden emblem of honor and then I put it away with the pearls and the Ceylon sapphire ring, forever. Or at least, until the next generation.

43

It is an odd thing to say but somehow that terrible war had brought me back to life. And to its responsibilities. The defeat of my country, my lovely Paris with jackbooted German soldiers marching triumphantly through its streets, arms held in a stiff salute in front of them, and steel helmets jammed over their heads so we could not see their faces. They were so young, most of them, like our own boys, called to serve their country. At first we'd had some sympathy for their youth, their bewilderment, but then not for the insane desire to obey commands that could mean the death of civilization as we knew it. Nor for their sadistic treatment of our men, or for raping our country. Of course, there are good men to be found any place, anywhere in the world, but then it was power gone mad.

It took that war to rouse me from my self-pity, my lethargy, my small home. I had never returned to the Villa Romantica, simply left it exactly as it was, with a housekeeper to clean and her handyman-husband to maintain things. No doubt it had been gathering dust since I left, because without the owner on the premises, nothing would get done.

The enemy officers who'd occupied it seemed not to care. I was told they held parties, smashed my fine wineglasses in the fireplace after mammoth drinking bouts, took paintings off the walls and threw them into the fire; they chalked over my youthful portrait, making a caricature of the fine work by Paul Cesar Helleu, painted just before he died. Many artworks were ruined this way. By the end, there was little left to remember the good life at the villa. Only memories. Which are, of course, forever.

I lived out my life with those memories to sustain me, on the small farm in the Luberon valley, where no one recognized me, a gray-haired woman, old but still erect with that dancer's posture that was to sustain me to the end. No one was left to care that the woman selling potatoes at the market, pulled by her hands from the earth that morning, was once the star who'd sung and danced on the stages of the world, whose lover was as famous if not more so than she herself. The woman who had killed him.

I, of course, remembered everything. Which is why I finally took up my pen and wrote it down here, for those that will come after me and who might have some curiosity, or think themselves related, or who might even be family, because, after all, I did have a daughter. Once upon a time. Isn't that the way every fairy tale begins?

In the end, I was simply Madame Matthews, though of course I was never truly that. I could sit unrecognized in the local café after the market closed for the day, sipping my glass of red, and nodding cheerfully to those who took the time to bid me *bonjour*.

I made my preparations. I went to the local *notaire* and made a will. I left the Villa Romantica to Jolie Matthews, known as "Jolly," though I was careful not to name her as my daughter.

The girl had been told the villa belonged to a distant relative. I knew she had visited several times and through the grapevine of local gossip, I also heard how she'd enjoyed it, how much she loved the villa, and how because of her, it had been restored gradually to if not glory, at least its former beauty. Simple. Pristine. Perfect.

It was all I could wish for. My daughter living in the villa I had created and built. They both had my love.

Of course I left her the pearls. And the sapphire ring. I liked to think of her wearing them, and of the pleasure they might give her, as they had given me.

I have also stipulated in my will that my beloved pets are to live in the villa. I am ready to go. The fact is, I have lived long enough anyway. I gave what I could, laughed, and have known the joy of being loved. It is, at last, enough.

My little brown dog lies on my lap, gazing soulfully into my faded blue eyes. My small gray cat sprawls his length against me. And the tiny canary sings its brave song.

Part IV

The Present

44

Verity

I don't like the way I feel. As though I am heavy when I want to be weightless. As though my brain has deserted me when I need to think. As though my chest is still heaving with water, my ribs aflame with pain.

I'm guessing this is the way you feel when you are drugged into a sort of submissive state, with no will of your own, no way to make your limbs obey the brain's commands. Or perhaps it's that the brain is issuing the wrong commands. How am I to know? I'm simply lying here, trying desperately to begin to think. To remember. If I don't, I think I might die and I don't want that. I have things left to do before I go, and besides I'm too young. I want to make sure that my cheating husband gets to know what I really think of him. I want Mirabella to know that I am so glad she found me on the train and made me her friend. And I want to thank the Boss for saving my life. At least I hope it's saved.

I do remember him lifting me from the waves, stroking my wet hair from my face, being held in his arms as he walked up the beach, calling out, "I found her." I remember he said, "She drowned."

So that's why my chest felt full of water. I recall now the immense weight of it, but more, I remember the waves surging over me, going down beneath them. They were black not green, as they were when I'd swam so happily in them earlier. Yet I'd felt the sand under me, knew I wasn't in deep water, I was merely resting there. Until the Boss came and hauled me up, lifted me in his strong arms the way the hero always does in movies. I almost expected him to be in the Superman suit, not dressed in a black turtleneck and running pants. God, I think I fell in love with him there and then. Never underestimate the attraction of power, whether it's strength, as it was at that moment, or importance and wealth, as he'd always had. A double whammy, in fact.

And then Chad Prescott had me on the ground and was blasting my ribs until I felt sure I heard them crack, only I couldn't speak to tell him it hurt. I could only hope he knew what he was doing.

He faded from my vision. Everything went black. I knew nothing until I woke up in the hospital, with Mirabella leaning over me, her face a picture of concern. I had no idea how much time had passed, what had happened, where I was, even. Mirabella understood at once.

"It's okay, my little Verity," she said, smoothing my hair from my hot head with a cool hand.

I've hated hospitals ever since I was a child and they took my tonsils out and never gave me the promised ice cream afterward. "Get me out of here," I said in what I thought was a quiet voice but somehow came out as a hoarse shout.

"Shh." She took my limp hand from where it lay immobilized like the rest of me, on the white sheet, and kissed it tenderly. "You had an accident," she said, still in that soothing voice people use on other people who are really sick, so as not to frighten them.

"I did not," I said, as forcefully as I could manage since my own voice had now retreated to a squeak. "Somebody hit me, somebody threw me in the sea, I could have drowned. . . ."

Realizing the horror of what I was saying, I suddenly burst into tears. Mirabella handed me the tissues and I mopped busily but still they came.

"It's the relief, sweetheart," she said. "That's all. Chad is looking after you, and he's the best you can get. And so am I, looking after you."

"You are the best I can get," I said, noticing the flowers displayed on every available surface. "I'll bet I know who those are from. There's only one man who could afford them and it's not my husband."

"Soon to be ex, remember? And you are right, of course. The Boss is distraught that this happened to you at his party, at his villa. He will do anything to help. In fact he wants you to stay at his home, in one of the guesthouses, where you will be looked after, as he said to me, 'Like royalty, only better.' "

I laughed. The Boss was a charmer, and cute with it. Sort of funny—there was always a little disclaimer where he was concerned. I don't know why because he had certainly never been anything other than charming and generous to me. Especially now with his offer.

"I want you to come to me, of course," Mirabella was saying. "But the fact is I have to be away for a couple of days, some business thing in London to do with Aunt Jolly's will and the property, that you know Chad Prescott says she deeded to him in a letter. Which in fact she did, but of course it's not valid. I have to straighten it out."

"Is Chad giving you trouble over that?" I was surprised.

"He did at the beginning, but he's backed off. It's his lawyers who won't let go. Still, you'll be okay there, at the Boss's place. He has an army of servants to look after you, which is more than I can do."

"I'd rather eat my breakfast in the kitchen with you," I said. "I'm pretty good at carving up melons, buttering toast . . ."

"We'll do just that, in a few days' time. Then you'll come home. Meanwhile, enjoy your flowers and get well. That's what I want most from you."

"You don't want my love then?" The squeak was back in my voice. She was already at the door and turned, one hand on the knob, to look back at me.

"You betcha, baby," she said with a wink.

45
The Boss

A couple of hours later, the Boss returned home to the Villa Mara from the hospital, where he'd left Verity in the care of several doctors, including know-it-all Chad Prescott, as well as the fuckin' Colonel, who was determined to get his hand in and would probably want to claim responsibility for saving her life and then later for arresting the culprit for what he was determined to call an "attempted murder." And he'd be right. It was only "attempted." The second Russian had also fucked up.

He stood, alone for a while, making sure his orders had been carried out. His party was still going on, the drama missed by almost everybody. A live group had replaced the DJ and the party-goers crowded around the low stage, clapping their hands to the new rhythm, or waving their arms over their heads, swaying. Champagne glasses were being refilled, and the scent of good steak mingled with the night jasmine, the lavender, the briny sea air.

The TV reporters had departed, and down by the sea the bunker was in darkness. Except, the Boss noted, for the red light of a burning cigarette. The Russian was waiting for him, expecting to be paid, no doubt. And for what? Fucking up? It did not work that way.

The beach was a madhouse, police dogs straining on tight leashes, sniffing every goddamn bush. It should never have come to this. How he had kept most of his guests unaware of it all was a miracle only he could produce. He was a sort of God, he knew that, but this had been tricky and the Russian was responsible.

"You're late," the Russian said, stamping out the cigarette under a booted foot.

"Late for what?" The Boss's voice was ice.

"Fuckin' late paying me. I've been waiting here half an hour. And anyway, the job turned out bigger than you said. I need more money."

"And how much more would that be?"

The Russian had not expected such quick compliance; he'd been prepared for a fight. "Ten thou." He took a flier on the amount, instinctively understanding the Boss was going to go for it. Why, he did not know, but he knew he would. He did not need to say, "or else." That was implied.

"You are blackmailing me," the Boss said. His tone was surprisingly quiet for a man who'd just realized he was being taken, and taken by a crook.

"You might call it that. I consider it payment for services rendered. Killing off a girl costs."

"But you did not kill her." The Boss sounded reasonable.

"She's as good as dead. Trust me."

Of course the Boss did not trust him. But he had something else in mind and right now it appeared the Russian was the only man who could carry out what he wanted. Anyone else would be too dangerous, but since the Russian was already attempting to blackmail him, why not give him the work?

"I'll give you five now," he said. "Five later. Plus another ten if you do what I ask."

The Russian lit another Marlboro, crushing the empty packet under a foot the way he'd crushed out the cigarette stub earlier. The Boss frowned; he did not approve of litter.

He said, "You already fucked up, almost killed the wrong woman. Now you can get the correct victim."

"Matthews?"

"Who else did you suppose it was? You had your orders."

"The girl got in the way."

"And you should have gotten her out of the way, not left her half-alive, you fool."

The Russian did not like being called a fool. Fists clenched, he took a step closer, then thought better of it. After all, he was looking at his meal ticket.

"You were supposed to kill Matthews and get

the painting," the Boss said. "When you've done that and brought the painting to me, I'll pay you. And not until then." He turned and walked back to the side of the bunker.

"And how the fuck am I gonna do that?" the Russian yelled after him, disregarding that anybody passing might hear him.

The Boss paused. "That's up to you," he said, pressing the button. "That's your job."

The ivy-clad wall slid aside and in a second closed behind him.

It was, the Russian thought, amazed, as though he had never been there.

46

The Russian knew it was true, the task was uncompleted. He still had to get that painting from Mirabella's room where it hung next to her bed. He had tried and failed twice. He was not a man accustomed to failure. He'd get it, one way or another.

He wasn't afraid of her, though it would be better if she were not there. Too many killings was like spoiling the broth somehow. It made for bad soup, and bad vibes could make someone like the Colonel or the everlasting doctor latch onto him. He knew they'd already noticed him.

Yet the Boss wanted her gone, he wanted her land, he wanted her villa, he wanted that fuckin' painting. God knows why, it was a dreary thing. But lust took many forms, as he himself knew only too well. When a man lusted after something, be it a woman or a painting, he had to possess it. And a man would pay well to do so.

It was easier to get into Mirabella's room than the Russian had thought. Hidden in the shadow\ of azalea bushes that grew six feet high, he walked along the path to her house, any sound masked by the music still wafting through the night: laughter, the occasional bark from the canine patrol still working the beach, the remaining guests too busy discussing the recent happenings, puzzled and more excited than scared. After all, they did not usually come to a party, especially a grand expensive one like this, and get the thrill of a police alert and a drowned girl thrown in as the entertainment.

"Trust the Boss," he'd heard one woman say, laughing as though it was an amusing experience. Yeah, he thought, you do that, bitch, trust the Boss and see what happens to you.

Of course Mirabella had left the french windows open. He'd tried to get in earlier but she was too alert, too frightened, it had been dangerous for him to linger. She'd slid out of there, her back to the wall, shoes in hand, unaware that he was watching her. Now, though, the place was all his.

He had the pearls in his pocket. All he had to do was get that friggin' painting, hand both over to the Boss, receive his payment plus bonus, and get the fuck out of there. For a few moments he allowed himself the luxury of contemplating where he might go, with all his money safely banked in that Swiss account. No small town where he would be noticed as being different, that was for sure. Something like a cruise maybe, on one of those big ships they had nowadays, thousands of people all eating and drinking and dancing and busy meeting and greeting. Easy to get lost in a crowd like that, especially with a new identity, and no hint of the Russian in him. He could speak English with the best, nobody could ever tell.

It took him seconds to enter Mirabella's room. A few more seconds and he'd wrenched the painting off the wall. The tack came out with it. Plaster fluttered in little white flakes onto his black sweater. He brushed them off, and shoved the painting underneath the sweater, careful to keep the paint side away from his sweat-damp skin. Which gave him thought that maybe he was getting too old for this game; he never used to sweat. Now, he could feel it trickling down his back. What the fuck? Enough was enough. He wanted his money and to get out of here. Killing old women and cat-burglaring were not his game. He was a street fighter, a man who killed other street fighters, men like himself who were working for what he'd always called, "the other side."

He left the villa, letting his eyes adjust. Of course he knew the terrain, knew the easiest and darkest route to the bunker where the Boss awaited him. His boots crunched on the gravel path and he hesitated again, wondering if he should take the longer way, across the grass. But no, there were dogs around and cops; the night's affairs were not finished. They would still be there at dawn, with the stragglers from the party, maybe even one or two they might have arrested, or detained on suspicion. Suspicion of what? Was that girl, Verity, dead? He smiled, thinking of her. If she was not, then she soon would be. The Boss would take no chances on her regaining her senses and her memory. He was quite certain of that.

He had no idea how to get into the bunker. There was no door where you might knock, no bell to be pressed. But there were tiny cameras and they were all pointing at him so he had no need to knock. A wall slid back, revealing a steel slab of a door. There was no handle, it simply opened as he stepped up to it. He glanced nervously behind him. He wasn't used to this high-tech shit, he needed a door he could open and close himself, he needed his escape route and he realized the Boss was not allowing him one. Too late to go back.

"Come in," the Boss said.

The Russian could see him, or at least the back of his head. He was sitting facing a giant bank of television screens that showed the entire property. The Russian realized that nobody could make a move in this place without being caught on one of those cameras. And no doubt those images would be kept in perpetuity for the Boss's use. With those cameras, those images, and with technology, the Boss could put any person anywhere on his property he wanted. Their image, that is. If he wanted, for instance, someone on the beach, throwing Verity into the sea, he had it.

The Russian's throat went dry just thinking about it. He had never had any compunction about killing, well, only the once with the old woman, Aunt Jolly, but that was because murdering old ladies was not his business and he had regretted it ever since. Especially as he had yet to receive payment. Fuck it, he was getting his money and he was out of here. Gone. The thought gave him sudden courage and he walked boldly up to the Boss and put the painting on the desk in front of him, awaiting the words of praise, or even thanks.

The Boss got up. He looked coolly at him, one brow raised. "So?"

Cocky fucker, the Russian thought. Believes he has it all, that he owns the world. Well, he doesn't own me. He said, "I got everything you want."

"You screwed up royally. One young woman is in the hospital, only half-drowned. The other is still walking around very much alive."

"Fuck them." The Russian was impatient, confident. He pulled the string of pearls from his pocket. They slid through his fingers and fell to the floor with a surprisingly noisy crash. Pearls were heavier than he'd thought. He bent to pick them up.

"Leave them."

The Boss's voice was ice. The Russian glanced up, surprised.

"And where is the ring?"

The Russian frowned. All the Boss had asked for were the pearls and the painting. No, wait a minute, there was also the big sapphire Mirabella wore, that's what he'd wanted too. Greedy bastard, as if enough wasn't enough for a billionaire like him who could easily go out and buy bigger and better. Why did he need all this shit, anyway? Especially that dreary little painting.

"It's on her fuckin' finger," he snarled. And then his head snapped back with such sudden force he thought his neck would break, and he was on the floor, with the Boss standing over him, dark eyes burning into his.

"Get up," the Boss said.

The Russian knew he'd better, though it was difficult to get his feet back under him.

"Now, get out."

The Russian had not lost all of his senses, though he was afraid. "I want my money."

"It's already in your Swiss bank. I don't cheat with money, though you cheated with your job. Now, go."

The Russian went. As fast as he could get his numbed legs to move, he went, telling himself he had to keep on going, get away from here, away from that crazy bastard who he'd swear to God would kill his own mother, if he'd ever had one. He had looked into the devil's eyes and he was afraid. It occurred to him to wonder why the Boss was letting him go. Wasn't he dangerous? Couldn't he go to the cops? Or simply the TV stations? Tell his tale to the world. Denounce the Boss.

Then he realized, understood more like it, you did not simply denounce a man with that kind of power. The Boss held all the cards. You would get nowhere. He wasn't even significant enough for the Boss to have killed, which he could easily have done, right there and then.

Relieved, he picked up his pace, walking across the grassy cliff toward the lights of the Villa Romantica.

The dog got him from behind. One of those police canines, they said later, though nobody seemed sure which one it was or why it had attacked him, other than he was a man walking alone in the dark in a place he wasn't supposed to be. And after all, that was what the cops had been on the alert for.

It did not kill him, though. They pried its teeth open, got it off him, but it had mauled his face badly, simply taken his entire head into its mouth. That's what it felt like, to the Russian anyway.

Later, in the hospital, his head completely wrapped in bandages so he looked like something from *Ghostbusters*, they told him he'd been lucky that Dr. Chad Prescott was around.

"One of the best neuro-cranial surgeons in the world," they said. "It's Dr. Chad you can thank that you not only have two eyes but you've still got some gray matter. Brains. If you ever had any to begin with."

The Russian wondered, over the next painful days, whether in fact he had.

47

Verity

I had never felt like a princess before, but I was rapidly sure I was becoming one. The Boss's guesthouse was small but perfect, a white villa with a coral tile roof. Double glass doors were flanked by pink oleander bushes. The whole area was surrounded by fields of lavender and the scent took my breath away. Inside, though, an almost-familiar perfume hung in the air. It was from another era, but still I recognized it. Evening in Paris. I remembered the cobalt-blue bottle from my girlhood, behind the drugstore counter along with lipsticks in bright pink, and nail polish in sparkly white. Drugstores had everything in those days, which after all were not so long ago. Now they seem more commercialized, with so few specialty brands a teenager can afford and feel she is "special" too.

Still, no need for a "princess" like me to worry about drugstore lipstick; the bathroom vanity had everything any woman could possibly need, or even think of, from Estée Lauder night cream to nail polish remover. Looking at my chipped fingernails I decided I'd better use it.

What was I thinking? Had my brain gone into

complete denial? Gradually last night's events floated back through whatever brain cells I might have left. I remember recognizing I was dying, wondering if this was what happened. Closing my eyes, I felt again the sensation of the waves washing over me, the icy chill of the water that was so pleasant in the daytime when swimming. But I had not been swimming. I could not move. And then I was plucked from that sea like some forgotten mermaid by a man whose kindness of heart, whose bravery I admired. And who I was now falling in love with. The Boss.

I lay back against the pile of sumptuous pillows, softer surely than any I had known before. If riches meant you could have pillows like these then I would like to be rich.

Of course, it also meant you could own a guest-house like this, a small villa in its own right, and far larger than most New York or London apartments. At the windows, thin white curtains swayed in the breeze, and the pale travertine floors were scattered with rugs of modern design. A white sofa and a huge chair were in front of the stone fireplace already set with kindling and a couple of small logs, in case, I guessed, I felt the need. Or simply wanted that comforting glow.

I was lying dead center in a bed so large it must have been made for giants. Perhaps for the Boss himself, who was a bit of a giant, with his great height and his broad shoulders, though I could not imagine him liking the silken sheets in a pale peach color. I scrunched them in my fingers. Were they really silk? I had never known anyone in my life who had silk sheets. Never would again either, I guessed.

I wanted to move, to get up, walk around but that weight seemed still on my chest and there was a definite buzz in my ears. Or was it in my head?

I also wanted badly to cry but my eyes were so dry I could not. There was a knock on the door. I was afraid to speak, to say, "come in," because I had no idea who might be out there.

The door pushed slowly open, and then Chad Prescott put his head around it and said, "Hi, are you awake?"

Oh God, I was so awake at that moment I almost could have leapt out of bed. And not only that, behind him came the Colonel. Later, I wondered if I could be in love with three men at once. The Colonel, the Boss, and Chad Prescott. Surely that was not normal. A girl fell in love with one guy and that was that.

Nevertheless, being a fair person, I gave both men equal smiles, or something I hoped approximated a smile. Recalling the cheating husband, I reminded myself warily, this was my own life I was talking about. One mistake was enough.

Then the Boss came in and I had all three charmers.

The Boss came and stood possessively at the head of the bed. He threw me a smile of such tenderness, I melted all over again. I wished I had lip gloss and a spray of that lingering Evening in Paris. One day I was going to find out who that had belonged to, who had lived here, who had left her reminder for me to enjoy.

Why, I wondered, had it taken this terrible experience to discover what life and love were all about, when women like Mirabella seemed simply to know it all by some feminine instinct that perhaps I did not possess?

It was the Boss I saved my special smile for, though. The big, handsome hero with his dark hair swept back from his forehead, his deep dark eyes that took me in as though he owned me; his cool hand that gripped mine as if he never wanted to let me go. When a man feels like that about you and lets you know it, subtly, but overwhelmingly, most women are sunk. I know I was. Right there and then. All over again.

But yet there was also my Colonel, my other hero. The family man, the one I knew I should fall for, not the bad boy I knew the Boss was at heart. Or even the beauteous Chad. But anyway Chad was spoken for, by Mirabella. Good luck to her. I was going to take what I wanted, and right now, it was the Boss, who had saved me, rescued me, looked after me like he loved me. How could I not?

Yet, somebody had also wanted to kill me, and I was afraid. I felt myself drifting backward again, into that dark place, where I did not have to deal with life and love and reality.

Somehow it was safer there.

48

Paris

Mirabella

In Paris, I wasn't surprised to bump into Chad Prescott. When I saw him, I felt that dangerous flutter in my stomach I recognized as a prequel to falling in love, a seemingly necessary process the body goes through to let you know, in your brain, where you're at. Or at least where you're going, because when that moment hits you, there is no going back.

"What a surprise," I'd said, though why I was surprised I did not know, since I was sitting at one of the overly small tables outside the Café de Flore at the corner of Boulevard Saint-Germain, where everybody in the world passes by at some time or other. Or so it appeared to me, a woman who had spent many happy hours there, over a glass of this or that, making a tiny bowl of peanuts last longer than anyone ever thought possible. I love the Flore because they never hurry you, and the waiters never give you that stare, unless you are the worst kind of tourist, the ones sneaking smartphone shots of celebrities or of quirky folks. The Flore is tailor-made for the quirky, and even in winter, it's the place to go.

Back in the day, I would sit inside on a red banquette with the snow fluttering against the window, knowing my flight out to wherever was doomed by the weather, making more than the best of it, nibbling on the tastiest herb omelette in the world, good eggs scattered with thyme, rosemary, and lavender. Hot from the pan, it slid down the throat like manna from heaven. Who cared about a missed flight when you were already in Paris and eating like a king?

"So," Chad said now, coming up sneakily from behind and putting a hand on my shoulder. "What brings you here, Miss Mirabella?"

That hand gave me a little shiver of pleasure and I gave him a quick once-over. Even better than I remembered: tall, tan, and lived-in, that's how he looked. Could I be getting the wrong message, or was that instant chemistry floating in the air between us ? If so, why had it waited so long to happen? Not that I had seen that much of him, but because of Verity our lives had become entwined.

He asked my permission to sit and of course I said yes. Then he went over Verity's story, shocking me so that I forgot all about myself, my own feelings, his attraction. I told him I was on my way back, waiting for the flight to Nice, and he told me he was on the same one.

"We might even get seats together," he said. "I'll see what I can do."

He wandered away, mobile phone in hand. He had a lazy walk that at the same time contained more energy than any man I've ever known, as though he were ready for anything. Because of his jungle experiences, I guessed. In that deep dark world anything might happen and usually did. In fact, he was probably lucky to have survived this long without getting a poisoned dart in the back of his head from some hidden jungle warrior.

When he returned, with new reservations for side-by-side seats, I told him exactly what I had been thinking.

"It's not as exciting as you imagine," he said. We were crammed into uncomfortable chairs at a too-small café table, surrounded by Parisians who as always, were so into each other they had no time for mere mortals such as us. And we had no time for the Parisians either. I no longer cared to note what they were wearing that looked so much better than my own usual sweater and skirt, though, under Verity's surveillance, I had abandoned the T-strap black leather shoes in favor of a pair of heeled suede booties with a bit of fringe around the ankle. Quite becoming, though I say so myself, and they definitely made my legs look longer. Actually, longer than I had ever thought they were, which just goes to show we girls should take stock of what the mirror tells us, look longer, see what we can do.

Verity always said that, anyway. But then, she was gorgeous with her young-girl blond looks. How she ever got involved with the cheating husband, I'll never understand. Still, that's being taken care of right this minute, as I speak, in fact, by my trusty lawyers. Before she knows it, Verity will be a free woman. But now, I'm listening very carefully to what else Chad has to tell me.

"Verity is enamored of the Boss," he said, as casually as if it were an everyday experience she went through.

Stunned, I took a slurp of my vermouth cassis, a tall, shocking-pink drink crackling with ice I had recently become enamored of. I said, "Verity and men are not good news. Especially with a powerhouse like the Boss."

"I warned you. And I warned her against him. He's all charm and generosity, but there's something lurking under that handsome face. And anyhow, where *did* he get all that money?"

"Does anyone ever know where rich men get their money?" I asked the question, knowing the answer. "No, we do not. "They just have it, that's all. And some of them lavish it around, like the Boss, all show-offy, while others keep it quiet and do good deeds. Of course," I added, "that doesn't mean he's not doing charitable things, in fact I've heard of some of them."

"Those charities are reported, very carefully in press releases, from the Boss himself. I told you before, Mirabella, and I'm saying it again now, I don't trust him. There's something in his eyes, the way he looks at a woman, that too-intense stare as though he would like to get into her soul. . . . Ah, I can't describe it, it's simply something I sense. . . ."

Despite his not being able to describe it, I knew exactly what Chad meant. In my bones, I knew. And yet, I had danced happily in the Boss's arms, thinking how wonderful he was, throwing a fantastic party for all his friends. But were we really his friends? Did we really know him? The person he was? I was merely an acquaintance, as was Verity, until he rescued her, the mermaid from the sea. He'd taken pity on her youth and vulnerability. . . .

"That's exactly it," I said to Chad. "Her youth and vulnerability."

"Her youth and vulnerability," he repeated. "And, she's there, alone in his guesthouse."

I felt a sudden claw of anxiety. "I mean, he couldn't, he wouldn't . . ." I did not want to voice what I was thinking, but Chad knew exactly what I meant.

"We have to get back," he said. "Lucky I have the tickets. We'll be there in a few hours."

I hoped it would be soon enough.

And then he got the phone call.

I watched him walk away from me again, mobile clutched to his ear, a concerned frown between his brows as he turned to look at me. He raised an eyebrow, lifted a shoulder in a what-can-I-do shrug. I heard him say, "I'll be there." And then he came back and put an arm around me.

"An emergency," he said. "A child, a car accident."

I nodded. I knew he had to go.

He tilted my chin with a finger, looking deep into my eyes. "I'm a doctor first and foremost. That's the way it will always be."

I nodded again. Of course it would. He was already shifting his bag onto his shoulder.

I said, "Then I'll go on alone."

He looked sharply at me. "I can't let you do that. It's dangerous."

"My friend's in danger. It's what I have to do."

I probably sounded as though I were putting him on the line for not going, but that was not what I'd intended. "She's all alone," I said, suddenly remembering how alone Verity had seemed when I met her on that Paris-to-Nice train, when she did not really even know where she was going, and certainly not why. Simply escaping, she had thought, only to end up in more danger than she would ever have faced from the cheating husband.

Chad nodded; of course he understood, and he

really wanted to go with me. But he shrugged again. “What choice do I have?”

He sounded resigned, he had to do what he had to do, and right now his priority was to attempt to save a small child’s life putting a broken head back together as only a brilliant surgeon like him could.

He grabbed my shoulders, pressing me tightly to him as though afraid I might disappear right that minute and only he could keep me there.

I gently disengaged him, took a step back, gave him a good-bye wave, hoping I was as brave as my words. I was quite suddenly terrified of the Boss, and of the fact that my friend was there alone with him, that she might be in his power, and I was the only one that could help her. Save her, more likely, because I knew somehow that the Boss had the kind of power over life and death that we, mere mortals, do not. I knew in my bones, as I usually did, that behind that charming facade was a man capable of anything.

As though he had read my thoughts, Chad said, “He’s capable of anything.” He grabbed my arm again as we left the café and he flagged a taxi down.

We looked into each other’s eyes. There were no smiles. Deadly serious, he said, “I’m calling the Colonel. He’s the only one that will understand. I’ll tell him you’re on your way and that he must protect Verity. I don’t know what he can do, with a man that powerful. The Boss has committed no crime, there's nothing to accuse him of. I just want the Colonel to be aware."

With a final hug, I got into the taxi. "You know what?" I said. "I think the Colonel is already aware. He is far more clever than he lets on. He doesn't miss a thing."

"But I'll miss you," Chad said.

They were the last words I heard as the taxi sped away.

49
The Colonel

The Colonel did not understand what it was that drew him to Verity, but it was certainly more than her blond good looks, her pert nose with the bump in it that made it look a bit off-side, her wide blue eyes, and a mouth that might almost, in another era, have been called "rosebud." But no, it was too large for rosebud, too vulnerable with its soft underlip that she had the habit of catching in her teeth when she was worried. Which, in fact she'd appeared to be much of the time. And the Colonel believed she had good reason. No one came that close to being eliminated, not once, but twice, within a couple of weeks, without there being good reason. Hers was, he was sure, that she was friends with the wrong people. In particular, right now, the Boss.

His research into the Boss delivered no more than he already knew: that the Boss was a self-made man; that he made his money mostly from property and mostly in far-flung locations, where the rules governing such transactions were not regulated and also where, for certain large sums, men might be bought. The Boss had moved on, of course, to more respectable places and people, and now a sort of cloud of goodwill surrounded him that guaranteed access to solid financial institutions as well as that part of society, that while not exactly "high," was certainly celebrity- and money driven. You had only to attend his party to notice who was there, and to understand. Money talked, that was why. And this man had more money than Rockefeller, or so it was said.

What was also apparent to the Colonel, when he was checking this information, was that dates and times and places were not mentioned. In fact it was impossible to know where the Boss was born. Sometimes it was said the Ukraine, while an alternative version claimed the Big Island of Hawaii, or even in the gambling center of Macau, off the coast of China. No interview the Boss had given ever raised the question of his beginnings, because he always laid down the rules of what questions might be asked and what subjects might not even be approached, which made it easy for him to have the appropriate answers to hand. In fact, the Colonel thought, reading through some of those interviews on Google, the man was a complete mystery. He was only ever exactly what he wanted to be right there and then.

The Colonel did not consider this normal. He told himself everyone had parents, everyone had a past, which might include wives and children, and probably brothers and sisters, aunts and uncles and grandparents. Nobody came into this life alone. So, where was the Boss's mother? His family? Did the Boss have a wife somewhere, kept out of sight, out of his social whirl?

Yet, to all intents and purposes, the Boss was a single man who lived alone, had no close personal friends, and maintained a staff that protected him like the Secret Service and who all had signed a pledge of nondisclosure, even the chefs who'd cooked the stupendous food for that party. Even, dammit, the bartenders.

From his long career as a gendarme, starting at street level and working his way up over the years to the top of his profession, the Colonel had learned never to believe in coincidence. If something bad happened, a murder for instance, there was never any "coincidence." It was purely and simply a criminal act.

Now, sitting at Verity's bedside, watching over her as though by sheer strength of will he could make her better, he thought if there ever was a woman that needed his protection, it was this one. It had been a long hard road after his wife was killed, taking on the role of bringing up two small girls alone, returning home to those endless evenings, his children secure in their beds, some favorite music playing, a bottle of wine opened, and no one to share any of it with. Especially his emotions. There had been nights, he would admit it, when he, a grown man, the tough, vigilant cop, had broken down and cried. But wine was better without tears and time moved on. Looking at young Verity Real, sleeping like she was drugged, he felt a tenderness he recognized as the first awakenings of love.

He got up quickly, told himself he was a fool, brushed down his uniform, adjusted the tie, patted the gold stars on his epaulettes. He should not be wasting time here. The girl—he always somehow thought of Verity as a girl, not a woman, though she was certainly old enough to qualify—did not need him. Of course not, she would never need a man like him.

Without so much as a knock, the door suddenly swung open. The Colonel's hand reached automatically for the weapon at his hip, so it was the barrel of a Luger the Boss faced when he walked in.

"Well, well," the Boss said, putting his hands up. "The Colonel is playing soldiers again. I thought we'd had enough of that at the party. Anyhow, I did not expect to see you here."

Embarrassed, the Colonel apologized. He took out a large white handkerchief and mopped his suddenly sweaty brow, feeling like a kid caught in some nefarious act, instead of the policeman acting on his duty.

He said, "Your men at the gate were good enough to allow me to enter." He knew he sounded like he was reading for a script, when all he'd wanted to say was the guys let me in, I came to check on the young woman who'd almost drowned and investigate the suspicious event.

There was just something intimidating about the Boss, an element the Colonel recognized from his years of investigating criminals, an invisible aura of darkness. This was a no-holds-barred man who would allow nothing and no one to stand in the way of getting what he wanted. And quite suddenly the Colonel understood that what he wanted was Verity. And he felt afraid for her.

The Boss said, "Well, as you can see, Verity is being very well looked after, right here. Anything she wants, or needs, will be hers." He sounded impatient, as though it was time the Colonel left.

The Colonel said, "Then I suggest you have Dr. Prescott examine her when he returns."

"Prescott?"

"The world-renowned neurosurgeon. I'm sure you'll recognize his name and his work." The Colonel was definitely sweating. He mopped his brow again, aware that the Boss was observing him. "Besides, he's your neighbor."

"I know him. He was nice enough to attend my party, as you were yourself, Colonel. I trust you enjoyed it. I'm a hospitable fellow, I like to share what small things I can offer to my neighbors and friends, like yourself. But now, my dear Colonel, I must ask you to leave. Let us allow young Verity to get what they call her 'beauty sleep,' though as you can see for yourself, she surely needs no sleep to make her beautiful."

The Boss was smiling at him, holding open the door. The Colonel wanted to hit him. He wanted to punch him right between those dark eyes that were staring so mockingly into his own. It took all his self-possession to simply put on his cap and walk past the man and out through that door.

As he hurried down the path, past the main house to where his car was parked, down the gravel driveway, for the first time in his life the Colonel was uncertain what to do. In the end, he decided he needed to get in touch with Chad Prescott, and with Mirabella.

Mirabella

The Colonel met me at the Nice airport.

"Madame Mirabella," I heard him call as I wandered from the labyrinth, dragging my wheeled duffle behind me, still lost in the gloom of leaving Chad, a man I had not so much as really even yet kissed, well, not properly anyway, let alone had a more intimate relationship with. Such as an affair. I was lost in gloomy thoughts of that, and of what I was going to do to help Verity, and now here came the very man I needed.

The Colonel took my bag and brought me up to date on Verity's welfare.

"We have to get her out of there," he said finally.

I told him what Chad believed had happened, and how he distrusted the Boss.

I had a vision of her in that enormous bed, her angelic sleeping face propped on a small mountain of pillows, the bedside table piled with books, magazines, the chilled bottle of Perrier, even a crystal glass to drink it from; the kindling in the grate waiting only for a match to light the log fire, soft music playing, the view of trees and flowering bushes and the scent of jasmine and lilac from the bowls of flowers. It did not take a genius to know how easily a girl might be seduced by such lavishness, by such overwhelming gener-osity, by such power and money.

"What shall we do?" I asked the Colonel, feeling completely helpless.

"I have to speak to the Boss," he said.

50
The Boss

The Boss had not gotten exactly what he wanted. He was a frustrated man, a grown-up child deprived of the promised treat, and it was his own fault. True, he had Verity shut away in his guesthouse, though now not quite "at his mercy" as she had been before. And true, he had received due recognition from the media by saving her life. The video of him walking from the sea holding the unconscious girl aloft had been featured on every newscast worldwide. *Her hero,* was the caption, along with cameos detailing his life, his homes, his wealth, his generosity, and the fact that he was single.

The party had been shown in all its expensive glory, lanterns glowing in the trees, champagne chilling in huge silver buckets, flowers trailing over walkways, over tables, over beautiful women's hair as they smiled for the cameras.

Yet here he was, alone as usual, in his bunker, sitting in his enormous leather chair, staring blankly at the wall of TV screens that showed his property. Empty now, but for the occasional patrolman with his dog. The German shepherds were intelligent, eager to be trained, to do man's bidding. Lovely dogs. He stared at the screens for a long time, frustration building up in him, twiddling a pen nervously between two fingers. Finally, he got up, walked into the bathroom, stripped off his custom-tailored black jacket, his fine pale gray flannel pants, and the blue Egyptian cotton handmade shirt that he always ordered by the dozen. Same with the shoes, Lobb of London had the wooden last, shaped precisely to his measurements. All he needed to do was call and they would get to work on a new pair, whatever he wanted. All his desires would be met. And that was at the heart of his problem. What to do to eliminate the boredom, the ennui of life, when nothing seemed to matter any more, when depression overtook like a dark dog of night? Not the beautiful German shepherd, but the great dog of darkness, the one at Hell's gate; Cerberus itself.

It was time for action.

He got dressed in the black velour sweats. He liked the way the soft fabric felt, and the fact that it did not make a sound when he moved; it never rustled or creased, in fact it was the ideal fabric for what he termed, "misbehaving." And the urge to misbehave was overwhelming right now.

Of course he had one woman, ready and waiting. Verity, all sweetness and light and imagining she was in love with him; probably also imagining the way her life would change as the wife of a billionaire. Might as well indoctrinate her into the truth of that, but first he had to call her friend Mirabella, who was the true object of what he might call his "affection."

Of course Mirabella had visited Verity already; now she needed to be convinced to return. He had her number. She answered right away.

"Hi," was what she said, in the sort of soft voice that made him guess it was someone else she'd been expecting to call.

"Miss Matthews? It's the Boss here."

"Ohh. Ohh, my goodness. Is everything alright? Verity?"

"It's Verity I'm calling about. She's safe here with me, on my property—I mean, because of course she is currently in the guesthouse. I confess to being a little worried, Miss . . ."

"It's Mirabella . . ."

"Yes, Mirabella. Well, as I was saying, I don't like her there all alone. I'm thinking of moving her into my villa where she can more easily be taken care of, and be less 'alone,' so to speak."

"So to speak." She was thinking of what Chad had told her, and said, frightened, "Oh, well, perhaps it's not good to do that. I mean, I can come over and get her. She can come back and stay with me now. I can look after her."

"I don't think there's any need for that, she will be perfectly well cared for right here. . . ."

The Boss had set the trap and Mirabella had walked right into it.

"No. No, I'll come immediately. I want her home, with me. I know she'll feel more comfortable."

"With her friend. Of course. Though I had hoped she might consider me a friend also." The Boss was playing the "friend" card to the hilt. "I've only tried to do what is best for her."

"And you have. Oh, goodness, yes, you have, sir. Boss, I mean."

He laughed then, genuinely amused. "You and I should get to know each other better. It seems we have a sense of humor in common at least."

Mirabella was dying with anxiety and not a little fear, thinking frantically of what to do, while trying to maintain the conversation with the Boss, who was being so sweet and nice, so charming she almost did not want to believe what she knew was the truth. That was the trouble with charmers, they could sweep you into their safety net and then zap you over the head, like a dead fish. Oh God, she had to go and get Verity out of there. . . .

"Well then," she said, quickly formulating a plan. "All I can say is thank you for caring so much about her. First you rescue her from the waves, and now you're saving her all over again, by giving her the best of care. I think that makes you a friend for life. Boss."

"Perhaps. Or maybe even more than that. After all, every savior needs a reward."

Mirabella froze. What did he mean by that? Did he *want* Verity? Did he mean to keep her drugged for good, in that high, wide bed, looking like a golden angel? That familiar response of anger and fear roused her.

"I'm coming over right now, to get her," she said. "Please have her ready. I won't need an ambulance, I'll just take her in my car."

"If I remember, your car went over the edge of the canyon. Quite a disaster, Mirabella. We would not want that to happen again, now, would we?"

Chills ran suddenly down her spine. Could he be threatening her? "I have another car, my little SEAT. She'll be just fine."

"You could always ask Chad Prescott to give you a lift in his beautiful Jaguar."

"Ohh, well, Chad is still in Paris. He had an emergency, a child, a road accident . . ."

"Ahh, yes. Good thing the surgeon was around. A man like that, a master of his profession."

"Dr. Prescott is one of the best neuro-cranial surgeons there is. The child was lucky to get him."

"I have no doubt." The Boss knew he had her exactly where he wanted her. He could almost smell it. It had worked for him all his life, that sixth sense, both in business and pleasure, and he was about to put it to use again now.

"Well, of course, my dear, I could send a car for you." He had no intention of sending a car for her, certainly not. He wanted no one to know she'd come here. Nobody would so much as see her. Of course he knew she would refuse.

"No, no, I'm already out the door, on my way."

He could hear her in the background, collecting her stuff, keys rattling. "Better arrive at the back gate," he said, smooth as butter that wouldn't melt in her mouth. "Drive up the first lane, make a right, and you'll come to a door. It's covered in ivy, the darn stuff grows like weeds, just can't seem to stop it. Anyhow the sensor will recognize you and the gate will open automatically. Just drive in."

Mirabella didn't even bother to put on lipstick, though she did put on her gloves. And the sapphire. It was like going naked without them.

She paused for a moment, her hands held out in front of her. She had worn gloves ever since the accident when she was twelve. She never showed anyone her hands. Not even lovers who had seen every other part of her. Not even Chad Prescott who as yet had never seen all of her. A surgeon like that, what would he think of the reddened objects with their ugly scars where they had been sliced open all those years ago? What would he think of the wounds with the imprints where the huge stitches had held them in place, so that one day she might use them again? As she did now. But never without the gloves.

How she envied women their pristine beautiful white hands, their shiny painted nails, made even more exquisite with bands of diamonds and gold. The sapphire, inherited from Aunt Jolly, had been her savior in a way, blazing under the lights so no one ever thought about what she might be hiding under its beauty, only about how remarkable it was.

The route to the Villa Mara took only a minute. Soon she was on the dark lane leading to the rear gates. A light came on as the car crunched to a stop. From the window she spotted cameras trained on her. She couldn't blame the Boss. A man like that, with all his money, was a prime target for kidnappers. He needed security.

More lights came on as she drove down a path that led to the sea, and a house, or some kind of building overlooking it. There were no lights, nor even any windows.

Then right in front of her eyes, the ivy-clad wall slid to one side, revealing a steel door. And the man behind it was the Boss.

"Welcome," said the spider to the fly.

51

Mirabella

I knew the Boss must have had set up his bunker especially to show me. At the press of a button, golden drapes lowered from the ceiling, masking all the walls. Then the huge bed was raised. Verity was in the very center, sunk deep into masses of pillows. Her golden hair was spread out like lace. The peach silk sheet was folded under her thin white arms that were carefully placed by her sides, hands flat, showing perfectly manicured, pink polished nails. A gardenia was tucked behind one ear, plucked, I had no doubt, from the great bowls of them on every surface, the scent of which threatened to overpower the air itself until I felt I choked for breath.

Dear God, I thought, she looks like a dead woman, made ready for her coffin. I turned to the Boss, who was standing right behind me. "What have you done to her?"

"What have I done? Why, Mirabella, look around, why don't you? Look at this palace I've constructed especially for your friend. I ask you, who could do more for Verity than I? Of course you are shocked to see her in this state but I assure you her medical care is the best. Better in fact than anything Prescott could have done. The machine you see next to her bed is feeding nourishment into her, even as she sleeps and the air is specially filtered to maximum purity."

The Boss spread his arms wide, the amiable smile reaching his eyes—generous, likeable, charming. "Trust me," he said gently. "I will make sure the old Verity returns to you intact. A girl does not almost drown without there being aftereffects, problems with the lungs, blood flow. I removed her from the hospital because I have the best medical help in the world for her here."

I wasn't buying it. Something was very wrong. I stared at him right back. "I'm taking her home with me now."

Arms folded over his massive chest, the Boss began to pace the room, glancing at Verity, then back at me.

"I'd like to know exactly how you intend to do that, my dear. In fact, why don't we share a glass of wine? Let Verity sleep while you and I figure out what is best for her. Of course it goes without saying that we both shall do only what is best."

He knew I was afraid, in fact he could probably read my thoughts almost before I had them. I wondered what to do. I had no clue, I was panicking. I refused the offered glass of wine.

"My dear, it's a Montrachet. I decanted it some hours ago, expecting your company."

"You expected me?"

"Of course. I knew you would come to visit your friend. It's natural. And as you can see, all is well."

I took the glass. I wished Chad were here, and the Colonel. I was afraid of this man, afraid for Verity. Yet he was being so nice, he was a celebrity billionaire, he did not need either me or Verity. . . . So what was I doing here, alone with him in this magnificent bedroom?

He took me by the hand and led me to a deeply cushioned velvet chair opposite the bed.

"Please. Taste the wine, I'm sure you are going to love it."

He came closer, bent over until his knees touched mine. He wasn't exactly threatening, but to me it felt like it. I took a cautious sip.

He towered above me. "Well?"

"Delicious. I'm not used to such elegant wine."

"Well now, why not sit back and enjoy it? In a few moments we shall see the show."

Mystified, I saw him press a remote, lowering a curtain and cutting us off from the bed, from Verity.

Alarmed, I got to my feet, but he was up at once, right there, in front of me.

"My dear Mirabella, when will you stop this panicking? I only want you to watch the show, of which, of course, Verity is the star. I have it all set up, electronically, but it will take a few moments. So, now . . ."

He pushed me back into the chair, and held the glass to my mouth, forcing me to drink. I knew I must not, knew what he was capable of. I gritted my teeth and wine dribbled from the corners of my lips onto my white shirt. I went to wipe it off, but he snatched my gloved hand. "Of course. Poor Mirabella, such a terrible accident." Then he squeezed my hand, hard, and I cried out in pain.

"Still hurts?" He was obviously enjoying himself. "Good. Well now, let's first see what I have to show you. And then we shall see what we have for the two of us. You always thought it was Verity I wanted, but it's always been you, Mirabella. From the minute I saw you, I knew what you were like. I knew you were my kind of woman. I know what to expect from you."

He came and sat next to me. I could smell him he was so close, a faint but heady old-fashioned masculine bay rum cologne that mixed somehow with his own male aroma. In one of those irreverent passing thoughts that came to me while under dire circumstances I bet he'd had it made specially, just for him. No one else in the world would ever be able to buy it. Only he would smell like the Boss. God, I couldn't even remember now what his real name was. Did anybody, I wondered? He was who he was, and that was enough. His very name, the Boss, reminded everyone of his power.

"Well now," he said, smiling. "Let's see the show."

52
Chad Prescott

Chad hopped a ride from Paris on a private jet carrying a rock group to a concert in Monte Carlo, an event given by the prince to honor some visiting president.

When he got to the hospital, he was told again that Verity had been moved to the Boss's guest-house, where she was guaranteed expert medical care. The Boss had told them it would be better than she could get there. And who were they to say no? Of course they'd taken his word for it. A man like that, how could they not? They would have left their own daughters in his care.

Of course they would, Chad thought. Anybody would. *A man like that.* He was walking out of the hospital when he saw the Colonel, also hurrying for the exit. He hailed him and the Colonel strode back, hand held out.

"My friend," he said. "I hope I can call you my friend, since we are in this together."

"And what exactly are we 'in'?" Chad had a feeling it was bad.

"Mirabella went to look for Verity. They told her she'd gone with the Boss. She has not come back, nor has she communicated with me. I'm on my way to the Villa Mara now. Two squad cars will follow me."

"Follow *us,* you mean. I'm coming with you." We should take a helicopter, get there quicker."

"Quicker but more noisy. We don't want to alarm him."

The Colonel saw Chad's shocked face and added quickly, "Alarm *anyone,* I mean. Mirabella also, as well as Verity who is just out of the hospital."

"And should not be," Chad added, grimly. "What is the Boss up to, anyway?"

The Colonel shrugged. "We are talking about a man who has everything money and power can buy. With some men this is not enough. There are things they cannot purchase. They feel the need to exert their power, to show it off, earn the kind of 'respect' from a woman they feel entitled to. They want the ultimate power, Doctor."

Chad did not have to ask what he meant. Ultimate power over life or death. He was a doctor, a medical man as he preferred to refer to himself. He was in the business of saving lives. But right then, he wanted a man dead.

The Colonel

The Colonel had disliked hospitals ever since his wife had spent her final hours there. More than dislike, it amounted almost to a phobia. The curtains closing off beds from passersby; the ever-present tick and purr of life-or-death machines, the squeak of rubber-soled shoes on nurses' hurrying feet, the sheer nervous energy of such places. He had not been happy therefore to have to be there to interview the waiter with his entire head bandaged and two blank fear-filled eyes staring back at him.

He knew the actions of criminals like the waiter were not motivated by brain power, by normal logic and reasoning. They were very simple, and motivated purely by need, or greed, or impulse. All three were what had sent the waiter to his—almost—doom, and certainly would end with him in jail. What he wanted from him now, though, was a simple clear statement. A confession, if you will. He wanted the waiter to tell him who had bought him. Who had paid him. And for how much. In the Colonel's experience it did not take a lot to buy a man like that. Under-the-table money, no tax declaration, then out of there fast as possible. Only this time it had not worked.

But the waiter was not talking. His eyes peered blankly out of those bandages. He did not even bother so much as to shake his head, to indicate he did not know. He simply sealed his lips and shut up.

The Colonel did not blame him; the reward for implicating the Boss would have been severe, and anonymous. This waiter, like the other one, would simply have disappeared.

Of course that possibility still existed but, with a shrug, the Colonel knew it did not matter anymore. What mattered was what Mirabella had to say. And Verity. Once he got her out of that bunker.

53
Verity

It was strange, mystical, almost, being held aloft over a stage on an ornately carved golden throne, as though I were the princess I had so often as a child imagined myself to be. Children have those kinds of daydreams, those fairy-tale fantasies they know in their hearts are not true, but in that moment they live them as though they were. Fond parents might call it a fertile imagination. They might say, "Oh, she's always playing games in her head, inventing things, you know." They called me a very "creative" child.

But now my head buzzed unceasingly, crammed with odd thoughts, memories, wishes . . . and how I wished I might be somewhere else, other than playing princess for the Boss. And, oh my God, could that be Mirabella with him?

The stage lights were blindingly bright but I knew it was she, I could tell by her fiery red hair, though I could not make out the details of her face. Yet I could see she held a glass of wine in her hand. Surely that meant this was a social occasion, that everything was alright and what was happening to me was a prank, some kind of joke. Yet I heard no laughter.

The lights were suddenly lowered, except for a spotlight aimed at me, on my throne, and at the objects on either side that I could not see because I could not move my head, which seemed imprisoned in a kind of collar. I tried turning my neck but it was impossible.

I called out, "Mirabella, help me." At least I thought I had spoken but no words seemed to come out. All I could do was look at her. She had saved me once, on the train, and again when the car went over the canyon. I had the sinking feeling that this time my luck had run out, because sitting next to her was the Boss.

"Well then," the Boss was saying jovially, rubbing his hands together in anticipation. "A little more of the Montrachet, I think, Mirabella, while you admire my show."

Mirabella

I am looking at Verity and I am living a nightmare. A horror story, some kind of theatrical event staged with real-live participants, and which I know with a cold feeling in my gut can only end in tragedy. I feel the Boss's eyes on me as I stare at his montage, his little "show," at Verity's blank face, and the golden halo that outlines her head. Her blond hair is pulled back so severely I feel sure it must hurt, but then so must the metal halo, and the wide matching collar, half hoops that I know must also be gold. The Boss would not have stinted on his show. The gold would be real gold, as would the large emeralds in her ears, and in the rings on her thin fingers. In fact Verity seemed so emaciated I didn't know how those rings stayed on. Her fingernails were enameled a deep red, as were her toes.

Then the golden curtain that had parted to expose Verity slid farther to the side, and there, mounted to the black wall beside her were the taxidermied heads of two donkeys. Each donkey wore a golden halo.

"So, you see, how lifelike it all is?" the Boss said. He was remembering the two donkeys he'd liked so much when he was a child, and how he'd ultimately had them executed, then sold them as fake "venison." He sat back in his large chair, rubbing his hands together again, in anticipation of more to come.

I was already on my feet. The fragile crystal glass smashed on the floor, wine went everywhere, rich as blood. He grabbed me and I shook him off with a strength I did not know I had. Verity's eyes were fixed on me. Her mouth moved but she was not saying anything, but I saw her bare toes curl and her thin fingers were gripping the arms of the throne as she tried to lift herself up.

I lunged at that small stage, took the two steps up in a single leap. Fear gave me a weird strength, an energy I did not know I still possessed. The horror of Verity up there, with the embalmed donkey heads on either side of her hit me, and I knew it was what the Boss intended for her too. He wanted to make his collection complete with the young blonde. He would place her in the center, all three wearing their halos, maybe even the emeralds. It was the way some very rich men paid to have rare paintings, Leonardos or Raphaels, stolen from the walls of museums so they might place them in their own secret "museum," a special place nobody had access to but themselves. And where they went to gloat alone over their stolen beauty.

I knew that place would be the Boss's bunker, and that Verity was destined to be displayed there, his ultimate trophy, on that wall and I did not know if I could save her. Nor did I know what was going to happen to me. I heard the Boss laughing as I ran toward her.

"Mirabella," she said, her voice a whisper. I saw that her eyes were dry as though she could shed no tears. I also saw fear in them. I gripped her hand in my gloved one. The sapphire sparkled in the strong light. Between the two of us we were at that moment worth a small fortune in jewels. And we would have given it up, everything, just to be free.

Quite suddenly all the adrenaline that had given me my fake strength drained from me. My knees gave way and I sank to the floor, resting my head on Verity's bare feet. They were so cold I feared the worst, yet I could feel a pulse beating, slowly, steadily.

She said, in a whisper, so soft she barely moved her lips, "Thank you."

I heard the Boss coming toward us, that solid tread of his, the sheer size of the man, a giant in the world of business, a physical giant in real life. He could crush each one of us with a single blow of his fist, and I was sure he had done that many times in his past.

"Well, well, my girls together. How lovely this is. I'll tell you what I propose we do first, before . . ." He paused for a moment, laughing softly, as though at a good joke, "Before 'everything else.' I think we should have tea. I ordered it specially. After that accident with the wine, I think a nice hot cup of tea is what any good English girl, like Verity, would need. Isn't that what Brits always say when in difficulty in wartime with bombs flying all around? 'Why don't we all have a nice cup of tea?' "

He laughed again at his own joke. I saw him take Verity's hand, very gently in his own large one. Then he turned to me, still on the floor at her feet, and said, "Come, my dear, we shall talk this over together. And then I'll tell you my plans for you." He freed Verity and helped her out of bed.

And that's how it was, with the three of us seated demurely around a table with a white linen cloth, with silver teapots and jugs and Limoges porcelain cups and plates of cookies and English jam tarts, stirring sugar round and round with silver spoons, afraid to drink that tea for what it might contain, when the door burst open. And Chad and the Colonel and a squad of uniformed cops came running toward us.

"Verity, it's the cavalry," I said.

54
The Boss

The Boss realized his mistake; a classic error. He had left the door unlocked. He did not wait for the cavalry. His own secret exit, hidden behind the paneling that held a Matisse of which he was particularly fond. Electronics fanatic that he was, it opened to the press of a finger, revealing a steep flight of wooden stairs, leading it seemed into nowhere but darkness. He had designed those stairs himself, used them many times for secret getaways, some as trivial as escaping unwanted guests or social obligations. But this getaway was serious and he knew it would be for good.

A touch of another switch revealed a small square room at the foot of the stairs. There was no furniture, only a stack of paintings leaning against the wall. He stopped for a second and looked at them, picked out the Turner, put it under his arm, and walked to the door that opened onto a wooden walkway, leading to a stone jetty and the sea.

His Riva was moored alongside the jetty. He clambered down the iron ladder and jumped into it. The boat rocked, almost sending him into the water, but still he clung onto the painting. He steadied himself, then took up his position behind the wheel, the captain as always, only this time there was no captain's cap trimmed with gold flaunting his position. And there was no one to notice, to admire. The Boss was, finally, alone.

The powerful engines roared at his touch, loud enough certainly to attract attention. He checked his watch. He reckoned he had fifteen, maybe twenty minutes before his hunters realized this was the logical place from which he would run.

He was well prepared. A man like him had to be ready for anything. You learned that young and it was a habit that never left you. A suitcase stashed under the backseat contained enough clothing to see him through a week or two. There were even a couple of pairs of the Lobbs. He could not manage without those shoes and saw no reason why he should have to.

When he was about a mile offshore, he stopped the boat and stood looking back at his own house, the Villa Mara, lit as though for a party. He could almost hear those police dogs yelping in excitement, and he could certainly see the torches held by the cops, maybe even by that bastard Chad Prescott. Or even worse, the fuckin' Colonel.

He stood for a long time, looking at his past. It was not easy to give it all up. The prestige, the celebrity status, the acclaim. The women. The power. Everything he had worked for. He hated all the intruders with a force that was almost physical in its energy. It took him only a minute, sixty perfect seconds, to set the battery that would start the timer that would blow his past and everybody involved in it into eternity. There would be nobody left to come searching for him, no Chad, no Colonel, no woman wondering where he was, no walls left holding the Matisses and Picassos. He had the only painting that mattered in the boat with him. The Turner landscape, shrink-wrapped and weatherproofed, exactly, though of course he did not know that, the way it had arrived in Iron Man Matthews's own hands, many years before.

The Riva purred down the coastline, heading for a small cove he knew well and had made his own. He used no lights, not even the starboard and port markers. He saw no other craft, no lights except for those dotted along the shore, marking homes or small coastal communities. When his instru-ments indicated he was close to his destination, he killed the engines.

The Riva rocked on the swell. The silence was total. In the darkness, the sky seemed to lower itself over him, pressing in a fine mist that immediately coated everything. Steadying himself, he stripped off all his clothing, stood, naked for a moment, then threw the garments into the sea. He watched until they disappeared. His old self had just died. The new self would begin.

Half an hour later, a man, slightly stooped, with too-long gray hair, wearing rimless glasses, a well-worn Panama hat with a brown band around it, an expensive blue short-sleeved shirt, khakis, and a pair of John Lobb loafers, docked at a small fishing jetty. Beyond the jetty was an asphalt airstrip, well-known to drug smugglers flying in under the radar from various points in South America. A large barnlike structure with a corrugated metal roof housed several small but powerful aircraft, many of which were capable of long-haul flights without refueling. Such as the flight to Columbia, where the Boss owned property. Under another name, of course. Another identity.

He grabbed his suitcase and boarded his expensive plane with its cream leather upholstery and its top-of-the-line equipment. He settled into the pilot's seat and checked the briefcase containing his papers: a passport with a foreign name, scattered with stamps from various cities around the world, and a photo of the man he had become. It would not have done to have a brand-new passport, though he did not expect to encounter any immigration officials, not where he was going to land, and flying under the radar as he would. Still, it had become a lifelong habit to be prepared for any eventuality. Any emergency.

He had flown planes since he was twenty years

old, been taught by a Russian pilot who flew an ancient propeller plane back and forth to tourist locations in the Crimean resorts. After that, when he'd started on his upward climb, he'd had a professional teach him all over again and afterward he had always chosen to pilot his own aircraft. It had been, he told himself now, facing the long journey ahead, a good decision.

He filed no flight plan, skimming the French coast under the radar, then soaring high above the clouds, away from the commercial jet routes, away from the world that knew him as the Boss.

He was smiling as he left all that behind, though he did still regret not making Mirabella his own woman. Still, there was always time for that. Maybe later. In some new life.

It was then he remembered the painting, the Turner landscape, the cause of all his troubles in the first place. He'd left it in the boat. He'd lusted after that painting, a man in heat for it. And he'd lost everything because of it.

The smile disappeared. And then the plane's engine began to stutter. The plane shook, wiggled its wings from side to side.

The Boss groaned. No problem, he told himself. Nothing I can't take care of. I always can. Can't I?

55

Verity

I'm a miracle, or at least that's what Mirabella tells me. I certainly don't feel much like a miracle, certainly nothing as grand as that. What I do feel is alive. If anyone had been intended for the other world, whatever that might be, it was me. I escaped that fate thanks to Chad and the Colonel, who I shall now call "my Colonel," and of course to my friend Mirabella's determination to save me, and to both Chad and the Colonel's own instincts about "the super man" himself. The Boss. The Colonel said even the police dogs, the German shepherds, bristled and sniffed and growled when out searching for him. A good dog knows a bad guy, my Colonel told me. I knew he was right.

When I was in that terrible room with the donkeys' heads skewered to the wall next to me, the intense light trained on my face, blinding me, too weak to so much as voice a protest or even to scream, I'd thought there was no way out. I'd waited for that burst of strength, the energy surge that would make me leap from my lofty place; waited to find "myself" in all the destruction heaped upon me, but it had taken my friends to save me.

How can I ever thank you, I asked Mirabella later, when it was all over and done with and the Boss was gone.

"Thank me?" she'd said, astonished. "Why, if you had not met me on that Paris-to-Nice train you never would have gone through all this. You never would have suffered . . ."

She'd burst into tears. My Mirabella. The brave one who never cried, except at weddings, as she told me, once again, when I passed her the tissues. And only then it was because it was not her own.

You can throw all the arrows fate can conjure up at Mirabella and she stands tall and strong and figures the way out, saves you from the certain hell that awaits if she doesn't. Now, that's a person you call a friend.

I'm sitting here, on the terrace of the Villa Romantica, where I never expected to be again, reluctantly tasting Mirabella's latest concoction. A vermouth-cassis she calls it. It's sort of reddish and clinking with ice cubes and tastes I think vaguely of paint remover, but I'm polite and I say thank you and sip obediently. I think maybe she got the proportions wrong, or used the wrong liquor. Ah well, she can't be good at everything. I think I shall tell her in the future to stick with champagne.

I'm not sure I'll ever get over the bizarre events that took place in the Villa Mara. Chad tells me it will leave an emotional scar, and Chad should know because he's a doctor. He's dealt with kids who have lost half their faces; he's put them back together as best he could, and he tells me that after a while they smile again, they talk and laugh and behave just like regular kids. Trauma is internal as well as external. Just look at Mirabella's hands, which finally, she has left bare. No more gloves. No more hiding the scars. But that is her story to tell, not mine.

Mine is very simple. I came here, to the villa, running away from a ruin of a life, not knowing what I wanted, believing I had lost everything that mattered, my husband, my home, my small amount of savings, my very identity. Mirabella took me in hand, she picked me up from the lowly place I had fallen, she saved my life in the car crash, she saved me again and again, ultimately from the Boss. An evil man.

I ask over and over how I could have imagined I was falling in love with him. I remind myself he was good looking, in that dashing, big man, important person, richer-than-thou way. I remembered the thrill of being on the Boss's arm, a woman to be reckoned with. Nobody would dismiss you or turn you away. Now, coming out at the other end of the story, with the truth known to the world, the Boss's reputation gone, his entire secret life exposed, my own story a media scandal that I'm lucky to have survived. I am thankful there are no more TV journalists with cameras, no more celebrity hunters thrusting cell phones in my face. I am anonymous again, and that is exactly how I want it.

Actually, that's not quite true. I'm sitting here, on the Villa Romantica terrace sipping Mirabella's awful concoction, waiting for "exactly" how I want it. Or rather "who" I want. I need to see him striding toward me, his cap, as always, clutched in his hand, his uniform immaculate, the gold stars shining on his epaulettes, his eyes alight with that special gleam that means "love." Anyone who has seen it knows exactly what I mean. It can light even an ordinary face, and in a man it's irresistible.

I am wearing a simple white cotton skirt that flares out from a narrow waist, tied with a black ribbon, fastened with a neat bow. I never thought I was a "bow" kind of girl but Mirabella informed me that I was. It was she who helped me choose this outfit on a recent shopping trip to Cannes, necessary because I've lost so much weight and am too skinny for my old clothes.

But I'm young, I'm healthy again, and I am much stronger than I ever was. That frightened girl running from "the cheater," and the bad marriage, is no more. Soon I shall move in with my handsome Colonel. We shall marry as soon as I am free, and I shall become stepmother to two delightful girls who are as needy for a mom as I am to be one.

If anyone needed a happy ending, it was me. (Or do I mean "I"?)

56

Chad Prescott

I find myself once again at the Nice airport, awaiting a flight to Paris, delayed naturally, and from there, flight to Rio de Janeiro, where I shall overnight, just long enough to take in its staggering beauty. Flying into Rio is a wonder in itself, over that green, green ocean, those white surf-swept beaches, those twin mountains and of course the most spectacular of all, Corcovado where the statue of Christ the Redeemer holds his arms wide in welcome. I shall dine there in some white-tiled hole-in-the-wall where you can get the best feijoada, a dish of black beans cooked with pork and other succulent bits and probably unmentionable pieces, and which will most likely be the mainstay of my diet for the next couple of months. In the Amazon villages where I am going, there are no supermarkets, no corner stores, no cafés and local bistros, where a glass of red and a fresh-cooked omelette can make your day. And there is, of course, no mobile phone reception. It is the latter I regret most.

In just a few weeks, I'd fallen in love. I have become used to Mirabella's soft voice, to her presence in my life, to opening my eyes in the morning and seeing her red hair spread on the pillow next to me, her sleeping face so tranquil, as though all the traumas and danger of the past weeks has finally disappeared from her mind. I've become used to thinking of the Villa Romantica as "home," the place I shall always recall with longing and to which I shall always return. It's no longer just "my land" and "Mirabella's land," the two are joined together as inextricably as we are ourselves.

How could this happen? I've asked myself a hundred or more times. Here I was, the long-range doctor, content enough with my hardworking lifestyle, the quiet times alone at the villa on the South of France coast, where omelets were offered at every café and wine flowed from carafes placed automatically on the table, along with the basket of bread, and the good Normandy butter, and the small bowl of olive oil from the mill around the corner. I'll still miss all that but, for the first time, I will miss a woman.

This is not just any woman. She is Mirabella Matthews, writer of detective novels of the kind I read myself with great enjoyment, in those free hours snatched from my work. She is Mirabella Matthews, the brave woman who faced up to life-threatening danger, took on a man so powerful, so clever and so ultimately evil, he would have sacrificed her along with the donkeys, and Verity, who had almost joined them on the wall.

Now, though, waiting for my delayed flight, the young man behind the bar offered me a glass of champagne. I refused. I was not in a champagne mood. No celebration. I was leaving the woman I loved behind. And I had not told her I loved her.

I ordered a beer instead, downing it, all the while staring morosely into space, not hearing the usual chatter, the gossip, the flights calls, uninterested in anything but my own thoughts. Which were all of a woman I was leaving behind.

I ordered a second beer, though I should have known better. Booze does not fix a broken heart. Not that mine was broken yet. But it was about to be if I got on that flight and ended up thousands of miles from where I was meant, right now, to be.

I canceled my flight, grabbed my old leather duffle, and made for the taxi line. As usual it was a mile long. It was also beginning to rain, that thin kind of rain that soaks you without you even noticing until it's too late to do anything about it.

I stood there, in my old parka, clutching my battered bag, my wet hair stuck to my brow, scowling at a world that for the first time I did not want to leave, ignoring the car horns, the honking, the buses skidding to a stop, the people standing in line grumbling. Then I heard her voice.

“Get in here,” she yelled, throwing open the door of the miniature car she drove these days. I guessed it was better than the blue Maserati she’d crashed over the side of the canyon.

I got in, slamming the door shut as she took off, escaping the threats and catcalls coming her way.

She was grinning from ear to ear. Her red curls had gotten wet in the rain and she looked young and kind of innocent, despite the cocky grin.

She threw me a sideways glance. “You didn’t think I was going to let you get away that easily, did you?”

“I was hoping you wouldn’t,” I replied.

57
Mirabella

It was much later, and we were still in my room, in the bed where we had made love. Chad took my bare hands and held them flat in his. He inspected the shriveled skin that without the gloves pulled my fingers down into the palms. My nails were perfect, but my hands curved like claws. I was ashamed all over again and I began to cry.

"Tell me about it," he said.

In all the years since the accident I had never spoken to anybody about it. Not even the psychiatrist who assured me I would be better, "cured" I guess he meant, if I unburdened my soul.

I did not then, or ever, but now I wanted no secrets between my lover and myself. He had to know what happened.

"I was twelve years old," I said. "I'd gone with my mother to a friend's farm. We were playing in the barn, as kids do, hiding behind bales of straw stored for winter feed for the cows. They had only a few cows, three in fact, but they were looked after like children, brushed until they shone, picked-up after like they were thoroughbred race-horses, so beautiful with their liquid brown eyes and long straight lashes. I was a city girl, I didn't know about farms and machinery. It was a play-ground for me. I climbed up into the rafters, you know the big king-beam a barn has, and all the others coming from it. Well one beam stuck out right over where I was hiding.

"There was a round metal machine at the end of it, sort of rusty looking, obviously something that had not been used in years. So of course, daredevil me, I had to give it a try. I thought I'd just grab onto the rope, swing out over all the kids below, and push the machine in front of me. Well, that's exactly what I did. The rope was old. The machine was old. Everything broke and I fell. I clutched at the rusty apparatus for some reason, trying to save it, I suppose. I landed on a cow. It probably saved my life, but I broke its neck. I was distraught. I had killed a helpless trusting animal. Don't worry, people said to me. Thank God you're alright. It was just a cow. Besides, look what it did to your hand. Of course the cow had done nothing, it was all my own fault. And yes, silly though it might seem, it has left a scar on my memory. I love animals, I take in stray dogs and cats, I help at the local animal shelter, I do all I can for them. . . ."

"To atone for the cow," Chad said.

"Oh, Christ, can you believe how ridiculous that

is? All those years ago and I still can't forgive myself. My arrogance and stupidity."

"That's all it was?"

I could see he did not believe me. I had to tell him. "I also landed on my friend. She fell off the hay bale. I thought she had died. I screamed to them to come help. She did not die but she had broken both legs and it was over a year before she could walk again. Years later, I was a bridesmaid at her wedding. She was still limping. 'You see, I'm walking on my own two feet,' she said to me with a big loving smile. It was then I learned about forgiveness."

Chad said, "And now it's time to learn to forgive yourself. Mistakes are made. We all make them. There are times when I feel I could have done more for my poor children out there in the wilderness, that I should have done for them, should not come back here and left them alone. Then I remember who I am. I do what I do, all I can do. I have my own life to live, my own world to live in. And so do you, my poor Mirabella. Can you leave it all now, and go forward? With me?"

It was the best question any man ever asked me. Apart from saying will you marry me, of course. But that came later.

And, wouldn't you know it, the canary sang.

Epilogue

When I think about Jerusha, I recall her sad story, but I remember also the joyous times she lived through and the success and the happiness that was hers, until it was all taken away from her.

I like to remember her as a lovely, smiling young woman, glad for the love she had, and glad to give that love. She was a true star in the firmament of life.

Now, Chad and I are able to enjoy the beautiful home she built with such hope and care. We think of her when we hear a voice echoing from the beach, or the great splashing roar of winter-night waves against the rocks, or smell the elusive scent that still sometimes lingers. We remember her, and thank her. She will always exist not only in our hearts, but in the way of life that she helped create, for those who came after her.

We would like you to know it was not for nothing, Jerusha.

Center Point Large Print
600 Brooks Road / PO Box 1
Thorndike, ME 04986-0001 USA

(207) 568-3717

US & Canada:
1 800 929-9108
www.centerpointlargeprint.com